PROTEUS

VOICES FOR THE 80'S

RICHARD S. McENROE

SF
ace books
A Division of Charter Communications Inc.
A GROSSET & DUNLAP COMPANY
51 Madison Avenue
New York, New York 10010

A Destinies Special
PROTEUS: VOICES FOR THE 80's

An ACE Book

First Ace printing: May 1981
Published Simultaneously in Canada

2 4 6 8 0 9 7 5 3 1
Manufactured in the United States of America

DIFFERENT STROKES
FOR DIFFERENT FOLKS!

Fourteen stories by some of the best and brightest writers of this or any decade, backed up by the finest, fanciest artists working today, in a special *Destinies* edition guaranteed to shake your conceptions of what science fiction is all about!

To the other charming
mixture of my acquaintance
Zienia Merton

TABLE OF CONTENTS

Frontispiece illustrations by Victoria Poyser
Endpiece illustration by Rick DeMarco

THE *DESTINIES* THAT ISN'T

Magazines and series anthologies are dynamic things, that change and develop over the course of their existence. They acquire an image, a tone, as the tastes of the editor and the readership become apparent.

Destinies, edited by Jim Baen, developed such a tone: it quickly became perhaps the best hard-science-fiction publication in the country, which was great—unless you were one of the authors who wrote one of the stories Baen bought that *wasn't* hard-science, before it was clear which course his series would ultimately follow. The early *Destinies* could publish the occasional Frank Herbert fairy-tale pig-story; the current *Destinies* just isn't the place readers look for such work.

So: PROTEUS.

Most of these stories were originally purchased for *Destinies;* to my mind they are some of the best material Jim Baen ever bought. They include work by some of the best-known writers in the field, people like Jack C. Haldeman and George Alec Effinger and Reg Bretnor, and by people you're going to be hearing a lot more from, like Eileen Gunn and Michael Swanwick and Andrew Weiner.

The rest are stories I'd heard of suffering a similar fate elsewhere, cast out into the cold to a litany of ''terrific, but it just isn't for us.'' It's valid for an editor to reject a story on those grounds; it isn't pleasant but it's unavoidable when there's a market for just so many short stories every year. You can't buy them all; you can't print them all—

But: PROTEUS. So we could at least print these. Work as good as you'll find anywhere, illustrated by a mixture of fresh and established artists from within the genre and without. Steve Fabian and Rick DeMarco. John Byrne and Lydia Moon. Broeck Steadman and John Barnes. Michael Wm. Kaluta and Viido Polikarpus. This is a good book. You're getting your money's worth, and change—and there's no denying that the thanks for that have got to go most of all to the writers you find here. They could have pulled out easily enough, with justification, and gone off bitching about another publishing nightmare. But they didn't. They gave us a chance to do right by them, to get their stories that deserved to be in print into print, and that was more than they had to do. So thanks, all of you, and I hope we've earned your patience with the result.

—Richard S. McEnroe
New York, 1981

Introduction to 'Terrific Park'

George Alec Effinger says he belongs to the generation of writers given to science fiction by the state of Ohio. He grew up not far from Roger Zelazny and Harlan Ellison. Andre Norton went to his junior high school. Perhaps for this reason the first man to set foot on the moon was from Ohio. No; the first man to orbit the Earth was from Ohio. The first American to orbit the Earth—

Since 1970 he has written more than a hundred short stories and the following books: WHAT ENTROPY MEANS TO ME, RELATIVES, MIXED FEELINGS (short stories), IRRATIONAL NUMBERS (short stories), THOSE GENTLE VOICES, NIGHTMARE BLUE (with Gardner Dozois), FELICIA, DEATH IN FLORENCE, DIRTY TRICKS (short stories), and HEROICS. Finished and due soon are: STEAL, BLOOD PINBALL (non-fiction), IDLE PLEASURES (short stories), and OBITUARY. He is currently working on a novel of World War Two intrigue.

Effinger has been nominated for most of the prestigious awards offered by the science fiction community. WHAT ENTROPY MEANS TO ME was a Nebula nominee, and a novelette, "The City on the Sand," was a Hugo nominee. When Effinger finished second in the first John W. Campbell Award voting he became the first sf writer to lose all three of these honors. He has been named the World's Most Non-Existent Author by a fan group in West Virginia. It all seems to stem from an innocent joke he made about the Masonic Order in the eleventh grade. He is very sorry and he hopes that enough is enough.

Effinger likes good books, good food, and good movies. He loves baseball and pinball, collects Depression glass, and is partial to some of the usual vices. He has been heard to claim that people are the same all over.

TERRIFIC PARK

George Alec Effinger

It had been almost two weeks since they left the last star behind. They were traveling on toward nothing. That was their purpose. Nothing. They were supposed to investigate nothing. They were very excited, a little afraid, very curious. Nothing has always had that effect on man.

Their craft was still accelerating, of course, and they fell farther and farther from everything they knew. They fell faster and faster toward their own complete ignorance. That, too, was their purpose.

There were only two men on board the spacecraft. They were very good friends. They had been chosen for this particular mission because their superiors were impressed by their credentials, and because the two men seemed otherwise unoccupied. To be truthful, the planners of the mission realized that it wouldn't likely take much technical skill to investigate nothing, especially as the marvelous and hand-made equipment on the spacecraft could do the job without them. Nevertheless, the essential quality in man that prods him toward foolish acts prodded these two men toward the very end of the universe. Such as it was.

There was very little to see. The humans aboard the craft had anticipated this, and had brought along with them litera-ture, music, and games, all in various forms, according to their individual preferences. Still, there had been a large amount of time to fill, subjectively speaking. As they ap-proached the speed of light, many paradoxes were involved. This was one of the main goals of the mission, that is, the two men were expected to record and document the paradoxes as they occurred. The men realized soon that this was much more fun than the toys they had brought along. Every morning they awoke with expectation. When the ship's clock told them it was time to go to sleep, they felt that same unfulfilled longing. They were becoming frustrated. They wondered how near to the speed of light they had to come before they would experience a genuine paradox.

They gave little thought to the idea that not experiencing the paradoxes they expected was in itself a major paradox. That would have made things confusing and tedious.

The stars were behind them. Nothing was ahead of them. A dark nothing that was supposed to curve in on itself or something. They were coming close to the limits of the universe, and as they did so they were simultaneously approaching the speed of light. There was nothing to see. Even the stars behind them were undetectable except by instruments.

Then, one day, the instruments registered something.

"Hey, Neil," said one of the men, "look at this."

Neil looked up from the screen of the book he was reading. "What's wrong?" he asked.

"Come and look."

"Just tell me, Buzz," said Neil. "I'm in the middle of something."

Buzz seemed slightly annoyed. "Really, Neil, you'd better take a look."

Neil was every bit as annoyed, even though he and Buzz were very good friends, and even though the two of them had shared many interesting adventures. He got up, sighing loudly, and went to the instrument panel that Buzz was studying. "What is it?" He couldn't tell what Buzz meant. There were too many things measuring and reporting.

"This here," said Buzz. He indicated a small digital readout.

"What's that?" asked Neil.

"This here manual says that it shows a large concentration of matter coming at us."

"That's impossible, Buzz," said Neil. "We passed the last matter in the universe a long time ago. The last star. You know that."

"This thing on the board doesn't," said Buzz. "Anyway, out at the very last extreme part of the universe, who knows what there is?"

Neil chewed his lip as he thought. He knew that Buzz wanted to slow their acceleration, to make the final stage of their journey actually decelerating. He was afraid that there might be some kind of physical boundary around the universe, and that they'd hit it at just under the speed of light. Neil thought that was foolish. Now, however, Buzz had the evidence of the instrumentation to support his fear. "What do you want to do?" asked Neil.

Buzz said nothing. He just punched out directives to the spacecraft to begin decelerating.

"All right," said Neil. "Figure out how far your little speck of trouble is, how large it is, and let the old machine get us there."

"Check," said Buzz.

"Leave me alone," said Neil. He was nominally the pilot, and aboard the ship his word was law, kind of.

"All right," said Buzz. He was the co-pilot, and his word was less than law, but only by a little. It was a significant amount, though.

It took a long time for the ship to decelerate. They had been moving at a rate of speed that increased along a hyperbolic curve which took them closer and closer to the speed of light. They would never reach that speed, but the difference became more negligible all the time. They had to back the ship down, and that stupendous job was rough on the physical framework of the craft. Both Neil and Buzz understood that, but it was part of the danger they had accepted when they took on the assignment. Like all pioneers, they had a very bad idea of what they were getting themselves into. There were better informed people, but these knowledgeable individuals refused to go along. Maybe the second journey, they said. If the first comes back all right.

Time passed at different rates inside the craft and outside. Inside, weeks had gone by. The ship had dropped its forward speed down to where stars could be seen behind them, back in the universe. There was more of a one-to-one correlation between what the instruments reported and what the men could see.

One of the things the instruments showed was a large mass ahead of them, a little to the left. Buzz had not been wrong. More warnings from other measuring devices had persuaded even Neil.

"It's out there, all right," said the pilot.

"Yeah," said Buzz. "I wonder if it's a paradox."

"Maybe. Anyway, it's a little to the left."

"Port side," said Buzz. "You want to head over that way?"

"Sure," said Neil. He was very agreeable most of the time. He made the correction. The ship's guiding computers were planning to make the correction in a short while, anyway.

Another couple of weeks passed before the mysterious mass became visible to Neil and Buzz. They took turns looking at it through a telescope. "Gee," said Neil. "It's a planet."

"Yeah," said Buzz. "I don't understand. What's a planet doing out here all alone and everything?"

"I don't know," said Neil.

"I know you don't know," said Buzz. "What do you think, though?"

"I don't know," said Neil. "What do *you* think?"

"I think it's too early to think," said Buzz. That sounded dumb to Neil, but the pilot didn't say anything. They just looked through the telescope and hoped that everything was all right.

The planet was not tremendously impressive, like some planets Buzz and Neil had visited. It was rather small in fact, and it was completely blue, except for what both men agreed were clouds. "It's a water world," said Neil. "Doggone it."

"Yeah," said Buzz. "I hate water worlds."

"Maybe there's some decent life in the water," said Neil.

"You want to kill it, right?" said Buzz, his expression showing some of the disgust he felt.

"Sport," said Neil. "It's sport."

"I have a question, Neil. Look at the planet again, and tell me what you see."

Neil looked, and described the world. "It's round, and blue, just like all the other times we've looked, and there are little streaks of white, like, uh, clouds. Polar caps. Don't see any moons. That's about it."

"Uh huh," said Buzz. "Can you see the daylight terminator?"

"The what?" said Neil, still staring through the telescope.

"The line between the day side and the night side."

"Sure," said Neil. "What about it?"

"Where's the light coming from?"

There was silence in the spacecraft. Buzz had stumbled onto something, and Neil didn't want to admit it out loud.

After a short time, Buzz said, "Aren't any stars any more. We passed the last one. Instruments show nothing but this planet. We have only faint indications of the stars we left behind. Just this planet out here, at the very end of everything, with sunlight coming from nowhere shining down on half of it."

"That's odd," said Neil. He had to admit that.

"What do you want to do?"

"We'll park the ship, take the shuttle, go down, and see what's up."

"I don't like it," said Buzz.

"Neither do I, Buzz, but what else can we do?"

Buzz shrugged. He thought they could skip the planet and go off in another direction. It would all lead toward the end of the universe eventually, anyhow. The planet complicated things. It wasn't one of the crazy possibilities they had been prepared for.

Neil saw Buzz shrug. It made him feel good. It meant that he was still firmly in command. Without a word, Neil directed the spacecraft to park in orbit around the water world. It would be several days before this was accomplished. Until then, they had nothing to do. Neil read, and Buzz wrote letters. All sorts of time passed.

The shuttle craft sped low over the waves of the water world. After an hour, neither Neil nor Buzz was afraid. They forgot the significance, the impossibility of their discovery. The familiarity of their flight over the water lulled them. They watched until they grew bored. The shuttle screamed on at two hundred miles per hour. Neil and Buzz started a game of cards. They played, bored by the game, too, for almost half an hour. They had reached a point where Neil was losing by a considerable amount. Buzz put down the five, six, and seven of hearts. "I knock with three," he said.

"Damn it," said Neil. "I was just going to—"

Several voices, singing, interrupted him.

"What's that?" said Buzz. He was very frightened.

"I couldn't make it out," said Neil. "It was coming over the g/a receiver, though."

"That's impossible," said Buzz.

"You want to forget impossible?" said Neil. "This whole thing is impossible. You can't explain any of it, can you?"

"What are we doing playing cards?"

"Just because the whole thing is impossible," said Neil, "doesn't mean it can't be boring."

"I want to take a look," said Buzz. Neil scooped up the cards and crumpled up the score sheet. He was glad that something had happened to distract Buzz from the game.

Ten minutes later, Buzz called to his friend. "Hey, Neil, look at this!" he cried.

"What now?" asked Neil, stepping up to the smaller telescope with which the shuttle craft had been provided. He looked. Far away, something interrupted the blue of the water and the blue of the sky. It was too far yet for details to be seen. It looked like a small island.

"An island?" asked Neil. "Did we see an island from orbit?"

"No," said Buzz. "This one, maybe, this one's too small."

"Maybe," said Neil. "We'll find out in a minute or two. Step on it a little." He continued to watch, while Buzz ordered the shuttle to speed up.

"The hammer is down," said Buzz. "Three hundred miles per. What do you see?"

"Something," said Neil. "I don't like it."

"What? Let me look." Through the windows all Buzz could see was the water, not far below, as the shuttle skimmed along. Neil left the telescope. Buzz stepped up and looked. There was definitely a small island ahead. Buzz saw what looked to be the outlines of a ferris wheel and roller coaster standing in dark contrast to the pale blue sky. 'H'ey," he said. "How about that."

Neil said nothing. There wasn't a whole hell of a lot to say.

The ground to air receiver crackled with static. Then the two men heard the singing again. This time they could make out the words. It sounded like a group of women singing, "Terrific Park has the rides! Terrific Park has the fun! Why not come out to *Ter—rif—ic Park!*"

"What the—" said Buzz.

"Shut up," said Neil.

A man's voice replaced the women on the receiver. He said, "Come on out to Terrific Park. Route One, just south of Rubbermaid, New Jersey. Pay one price and stay all day. Terrific Park."

"You want to go?" asked Buzz.

"Rubbermaid, New Jersey?"

"Near Metuchen, isn't it?"

"I don't know," said Neil. He was a little dazed.

"You want to go?"

"What day is it?" asked Neil.

Buzz asked the shuttle's computer, which got the information from the mother ship in orbit. "Lorenz-corrected, it's Tuesday."

"Shouldn't be a lot of kids," said Neil.

"You want to go?"

"I guess so." Neil sat down. He felt very frightened. He watched Buzz prepare their silver EVA suits. Neil was a little angry that Buzz wasn't frightened.

Neil and Buzz landed the shuttle craft in a vacant lot behind a chrome trolley-shaped diner. From above, the small island looked like a small chunk of commercial America. The land area was small, so small that it had gone unnoticed by the human space explorers and their sophisticated electronic devices. Nevertheless, the island was crowded with buildings, parking lots, apartment houses, and motels. From the ground, still inside the shuttle, Neil could see the back of the diner and an alley that led to the island's single thoroughfare.

"All right," said Neil, feeling the warning signs of an anxiety attack coming on. "Where are we?"

"We're on a water world at the very end of the universe," said Buzz. "By a remarkable coincidence, the inhabitants speak English and have built their civilization in an amazing copy of Route 1 in New Jersey."

"It is a remarkable coincidence, isn't it?" said Neil. The skepticism in his voice was lost on his friend.

"What time is it?" asked Buzz.

"I don't know. Ask the ship."

"The ship will tell us what time it is on the ship. I want to know what time it is here."

"Look at the sun," said Neil.

"All right," said Buzz. He looked out the side window at the sun. It was about fifteen degrees from directly overhead. "It's either about eleven in the morning or one in the afternoon, depending on which direction the sun is moving.

"Call it noon," said Neil.

"Sure," said Buzz. "No problem there. Lunchtime. You want to eat in or go out?"

"What do you mean, 'go out?' "

"There's plenty of diners, Neil."

Neil gook a deep breath and let it out in a loud sigh. "We're on an alien planet, moron. This isn't Earth, no matter how much it looks like it, here on this tiny island. There's no reason to believe that the air is breathable, that the inhabitants are humans, or that the food they eat is safe for us to eat.''

"Let's find out," said Buzz. "That's what we're getting paid for.''

"I was wondering what we were getting paid for," said Neil. He put on his silver helmet, checked his oxygen supply, ran through the preliminary routines according to his EVA manual, and waited for Buzz to put film in his camera.

"You know what I think?" said Buzz.

"No.''

"I think these people down here are the descendants of some lost interstellar probe. A lost colony. Maybe they stumbled through the same interstellar space warp that we used.''

"There's never been a lost interstellar probe," said Neil.

"Well," said Buzz, "maybe one that wasn't lost. One that hasn't been missed yet.''

"You're crazy," said Neil. "Are you ready?''

"Yeah, I'm ready now.''

Neil began the EVA cycle. The shuttle went dormant until either Neil or Buzz roused it by setting the exterior color locks in the proper combination. The two explorers walked out of the shuttle. Behind them a silver door hissed shut. A bright sun shone above them. A light breeze rustled the branches of the trees in the lot behind the diner.

"The air's okay, Neil," said Buzz.

"That's swell," said Neil. "I'm keeping my helmet on.''

"The computer says there's no poison and no harmful bugs.''

"Take yours off, then. I'm keeping mine on.''

"All right," said Buzz sulkily. "I'll keep mine on, too.''

The two explorers walked up the alley to Route 1. They stopped on the sidewalk. Neil was still frightened. Buzz was amused.

"It looks just like home," said Buzz.

"I know," said Neil. "I hate it.''

"Why?"

"Because it shouldn't look like home, that's why. It should look scary and weird, that's why. I could handle that. But looking like New Jersey . . ."

"I read a story once," said Buzz. "About these guys who go to Mars—"

"I read it, too," said Neil. While they talked, Neil and Buzz watched dozens of people walking along the sidewalks, staring in the store windows, getting out of cars, going into and out of diners, and generally not noticing the astronauts.

"They look all right," said Buzz.

"That bothers me, too. I don't like it."

"What do you think?"

"There are a couple of explanations," said Neil. "One is that these aliens have constructed this whole scene to allay our fears, and they're just waiting for us to be allayed enough to walk into their trap. And then again we may just be dead. Or we're dreaming. Or going through a space warp makes you see things. Or something."

"It seems okay to me," said Buzz.

"That's why you're only the co-pilot."

"You hungry?"

"Sort of," said Neil.

"Want to go into the diner?"

"No way."

"Then let's go to the park instead."

"Where is this park?" asked Neil.

"Route 1," said Buzz. "Just south of Rubbermaid, New Jersey."

"Terrific," said Neil.

"Yeah," said Buzz. "Terrific Park. Let's go."

The two space travelers started walking. After four blocks, Route 1 curved to the right. As they went around the bend in the road, Neil and Buzz could see Terrific Park. The ferris wheel was spinning, and a train of cars went rocketing down the steep first hill of the roller coaster. Neil and Buzz could hear the shrieks of the people.

"Come on, Neil, let's go."

"All right, all right." Neil felt like a tired parent. Buzz was behaving like a kid.

When they got to the gate, they saw a sign that told them that admission to the park was two dollars, after which they would have to pay for ride tickets and food tickets; or, as an alternate plan, they could pay four and a half dollars and go on as many rides as they wanted, having to buy only food tickets inside.

"What are we going to do?" asked Buzz.

"How much money do you have?"

"Nothing," said Buzz, disappointed. "But they gave you gold and fissionable stuff to trade, didn't they?"

"Sure," said Neil. "Ask the lady in the booth how much plutonium she wants to let us in."

"Aw, come on, Neil." said Buzz. "I want to go inside."

Neil was more frightened than ever. He couldn't understand why Buzz didn't see the horror of the situation. Everything about the place—the town, the street, the people, the park—pointed to some terrifying explanation. Buzz wanted to go charging right down the gullet of whatever was waiting for them. Neil didn't know what else to do. This is what they had been sent to investigate. This was the end of the universe. Neil and Buzz had been prepared for monsters and disruptions in reality and time paradoxes and space paradoxes and death by evanescence. They hadn't been prepared for New Jersey.

Buzz stepped up to the booth. Before he could say anything, the woman waved him inside. "Come on, Neil," he called. "It's all right."

"Another sign of strangeness and danger," thought Neil. He remembered the story about the men on Mars, and how they were seduced by familiarity. Neil shuddered. He watched Buzz hurrying ahead of him, walking beneath the wooden structure of the roller coaster. Overhead, the ride's cars rattled around a tight curve and down three quick hills. People screamed and laughed. Buzz was already at the entrance of the main amusement arcade. He turned around and waved to Neil. Neil looked down at himself. He looked at the

silver pressure suit. He listened to his own breathing. He heard the blood beating in his ears. He heard Buzz calling to him.

Neil thought of the sirens luring sailors to their deaths. He thought of Lorelei. He thought of the will-o'-the-wisp.

Buzz had stopped in front of a fun house. It was called The Wacky Shack. On either side of the turnstile was a dummy, shaking with electronic laughter. There was a fat man on the left, and a fat woman on the right. "Ha ha ha ha ha ha ha ha ha ha ha ha ha ha ha ha ha ha ha," they said. They never stopped. The sound made Neil shiver. The ugly faces on the dummies made him look away.

This is Hell, thought Neil. We've died, and this is Hell.

"We need tickets," said Buzz. "It's five tickets each."

"Go get them," said Neil. "I'm going to sit down on this bench. I'll be right here. Go get the tickets." Neil sat down and tried to ignore the humorless laughing of the dummies. He turned around and looked at a merry-go-round.

In a few minutes Buzz returned. "They let me have these," he said, holding up strings of orange tickets. "I didn't have to pay or anything. Before I could say anything, the man in the booth just punched out these tickets and gave them to me. They should last us all day."

Hell, thought Neil. We're in Hell.

"I want to go in the fun house," said Buzz.

Neil shuddered. "Sure," he said. He took five tickets from Buzz and followed his friend to the turnstile. They gave their tickets to a young man and went into the fun house. After three steps they couldn't see a thing. "I'm going to put on the helmet light," said Neil.

"Don't be silly," said Buzz. "It's supposed to be dark."

Neil walked forward hesitantly. There was an open pit waiting for them. Satan was waiting for them. Ugly silicone life forms that ate people were waiting for them.

Buzz stepped on a board and a grotesque face lit up behind a glass window. It leered and wobbled at them.

"Wah," screamed Neil.

"Isn't this fun?" asked Buzz.

"Terrific," said Neil. He was still shaking.

"I haven't done this since I was a kid," said Buzz. Neil didn't answer. They walked on in the dark. Every once in a while there was a step up or a step down. Neil hit his shin or fell off the step. He was cursing under his breath. Five times he walked smack into a wall. He began walking with his arms outstretched, feeling in front of him with his foot. He moved forward very slowly. Buzz was hurrying on ahead like an excited child. Soon Neil was alone. Damn it, he thought, don't leave me. He didn't call Buzz on the belt radio because he didn't want Buzz to know the pilot was scared.

They came to a large, well-lit room. In the middle of it was a slowly turning barrel. To get across the room they had to walk through the barrel. "I love these," said Buzz. He went halfway into the barrel and stopped. He started walking up the side of the turning barrel. He fell down and laughed. "Come on," he said.

"Why do I want to fall down and laugh?" asked Neil.

"It's fun."

"It's not fun. It's falling down."

"Falling down can be fun," said Buzz.

"You're not on a picnic," said Neil. "You're in a desperate situation. Remember that."

"I'm sorry," said Buzz. "I keep forgetting."

"That's another reason why you're not the pilot." Neil walked into the barrel and immediately fell down. "See?" he said. "That wasn't fun." As the barrel turned, Neil slid down the wall. Buzz tried to stand up, and fell down again on top of Neil.

"See? That was fun," said Buzz.

"No it wasn't," said Neil. "Get up and get out of here."

Buzz obeyed. They continued through the fun house. There were steel rollers on the floor that they slid across. There was a crazy tilted room, where Buzz ran back and forth. There were wobbly floor boards and little holes that blew air up at them. There were plenty of things that lit up and grinned. There was a snake that popped out of a tree, and mice that ran on a track, out of a hole in one wall and into a hole in another. All the time there were recorded howls and laughs around them. Neil couldn't relax. Buzz ran ahead, anxious to see what was coming next. After a while they stepped into a room with a large sliding board, they slid down. Neil felt like a fool. They bumped their way through a mirror maze and came out next to the laughing fat man dummy.

"That was fun," said Buzz. "Want to go again?"

"No," said Neil. He was looking at someone dressed up in a huge papier mache head. "Who is that supposed to be?" he asked.

"I don't know," said Buzz. "I'll go and find out." A moment later Buzz came back. "He's Adlai Stevenson," he said. Neil only nodded.

They walked to the concession stands on the boardwalk. There was a sign that said: FINEST BEACHES IN THE WORLD! FORTY EXCITING YARDS OF BOARDWALK! TERRIFIC PARK—FUN FOR THE WHOLE FAMILY!

"Forty yards of boardwalk," said Neil. "Wow."

"I want a frozen custard," said Buzz. "I have food tickets, too."

"You'll die of alien crud in your system," said Neil.

"Not in frozen custard."

"Cholera," said Neil.

"I've had my shots." He went up to an ice cream stand. Neil shrugged and followed. "I want a vanilla cone," said Buzz. "You want one, Neil?"

"Ain't got vanilla," said the man behind the counter.

"You don't have vanilla?" said Buzz.

"Look at the sign. You want vanilla, you go to Sid's."

"Neil read the sign. It said: ICE CREAM CLONES. THIRTY-SIX IDENTICAL FLAVORS. "Ice cream clones?" asked Neil.

"You got it," said the man.

"What flavor are they?"

"All thirty-six are rum raisin," said the man.

"Feh," said Buzz.

"Go to Sid's." The man pointed to a stand across the boardwalk. A sign on it said: SID'S KING-O-TAFFY. CORNMEAL TAFFY. FROZEN CUSTARD. SOFT DRINKS.

"Cornmeal taffy?" said Neil.

"Don't question it," said Buzz. "This is a foreign civilization."

"I'm glad you're beginning to realize that."

"I'll be right back." Buzz went over to Sid's and got himself a cone. Neil saw that Buzz had taken off his helmet to eat it.

"You're still alive, I see," said Neil.

"Yup. It's good."

"Maybe you'll die any minute now."

"I won't die," said Buzz.

No, thought Neil, because we're already dead. But I'll keep my helmet on anyway.

After Buzz finished the cone, they went on a merry-go-round. Neil had always hated merry-go-rounds. They bored him. But this one had brass rings to grab at. Neil collected a dozen and wore them on an index finger. At the end of the ride he tossed them into a box. They made a nice clatter.

"Swell, huh?" said Buzz.

"Yeah," said Neil. He was looking at someone dressed in a papier mache head of John Foster Dulles.

They went in the Laugh-in-the-Dark, and saw evil things that glowed at them. There were strings hanging from the ceiling that brushed against them. Neil couldn't feel them because he still had his helmet on, but Buzz didn't, and he told Neil how it felt. Buzz laughed and Neil rode through with his teeth clenched. He waited for the car to tumble into a fiery crevasse. Sirens went off and unseen forces cackled. Neil felt marked for destruction.

"You know," he said, after their car had reemerged from the Laugh-in-the-Dark, "an amusement park is the perfect symbol for limitless evil, deadly peril, and like that."

"Sure," said Buzz.

"What are we doing here?"

"Having fun," said Buzz.

"Besides that," said Neil.

"I don't know. Nothing."

"That's not the way it's supposed to be. This is like *Waiting for Godot*. It bothers me."

"Forget it," said Buzz. "I want to get some cotton candy."

The afternoon passed quickly. They rode on the roller coaster. They played pinball. They walked in the sand beside the ocean. They walked out on the rocks and looked into the brown water. They watched beautiful women in bathing suits turning slowly in the sunlight. They watched animated dummies bending, beckoning, laughing, threatening. They saw lions and gorillas rolling their eyes. There were flags and whistles all over. There was a ferris wheel, a huge ferris wheel. They took a ride on it. Every car had the name of a different town painted on the front. Buzz and Neil rode in one that said K-Mar, Ohio on it. From the top of the ferris wheel they could see the entire island. They could see the whole length of Route 1. They could see the diners and the motels. They spotted their shuttle. They saw the whole forty yards of boardwalk.

The sun was going down. Neil was getting frightened again. He knew somehow that a crisis would happen when it got dark.

"The sun's going down," he said.

"Yes," said Buzz. "Maybe they'll have fireworks."

"How can we see the sun on the planet, when we couldn't see it from space?"

"Diffraction," said Buzz.

"You're crazy," said Neil. Their car came to rest, and a man opened the gate for them. They got out, and a person dressed in a papier mache head of Thomas E. Dewey handed each of them a piece of paper. They were handbills advertising a massage parlor in town.

"That's something they didn't have when I was a kid," said Buzz.

"Don't be silly." Neil knew that it was a temptation, a test of their moral character. If they went to the massage parlor, they would be damned for all eternity. They would never be allowed into Terrific Park again. Or else they wouldn't be allowed to leave it.

In the Penny Arcade, Buzz played skee ball. Neil watched. Buzz won a bunch of coupons.

"What are you going to do with these?" asked Neil.

"If you win enough, you trade them in for terrific prizes."

"Like what?"

"Like a blender or an electric frying pan."

Neil snorted. "How many do you need for a blender?"

"Thirteen thousand five hundred," said Buzz.

"How many do you have?"

Buzz smiled sadly. "I got forty-five," he said. He went to the counter and traded his coupons for a rubber snake, a plastic back scratcher, and a Chinese finger puzzle.

It was dark outside. Neil looked up timidly. He didn't want to see the sky, but his scientific curiosity made him look. He was sorry that he did. "Hey Buzz," he said in a strained voice, "look at the stars."

"What about them?"

"There's twice as many as there were in the ship last night."

"How come?"

"I don't know," said Neil.

"Let's play miniature golf," said Buzz. Neil knew that they were both dead. Apparently there was miniature golf after death. Sunday school had never even hinted at that possibility.

They played golf. Ahead of them were two teenage couples, giggling and playing slowly. The girls hit the gold balls all over the place, and they giggled. The boys tried to demonstrate their skill and ended up taking two or three strokes more than the girls every hole. They giggled, too. Neil was impatient. "Let's play through them," he said.

"What about the sixth hole?" asked Buzz.

"We'll come back to it," said Neil. He didn't like the sixth hole. They had to putt the ball through a human skull.

"Is that real?" asked Buzz.

"Of course it's real. Everything's real."

"There are twice as many stars as there should be," said Buzz.

"And a sun that shouldn't be," said Neil.

"Look." said Buzz. He was pointing to the seventh hole. There was a windmill to putt through. Buzz was already bending over his green golf ball. His putt hit one of the vanes of the windmill. He muttered a curse.

"We'll never get out of here," said Neil. They had finished playing miniature golf. They were eating hot dogs; Neil had eaten half of his before he realized that he had taken his helmet off. He was terrified. Someone with a giant head of Everett Dirksen was shaking hands with children nearby. The stars above were flickering, mocking Neil's fear.

"Sure, we will," said Buzz. "They'll throw us out at closing time."

"Closing time," said Neil. "Does Hell have a closing time?"

"Hell?"

"That's where we are. Hell. *No Exit*. A cheap Hollywood Hell. Cheap, but good enough. We'll go crazy. The tortures are subtle. An eternity of Terrific Park."

"I should have saved my coupons, then," said Buzz. "I'll be able to get the blender."

Neil gritted his teeth. He didn't answer.

Buzz led him away to a stand where plastic fish bobbed in a tank of water. Buzz gave the proprietor some tickets and picked a fish. The man looked at the number on the belly of the fish and tossed a small package at Buzz.

"What is it?" asked Neil.

"It's a mood condom," said Buzz.

"What's that?"

"I don't know." Buzz gave it to a kid, along with the back scratcher.

They walked along. Buzz was getting tired, and Neil was getting more and more anxious. He wouldn't even look up at the fireworks. The night sky frightened him.

"We're closing in five minutes," said a man in the Penny Arcade.

"Here it comes," said Neil.

"Here what comes?" asked Buzz.

"I don't know," said Neil. "Judgement day."

"They're just closing the park."

"They're closing the world," said Neil. "There isn't anything on the planet except the park."

"There's motels. There's diners."

"There's Rubbermaid, New Jersey," said Neil. "Isn't that too crazy to be true?"

"It is true, so it isn't crazy," said Buzz.

Go to hell, thought Neil. Buzz stopped by an old machine. There was a wrinkled gypsy lady fortune-teller inside. Buzz dropped a token in the slot. The gypsy lady's hand wavered above the dusty cards in the glass case. A card with Buzz's fortune on it was supposed to come out of a larger slot; nothing happened. "Ha ha," said Buzz. "I don't have a fortune."

Neil shuddered. "I'll believe that," he muttered. It was becoming unbearable. The tension was too great. Neil was so frightened that he would have done anything to be back on Earth. Still, though, he was the pilot, and he couldn't let Buzz know that he was afraid.

"The park's closing," said an old black man, sweeping the litter on the floor of the Penny Arcade.

"TERRIFIC PARK WILL CLOSE IN FIVE MINUTES. THANK YOU FOR COMING TO TERRIFIC PARK. TERRIFIC PARK WILL BE OPEN AGAIN TO-MORROW, FROM NOON UNTIL MIDNIGHT. BRING THE WHOLE FAMILY TO TERRIFIC PARK. TERRIFIC PARK WILL CLOSE IN FIVE MINUTES."

The park is closing, thought Neil. That's death.

"I guess we have to go," said Buzz.

"Sooner or later," said Neil. He was cold all over. He shuddered. He felt like he wanted to cry.

"Well, come on," said Buzz. He started walking out of the park.

"Where are we going?"

"Home," said Buzz. "The shuttle."

Neil was afraid to go back to the shuttle. He was afraid it wouldn't be there. "Let's not," he said.

"Well, where else can we go?" asked Buzz.

"A motel."

Buzz smiled. "That's a great idea! We can sleep late, and get up and eat breakfast in a diner, and everything."

"Sure," said Neil. They walked along Route 1. Neil turned and looked behind them. Terrific Park was dark. It looked like the mouth of Hell. The stores along Route 1 were dark. There was no traffic. There were no people.

"Let's stay here," said Buzz. He pointed to a motel sign. It was the Sea-Ray Motel. The *Vacancy* sign was lit. They walked up to the office. Neil looked through the screen door. Buzz opened the door and went in, and Neil followed.

"Can I help you?" asked the desk clerk. He put down a pink-spined pornographic novel.

"A room for tonight," said Buzz. "A couple of twin beds."

"Sure. Room Thirteen." He put the key on the counter.

"How much do we owe you?" asked Neil.

"Owe me?" asked the desk clerk. "You don't owe me anything. What do you mean?"

"Come on," said Neil, taking the key. He left the office, followed by Buzz. "Room Thirteen, huh?" he said. He looked at the key. Where would that key lead him, he wondered. The desk clerk—who was he? St. Peter? The motel room—their private hell, their personal eternal torment?

Neil opened the door to room Thirteen. Inside, the room smelled like artificial pine. Neil saw himself in the mirror. He was surprised. He had forgotten that he was still wearing his silver EVA suit. He looked like a spaceman. It was incongruous in the motel room.

Buzz switched on the television, but the set didn't work. "Hell," murmured Neil. "We're in Hell. That's why the television doesn't work. The telephone won't work, either. In the morning, we won't be able to leave the room."

They went to sleep easily. They were exhausted. In the morning they got up, showered, checked out, and had breakfast in the Crisis Cafe. Then they walked to the shuttle, boarded it, and lifted off.

"I'm glad to leave that place," said Neil, as they listened to an advertisement for Terrific Park on the ground to air receiver.

"Why?" asked Buzz. "We had a great time."

"Sure, but I'll be happy to get home."

"It's going to make a funny report," said Buzz.

"They'll never believe it."

"I still have my Chinese finger puzzle."

"Right," said Neil. "It wasn't all a dream." They remained in orbit for several hours. Then, during a routine check prior to leaving the sector, Buzz noticed that the water world had disappeared.

"It's gone, Neil," he said.

"You're kidding."

"Nope. The planet's not there anymore. The star is, though."

Neil went to the window. Just as Buzz had reported, the planet had vanished, and the sun blazed brightly in the black sky.

"What does it mean, Neil?"

"I wish I knew, Buzz. I wish I knew."

"I'll ask the computer."

Neil stayed at the window while Buzz worked at the problem. Neil was completely baffled. He wanted to forget the whole matter. He wanted to write it off as a paradox, or rapture of the void, and go home. He hated it when strange worlds complicated his life.

"Here's something interesting," said Buzz. "Look at these."

"What is it?" asked Neil.

"The first one is a picture of the sky taken from orbit around the water world. The second one is a picture of the night sky taken while the shuttle was on the ground. The third is a picture of the sky taken just a few minutes ago. Look. In the first one there is just a sprinkling of faint stars, as you would expect. In the second, there are twice as many stars, like we saw in Terrific Park. In the third, there is just another sprinkling of faint stars. But that sprinkling is different from the first one."

"So?"

"Look at this picture," said Buzz. "I had the computer do it for me. I had the machine do a picture of the first photo superimposed on the third. It's the same as the second."

"What does that mean?"

"It means that we're in a different part of space than we were when we were in orbit before landing on the water world. It means that we saw the stars from both parts while we were on the ground."

"I don't get it," said Neil. "How could that happen?"

"Only one way, says the computer," said Buzz. He sounded serious, like a college lecturer before a mid-term exam. "You have the water world at one end of the physical universe. Just beyond it is the curving-in-on-itself boundary. At the very farthest part of the universe, incredibly distant, all the way across, billions of billions of billions of light years away, is this star. It's at the opposite boundary of the universe. The water world is circling it. It's orbiting a star on the other side of the universe. The light from the star travels through the Einsteinian curve and falls on the planet. So does the light from these stars. On the planet itself, you get the light from its own stars plus these. Twice as many stars. See?"

Neil didn't see. "You're crazy," he said. "The computer's crazy. We're just dead, that's all. Why do you have to make a big song and dance out of it?"

"I'm not," said Buzz. He looked hurt. He took his photographs and went back to his table.

"Look, Buzz," said Neil, "I'm sorry. I was a little—"

"Terrific Park has the rides—"

"Oy," said Neil. He looked out the window. The water world had popped through the relativity curve and was now below them. The spacecraft's orbit had pushed them through ahead of the planet. Below them, the sunlight sparkled on the blue water.

"What now?" asked Neil.

"Pay one price and stay all day," said the man's voice.

"I still have eight ride tickets left," said Buzz.

No Exit, thought Neil. We're dead.

"Fun for the whole family," said the man.

Introduction to ' 'Til Human Voices Wake Us'

For the life of me, I'll never know why this didn't go right straight into DESTINIES. Quantum mechanics make this story not only possible, but likely. But be that as it may, it's here now and I'm lucky to have it—and to have Michael Swanwick say a few words about it:

'Til Human Voices Wake Us was my first sale, and as such will always have a special place in my heart. The subway-surface line exists pretty much as described in the story. I was in a trolley that caught fire midway through the tunnel under the Schuykill River, so I can testify that the evacuation scene is plausible. I was impressed by the quiet calm and courtesy of the passengers—most unexpected in city-dwellers.

Swanwick's first published work was *The Feast of Saint Janis* in NEW DIMENSIONS 11. Other sales include *Ginungagap* to TRIQUARTERLY and *Mummer Kiss* to UNIVERSE 11. *Mummer Kiss* is an extract from a novel-in-progress, tentatively entitled THE DRIFT.

If *'Til Human Voices Wake Us* is any indication, it will be a book to look forward to.

'TIL HUMAN VOICES WAKE US

Michael Swanwick

I was drowning.

My legs cramped and churning water poured over my head. I slid deep below the white surface, struggling. My movements were slowed, muted; they created small bubbles that spiraled upward. Pressure grew and became a universal roar. Water poured into my mouth.

I gasped, choked, and flung a grasping hand into the air. It clutched the side of the bed and I awoke. The apartment was silent except for the refrigerator's whine, but a sense of unease remained, a gathering tension.

"Sally?" I reached awkwardly behind me and touched her for reassurance. She had pushed the blanket aside and lay exposed to the night air. Her muscles were tensed and quivering.

I rolled over. "Honey?" Sally was lying on her stomach, wide awake and urgently noiseless. She was biting her lower lip, and her face was screwed up in childlike fear. "Sally, honey, what's the matter?" Unconsciously I started to stroke her back, the way you do to calm a cat or some other small, frightened animal.

With a choked-back sob, Sally turned and seized me in a desperate, bruising hug. She dug her face into my shoulder, shaking her head fiercely. Hot tears slid down my back.

"Sally?" And then I realized what was happening; my mind doesn't work too well when I've just awakened. "There, there," I whispered. "Take it easy." Stupid words, but all I could come up with. Then I said, "It's the aura, isn't it?"

Sally nodded, jabbing me with her chin. Meaning that she did feel the aura, the fear and nausea that precede an attack. I stroked her back and made hushing sounds.

"Take it easy," I said, speaking slowly. "It's okay. I'm here, just hold on."

She must have lain beside me for hours, feeling the aura grow, fighting it and knowing how useless the struggle was. But even with the despair that accompanies the fear, she had tried not to wake me up. Bravery takes strange forms sometimes.

A thumping came from under the bed.

Pans rattled in the cupboard.

Sally shuddered, a racking spasm that jolted her whole body. I clasped my hands behind her, then shifted my grip so that I held one of my own wrists. She gasped and her nails dug into my back. Her teeth ground together horribly. "Don't worry," I whispered, although I knew she couldn't possibly hear me. "Take it easy."

A shoe skittered across the floor.

Sally's back arched. Her arms flew wide, she jerked from side to side, and would have fallen off the bed if I hadn't been holding her. I grasped her as tightly as I could. Somewhere inside me, my private imp of the perverse noted the similarity of posture between this and lovemaking, and I grinned involuntarily—the sort of thing you pay for every time you think of it.

There was a crashing.

A pounding.

The sound of a curtain ripping.

An ashtray hit the wall, then there was a flurry of poltergeist activity that washed through my apartment like a rip tide. I heard a phonograph needle scratch across a record album. Hard.

It could have lasted any amount of time. Subjectively it was forever. Through it all I held Sally and made my idiotic soothing-and-hushing noises.

Then she went limp in my arms. She was crying. "I'm

sorry," she sobbed. And then, "I'm so sorry you had to see."

"Hey now, I'm just glad I could help." It occurred to me that I was taking a lot for granted. "If I *was* any help at all."

"You were," she whispered.

"So I got to do something for you, and now I can feel big and *macho* about it. Since when does that rate an apology?"

"I'm just sorry."

"Don't be." I changed tactics before she could ask whether she'd done much damage during the attack. "Look, get some sleep, and if you feel bad about it in the morning, we'll talk then. But right now we both need sleep." I kissed her on the forehead, big brother style. "There's nothing to feel ashamed of, and in the morning I'll fix English muffins, okay?" So help me, that was what I said.

"Okay." She smiled faintly. "You're nice." She turned her back on me and pulled up some of the blanket. I gave her more, tucking her in.

When she was asleep, I got up, lit a cigarette, and sat smoking in the dark. I had a lot to think about.

Parapsychology is a subject about which little is known and a great deal is said; epilepsy is just the opposite. Pay attention, and I'll explain.

The mechanism of an epileptic seizure is fairly well mapped. It starts with a rift in the brain, a physical gap which prevents the cells lining it from discharing properly. The charge they build up grows steadily until it's triggered by stress or fatigue or pain. Then the charge grounds itself in a sudden flash that overwhelms the brain. Result: loss of control over cerebral and motor functions.

Interestingly enough, the fissure in the brain doesn't *cause* epilepsy, but simply dictates that it will take the form of convulsions. For every convulsive epileptic there are twenty nonconvulsives, whose disease can work itself in strange ways, usually some manner of irrational behavior—anything from the trembling of an eyelid to a stabbing pain or a ten-day fugue where the victim grabs his coat, leaves the house, and reappears much later with no memory of where he's been.

Now listen carefully, because this is *gnosis,* secret knowledge, that I share with you: psychic powers and epilepsy are just two sides of the same coin, inseparable. ESP is nothing that couldn't be cleared up with a little Dilantin.

And all you zodiac followers, dream analyzers and paperback mystics should ask Sally how *she* feels about her telekinetic "gift."

I put most of this together some three years ago (unaware of the unpublished works of Drs. Scarlotti, *et al*), just in time to drop out of college a semester short of my Masters. I came to the theoretical conclusion that there was no cure for my own psychic gift (recurrent precognitive nightmares), then proved it empirically by trying to ease off of my medication. After a rather spectacular failure, I drifted awhile before coming to rest in William Penn's "greene country town"— Philadelphia. I wound up at the Institute, at first because I thought they were looking for a cure, then because it was as easy a way of earning lunch money as any.

Sometimes, though, at night (perhaps after my latest girlfriend's had a seizure), I had to wonder what I was supposed to do with the rest of my life.

I'd cleaned up the morning aftermath and was buttering the English muffins, when Sally wandered out of the bedroom and sat down at the table. "H'lo," she muttered, not looking at me.

"Good morning, good morning, and again good morning," I said brightly. I had nothing to lose; she was already in a sullen mood. I bowed and kissed her neck below the ear. She jerked away.

"Please don't."

"Okay, okay." I took a chair, projecting profound hurt and rejection. When Sally didn't notice, I swatted the newspaper on the formica table top beside her plate. "Hey!"

She jumped. "What?"

I put on my best sick puppydog face. "Oh, nothing."

Sally came around the table and hugged my head. "Awww," she said, amused, "I've hurt its feelings."

I took a nonchalant sip of coffee. "Okay, that's all I wanted; you can go back to staring at your food." Sally cradled me a moment more, then kissed the top of my head before returning to her seat.

"You're funny," she said. Her eyes intently searched my face.

"How so?"

"Underneath, you're basically a nice guy. You're thoughtful and patient and understanding." She hesitated a moment, seeking the right word. "Sweet. You're very sweet."

"Actually, I wasn't looking for a serious answer."

"But most of the time you're either frivolous and joking or else moody, intense and secretive. Any display of your true feelings has to be practically dragged out of you."

"Hey now!"

"In fact, if I didn't know you better, I'd think that you didn't give a good goddamn about anybody, including yourself. Especially yourself."

"Does this breakfast-hour Esalen lead up to some devastating point?"

"I just thought that maybe there was some problem you have that you could share with me." A rising inflection at the end of the statement made it a near-question. I was briefly tempted to tell her all my problems on a serve-you-right basis. But I controlled the impulse.

"Nonsense," I said. Or a word to that effect.

"I won't push it."

The conversation lagged for a good while.

"Going to be dropping by the Institute after work?" I asked eventually.

"Maybe. Probably." She didn't sound too enthusiastic. I commented on this. "Well," she said, "I'm getting tired of the tests, and I don't get all that much out of them."

"It's a good chance to spend time with me." I waited for a complimentary reply.

Sally stared at the wall clock. "The time! I've got to hurry."

Swallowing a mouthful of coffee barely in time to avoid giving Sally a more interesting kiss than she expected, I tagged along as she headed for the door. She rummaged in her purse, pushing toothbrush, contraceptive foam, and yesterday's panties to the bottom.

"Bye-bye," I said. "Have a nice time at work."

She paused in the doorway and looked at me worriedly. "Oh, this is such a bad idea," she said.

"What is?"

"Falling in love with you." Her voice almost broke. She fled down the stairs.

Some time later I noticed that the door was still open. I shut it.

The observation room was created by panelling off a third of the lounge that served as a behavioral lab. I arrived early to sit in the dark and stare at the joists and braces. Through the one-way mirror, the empty lab was bright, remote and unreal. Soothing. I'd had a run-in with Doctor Scarlotti the day before, and I really wasn't looking forward to today's session.

The good doctor had been running a control on a new kid, a teenaged nonentity named Stringy. All I can clearly remember of him was the way the four-tined comb stuck in his hair bobbed whenever he shifted on the couch.

Scarlotti ran the Rhine deck through a shuffling machine crisply, giving it her total attention. She was in her late fifties, with mottled skin, short hair, and an air of doctrinal intolerance. However, it was she who had first connected ESP with epilepsy. She was the one who dug out the guinea pigs from our obscure hidey-places. And it was her proposals that had wangled funding from the Feds for the project. In the scientific community, she has beaucoup brownie points.

Scarlotti hit an intercom button, filling the lab with a

flattened version of her voice. "We'll be running the Rhine test again, Thatcher. Is that all right with you?"

The kid bristled at the use of his first name. Angry eyes glared at the mirror, but he said, "Yeah, sure."

The intercom-and-headphones (in triplicate) set-up in the observation room was kind of silly, since anyone lying on the couch could hear if you spoke loudly. But it's scientific dogma that an experiment's validity increases in direct proportion to the number of machines used.

"Now, try." Scarlotti slid out the first card and glanced at it. It was a green circle.

"Blue square."

"I'll be changing cards every ten seconds. Just keep on guessing," Scarlotti told him. She released the intercom button, cutting Stringy off from our conversation, and said, "I've been meaning to have a talk with you, Calvin."

I shrugged. "Okay by me."

"I'm not at all happy with the set of dream summaries you turned in last Friday."

"Yellow waves."

"Nothing wrong with them. I mean, five may not seem like a whole lot, but the week before I gave you a dozen. It evens out."

Scarlotti was holding the earphones to one ear, so that they dangled loosely. "I understand that you and Sally have been sleeping together."

I took a deep breath. "Need I remind you, Mae, that this is the Twentieth Century? The mores of your childhood no longer apply."

"Blue waves." Stringy got the color right this time, anyhow. Scarlotti made an exasperated noise and a small mark on a pad of yellow paper.

"How long has this been going on?"

"Why do you want to know?"

"Red waves."

"What is this thing he's got about *waves*, for Chrissake?" I demanded, suddenly annoyed.

Scarlotti rapped my hand. "Shush, Calvin." She switched

on the intercom. "Thatcher, did you hear any of that?"

Stringy looked embarassed. "Uh, yeah. Just a little."

"Never mind," Scarlotti told him. "Just go on with the test." She frowned at me, and wrote 'N.V.' on the top of the legal pad, her shorthand for Not Valid. I guess I *had* been kind of noisy.

"I ask because psychic abilities do not operate in a vacuum. In your case it's especially important that I know what you do outside the Institute, because you're our only precognitive and I'm trying to test out Dunne's theory."

"The business about future memories?"

"A square of some sort. I don't know what color."

Scarlotti pushed the intercom. "Guess."

"Blue."

"Yes. So far as I've been able to determine, all your visions are of events that you later either experienced or heard about."

"So?"

"This fits right in with Dunne's ideas. A true precognitive vision would not necessarily be limited to situations of which you have direct knowledge. And it would be infallible, rather than based on faulty half-memories and later misunderstandings."

"If I recall," I said, "Dunne went on to say that these visions came from an awareness of parallel time-tracks. Each of varying probability. So that by dreaming I'd be choosing from possible futures and making one of them real."

"I don't think we need go that far yet."

"Thank you."

"Green star."

"So you can see where my line of thought is leading."

"Not really, no."

"If your visions really are a loose weaving of future memories with past and present events, I need to have a clearer idea of what your past and present actions are."

"Just what are you suggesting?"

"Green star again."

Scarlotti drummed her fingers impatiently. "That you

keep a control diary, of course.''

"No *way*, Scarlotti. My private life is my own.''

"Red waves.''

"Thank you, Thatcher.'' She hadn't looked at a card for his last two responses. I was really making garbage of the session. She sighed, gathered up the discards and put them through the shuffler again. "All right, my young friend, let's see you trigger a *petit mal*.''

There's a simple test for convulsive epilepsy. Hold a pencil between the first two fingers of each hand. Sit down and hold your arms out before you. Hyperventilate for a minute or two, then hold your breath. If you're subject to seizures at all, this will trigger a small attack, a *petit mal*, and one or both of the pencils will fall from your hands.

This is what Stringy did, only without the pencils. Scarlotti slid out the first card. A red star.

"Red star.'' His voice was blurred.

She held up another. "Blue circle.'' Right again.

A third, then a fourth and fifth. Then Stringy shook his head and looked about dazedly. I sympathized with his confusion. "Hey, man,'' he mumbled. "Don't worry about me, I'm all right.''

I trailed Scarlotti into the lab. She patted his hand clumsily. "Of course you are, Thatcher. You did very well.''

"Oh yeah. Right.'' He didn't sound convinced.

"Rest for a while, why don't you, then go to the lounge and have a coke.'' Stringy sat up and stared for a while, then shuffled away, still looking groggy. "Calvin, come into my office.''

What followed is somewhat embarrassing to relate. Scarlotti opened by demanding a day-to-day diary, and a minimum of fifteen pages of autobiography per week. I countered by offering to tell her anything that was relevant to my precognition. She lowered her demands to a diary of events with pseudonyms for anyone I wished not to identify. I offered to tell her anything that was relevant to my precognition.

At which point the conversation degenerated.

Ultimately, though, I won. After all, I was the only pre-cognitive she had.

It was my shift on the couch. Doctor Scarlotti chased me out of the observation room, noting as she did my bloodshot eyes and generally haggard appearance. "Did you have another nightmare?"

"No."

"Don't lie to me."

It was a low point in our professional relationship. I ran through the hyperventilation ritual, thinking poison thoughts.

Breathe *out*, in. *Out*, in. *Out*, in. *Out*. The world opened before me and I fell in. Ego loss. White noise made visible. A spiraling, pinnacling babel of voices. Grade B snake-pit movie sound effects, and cue up the organ to a climactic break.

Demon voices resolved themselves into the clashing of metal wheels echoing off subway walls. I found myself on a trolley on the sub-surface line, somewhere past Thirtieth Street Station where the tunnel dips below the Schuylkill River. The passengers' faces were pasty white and sluglike. One of them looked oddly familiar, but my attention was fleeting. I had no memory of how I'd gotten there, and I was filled with a sourceless fear. Fear is the main component of an aura, and I was sure I was in for a seizure. I stared out the window, trying to distract myself.

Gray concrete walls rushed by. The tunnel was a depression-era public work, and its age showed. Great dark stains mottled the walls, and occasionally water dripped down from overhead. The lights flashing by dizzied me, so I craned my neck forward, afraid that they might accidentally hit a four Hertz rhythm and trigger the seizure.

Another trolley bounced and swayed a constant distance ahead. Blue sparks crackled from the overhead power line. Alongside it the B train subway tracks running level with the

trolley tracks dipped down lower, making the tunnel seem cavernous. A chunk of the ceiling fell, spattering softly just behind the forward trolley.

The trolley lurched abruptly as the operator hit the brakes. I turned to him, puzzled, not making the connection between his actions and the soft fall ahead. His face was an ashen gray and he was staring forward, where the roof was giving way. The concrete was followed by a flow of mud, and then a sudden gout of water. More fragments of the ceiling fell. The import of what was happening finally sank in.

Staring wildly about, I caught the expressions of the other passengers: fear, incredulity, puzzlement. Somebody in the back snickered disbelievingly, thinking somehow it was all a wild joke. My attention centered on a fat-cat businessman, the type I normally despise on sight, and I thought: *He's scared witless, but he's not giving in to hysteria.* I remotely admired him for it.

The driver leaned out of his window as he reversed the trolley and let it barrel full-steam backwards. Ahead, more and larger chunks of the ceiling were falling. The trolley began moving upgrade, and for a moment it looked like we might make it. Then a spume of water hit the overhead power line. There was a tunnel-wide *flash* of blue, and all the lights went dead. The trolley coasted to a stop and the driver yanked open the front door manually. "Everybody *out*!" he yelled. "One at a time!"

We got up from our seats and milled forward. Somebody muttered "Excuse me," and somebody else said, "Quite all right." I scuffled to the steps, where the driver yanked me off and turned me away from the water, toward Thirtieth Street Station. "Run!" he told the person behind me. I ran.

The roar of water grew louder. I ran stumbling over the ties and sensed rather than heard or saw, that others were doing the same. We hadn't gone more than a hundred yards when the tunnel collapsed behind us, and a great wave of water struck.

I was slammed forward. It was cold and it hurt immensely. I was tumbled head over heels and twisted about. I lost consciousness.

I came to, not quite sure of where I was. I was lying on a couch and someone was leaning anxiously over me. I thought maybe I was in a hospital emergency room, and I wasn't sure whether it was for the tunnel disaster or I'd had a seizure in a public place.

"I'm all right," I managed to say.

"Of course you are. Do you want to talk about it?"

"No," I said. My thoughts were all in a jumble. Mangled corpses swam before my eyes, and I thought of all the people who had died. The trolley driver must have been one of them; he'd stayed behind to help.

"Of course you do." It was such a stupid statement that I had to open my eyes and see the idiot who had made it.

Scarlotti peered down at me.

"Oh," I said. "Right." So *that's* where I was. I felt dizzy and nauseous.

"You said something about trolleys, Calvin," the doctor prodded. Somewhere in the observation room, a tape recorder was taking down our words.

" 'Scuse me," I said. "Sick." I rose from the couch and ran out.

I honestly thought I was going to the john to throw up. But I went past the bathroom to the lobby, where there were pay phones. I fumbled out a quarter and dialed a number I knew.

"Shaw and Dunning," said a familiar voice. "May I help you?"

"Sally, listen. I love you! Do you hear me? I love you, I love you, I love you!"

"Cal?" There was stark amazement in her voice.

"Yes, me. You've won me over with your cruel, sardonic good looks and the rakish way you comb your moustache. See? It's me, flip and glib as hell, and I love you." This was all one spout of words. "Honey?"

"What?"

"I love you. Do you like me even a little?"

"Oh God, Cal, I've loved you for a long time." Her voice faded back and I faintly heard her say, "I don't care—go away," and, even more faintly, "Cram it up sideways." Then she was back on the line. "That was Fatty Shaw. He was ribbing me, but I don't care. Cal, why on earth did you call me at the *office* to say this?"

"I had to. I couldn't wait. I've loved you since forever and I'm just now sure of it." Doctor Scarlotti was hovering nearby, listening with frank interest. I jerked my thumb angrily and she left. The conversation settled down to a less frenetic but no less intense level.

Finally Sally said, "Cal, I can't go on talking like this. Shaw is going to rip the phone out of my hands. Why don't we meet somewhere for lunch?"

"Why don't we? I'll meet you here and you can take me away from the people in the white coats."

"Okay." Her voice was happy. "I love you."

"I love you too. More than you'll ever know."

"You've made me so very happy," she whispered. There was a click and the line went dead.

I slumped to the floor, letting the receiver dangle over me.

I was sweating and breathing heavily in adrenal aftershock. I remember thinking, *Now what the hell was* that *all about?*

Eventually I hauled myself up, went back to the labs, found a couch, and crashed.

Dreamless hours later I realized I was asleep, tried to wake up, and couldn't. I felt the vinyl ribs of the cushion dig into my back, but I couldn't open my eyes or sit up. It was like being paralyzed. When I tried to move my hand across my face, it just lay there, inert and tingling. Someone was moving about nearby; there was the scuff of shoes on carpet. I tried to speak, but my mouth wouldn't work. I concentrated on a finger, willing it to move. Nothing.

Panic rose within me. I recognized the symptoms as an aura, and I wanted desperately to wake up. I tried to move my body again, then my arm, then a finger. Body, arm, finger. Body, arm, finger. On the ninth try, I surged to my feet.

My head swam, and my ears buzzed. Someone came by, said something I couldn't make out, guided me to Scarlotti's office. I shambled in.

Scarlotti spoke and I couldn't follow what she was saying. My eyes wouldn't focus. Something about an accident. Her face was wrinkled with concern. "Do you understand?" she asked. I nodded. Something about death.

"This has to do with your research?" I asked. She seemed upset, which was odd. I wasn't used to seeing her in a flustered state.

"It has nothing to do with my research," she said. "It's Sally. She was on one of the trolleys." Her face loomed large, grew small and distant. "Don't you understand?"

Sally.

"Dead," I said.

I told you about the nonconvulsive who grabs his hat, walks out, and disappears into a week-long fugue.

I grabbed my coat and walked out.

The water under the Market Street bridge was brown and dirty. It swirled in a slow, irregular eddy. Bits of this and that floated on the surface, probably garbage from upriver rather than flotsam from the disaster. I stood with the other idlers, jockeying for a good vantage point, and tried to come to grips with my guilt.

I didn't do it, I thought. It didn't help. I wanted to howl, to tear open my flesh with my fingernails. I wanted to grovel and eat dirt. But I just stood there. Thinking of how I'd seen Sally's face among those of the trolley passengers and suppressed that knowledge.

If I'd warned her, she'd be alive now. Subconsciously I'd known; I'd phoned her, said I loved her, the way you'd drop flowers on a loved one's grave. A cheap attempt to buy off guilt. But no matter how it was rationalized, I was guilty. I turned away from the river, nauseated because I was still afraid of death, and didn't have the courage to jump.

It didn't happen, I told myself. *I don't believe in it.* And it was true; I didn't. I strained against the bridge, picturing the trolley just before the disaster. Unreal. My hands slid on the cement handrail, and I glanced down to see them red and sticky with something, maybe blood. I pushed them down harder, watched them grudgingly move further, and sure enough I felt a distant pain. "It didn't happen," I whispered, figuring that if I could deny it aloud it would cease to be. Some guy next to me glanced my way, suddenly concerned. I locked my elbows and leaned forward and screamed, "It didn't! It didn't!", unable to finish the sentence. People nearby backed away. Somebody said, "I think he's—" and I began to fall to the pavement.

The pavement fell away from me, and there was an upsurge of demon voices. I realized I was in for a bad episode, and it seemed terribly unfair. The howling grew shriller, and I was back on the trolley.

I opened my eyes. Fear mingled with an overwhelming sense of *déjà vu*. I glanced about warily, seeing the pallid, strangely familiar faces of the passengers. Sally was among them, engrossed in a newspaper, and I wondered why we weren't together. My hands gripped the seat moistly. Nausea rose, and I glanced out the window to distract myself.

Maybe I had a precognition of this, I thought. It tasted both right and wrong at the same time. Lights flashed by outside, and I shuddered and looked away, afraid that they'd accidentally hit a four Hertz rhythm and trigger a seizure. *Sally might help,* I thought, *she can keep me calm 'til the next stop and we can get off there.* I started walking down the aisle to where Sally sat.

And stopped. Because there'd been a discontinuity there. One instant I was sitting, the next, standing. But I hadn't stood. There'd been no transition.

Which meant that I was dreaming.

The trolley swayed, as if to deny my reasoning. My gorge rose and I had to clutch at a seat for support. It didn't *feel* like a dream. But as I hesitated and tried to calm my stomach, memories came flooding back. I remembered my dream, the telephone call, the seizure on the bridge, Sally's death.

I convulsively turned away from Sally. Facing her dream-image when she was dead, was more than I could handle. I fell heavily into a seat, thinking that maybe I'd stay on the trolley when the water hit, not knowing what would happen if I died in a trance state, nor especially caring.

But as I dropped onto the cracked plastic seat covers, I was suddenly filled with a deep disgust and revulsion at my helpless attitude. I don't know what caused it; maybe it came from the repetition of the same pathetic and pointless disaster. Whatever, I realized that all my life I'd let the sad events of being human grind me down. I'd always given up in the face of the facts. I'd never tried to fight back. It seemed like a sick, possibly insane attitude to me now.

I stood, reeling, determined to at least make a gesture. To at least try.

"I don't believe!" I yelled. Heads swiveled in my direction. The driver slowed. Sally opened her mouth in recognition. Before she could say anything, I screamed, "You're all figments of my imagination!" Anything to keep her from speaking.

The trolley wavered and patches of white drifted across my vision. I concentrated on the trolley again, picturing it as

clearly as I could, and it came back into focus. I pictured the
tunnel walls flashing by and slowed them, bringing the
trolley to a stop. It sounds easy, but it wasn't.

Ahead I envisioned the forward trolley, sparks shooting
from the overhead line. Behind it a piece of the ceiling fell,
tumbling slowly and ponderously. *No!* I thought/howled,
and pictured it suspended in mid-air. It stopped, but it took all
my will to contain it, and I couldn't make it disappear.
Images have a natural flow, and it's not easy to impose your
will on them. Try, for example, imagining a bull loose in a
china shop. Now imagine him running through narrow aisles
and not breaking a single fragile piece of porcelain. *That*
gives you an idea of what I was up against.

The image of the trolley grew indistinct, and I recaptured
it, smaller this time, below me, as if I stood astraddle it. The
tunnel walls shifted loosely as my attention wandered. I
looked down through a roof become transparent at doll-sized
people gaping in awe, yet somehow accepting my altered
appearance. Classic dream-logic, I suppose.

What am I going to do now? Doubt assailed me suddenly,
and I roughly shoved it aside. A corner of my mind was
churning, working out a rationalization for my actions.

Since my early teens, I'd felt guilty over my precognitive
dreams, even though I knew such guilt was irrational.
Whenever I dreamed of something bad, I'd felt responsible.
I'd never confided this with anyone because I *knew* the guilt
was based on a fallacy, the reversal of cause-and-effect.

But suppose the theory Scarlotti had so offhandedly dismissed was right. Suppose I did choose among possible
futures and make one of them real. Then my guilt was
genuine. And maybe, just maybe, I could change the past as
well as the future. Nobody really knows what lies behind
precognition anyway. It was worth a try.

I struggled to hold the images steady. It didn't work too
well; they slipped and slid away from me, as if they had wills
of their own. Casting about frantically for ideas, I decided to
play along with the dream, to make use of its unreality. To
employ dream-logic.

I pictured myself suffused with a golden radiance, tower-ing over the trolley like a god. There were appropriate gasps from below me, and the walls flickered with reflective light. I smiled. It just might work.

I lifted my hand in benign blessing, and a glory shone forth from me. *"Bless you, my children,"* I dream-said. *"I am your Dreamer, and I just came by to tell you that everything's okay. None of this is real. It never happened. It's all a dream. And you're all right, every one of you."* Which was bombas-tic nonsense, sure. But it was all spur-of-the-moment. I pictured the faces smiling, then let them fade. I slowly shifted my attention away from the images I'd been holding so rigidly in my mind, and let them dissolve, like any other dream.

The world went away, but gently this time.

A hand touched my shoulder. "And then what?"

"Hey!" I sat up reflexively; I was back on the couch. Vinyl creaked beneath me, and a hand on my chest forced me back.

"How'd I get back here?" It seemed like a reasonable question. The lab room was harshly lit and one of the fluores-cent fixtures was failing, flickering garishly.

"You never left," Scarlotti said. "You've been on the couch since I told you that Sally died."

"Sally died," I echoed flatly. So much for the almighty God of Dreams!

"Not really." A small smile quirked Scarlotti's mouth. "Do you remember me telling you I thought your precogni-tions might be based on future memories, subject to misin-terpretation and misinformation?"

"Not really? What do you mean, 'Not really'?"

"I decided the simplest test of this would be if you had a precognitive dream that didn't fit the *facts*, but did fit your future *belief* of what the facts were. If at some point you believed Sally were dead, you could well dream of her death beforehand without its necessarily coming true."

"Don't jerk me around, Scarlotti! I really want to know."

Scarlotti blissfully ignored my anger. "So when you made

your telephone call, I deduced that you'd envisioned Sally dying. I had Thatcher bring her here by taxi, and when she was safe in the lounge, I told you she'd died in a trolley accident.''

I shoved Scarlotti aside in my haste to get to the lounge. Sally was sitting at a card table, playing three-handed pinochle with Stringy when I burst in. She looked up and smiled at me. "Well!" she said. "What's the matter with *you?* ''

There's been an interesting shift in the quality of my induced-seizure visions in the year since then. More often than not, they're trivial; gone are the recurrent precognitions of disaster. A few are even positive. In one of them I had my degree, which encourages me whenever night school gets to be a bit much. And there are visions involving myself and Sally which I don't share. Scarlotti wants desperately to know about them, but I still hold that some things are personal and private.

The only trouble is that I can't accept Scarlotti's theory of memory-transference. I keep thinking how she lied to me, sent me into the most terrifying episode of my adult life and risked my sanity, all for what was basically a whim. And it doesn't wash.

It was a callous, insanely reckless thing that Scarlotti did. It's something I can't believe her capable of. Despite an occasional insensitivity she's not the type to play dice with another human being's mind.

Dammit, it just isn't like her.

What frightens me is the suspicion that I actually *did* change the past. That Sally actually died and that I made her live again. That my vivid dreams of past events create those events, and make the past over into something it wasn't before the dream. It's no harder to believe in than that a professional like Scarlotti risked my sanity on a sudden whim.

If psychic epilepsy alters reality, then Sally's telekinesis is simply a mild form taking immediate effect on nearby objects. Stringy has an even milder form; he remakes the cards into whatever he guesses.

It fits too well.

It scares me.

Sometimes I wonder how many other people have my gift. How often my world is shifted around by people who don't know what they're doing, people I don't even know.

And sometimes at night I have nightmares I never remember, and I wake up crying. Then Sally holds me and makes calming noises, until the aura fades.

Introduction to 'Acute Triangle'

Rob Chilson's novels have been released by DAW and Popular Library; his short fiction has appeared in *Galileo*, *Cosmos* and *Whispers*.

In *Acute Triangle*, Chilson expands on the old maxim: not only can money not buy love; it can't even purchase honest hatred. . . .

ACUTE TRIANGLE

Rob Chilson

It was a large room, and every square meter was occupied by a beautiful, active, bright-eyed young woman: blonde, brunette, redhead; short, tall, medium; slender, medium, full-figured. All were energetic, happy, nude. Ardley Mendoza's head spun as he followed the salesman. The girls made way for the two of them, waving or calling to them good-naturedly, turning back to their games but clearly remaining aware of their presence.

Ardley saw Eda Bergen playing badminton with two of herself and Paula Mock, serving with a characteristic frown and pout that caught his breath. Then a little rush of dancers engulfed them, nearly every one with a famous face and figure, both invariably superb. The faint, compelling *odor* of them all was pervasive.

The salesman, a Mr. Wen, led him up to a door in the transparent wall of the recroom. Three of the girls stood here, identical, tall, with platinum hair down to their hips. They swung around, stepping out of the way of the men, smiling at Wen—three identical famous dimpled smiles.

"Our latest model," said Wen proudly, patting one on the back. "Terry Louvain, Miss Teen-Luna."

Ardley felt a flash of—he didn't know what. Irritation. They smiled at Wen as if they knew him. Surely the man couldn't know all of them. Of course not. There were hundreds of them in this room, and this could only be a fraction of the company's biosomatic robots.

Inside the little office, Ardley breathed more easily as the door was closed. The crowd of beautiful, active robots was

51

still visible through the transpex wall, but the happy uproar was muted. Ardley was perversely pleased when Wen also sighed in relief. Apparently you never got used to it.

"Now, you mentioned Dorothy Dorne?" repeated the other, seating himself behind a desk so small it was more token than desk. "One of our more expensive models," he said, making no other move. "The fastest-selling biorobe in existence, available only from Unlimited Systems. Guaranteed identical to all normal tests, except in personality."

The door opened and one of the girls entered. It was Dorothy Dorne, wearing nothing but a shoulder-length wave of caramel-colored hair, lightly-tanned skin glistening faintly with perspiration. Ardley stood up automatically and she smiled Dorothy Dorne's personal, possessive smile, still breathing rapidly from her game.

Ardley Mendoza sat slowly, legs weak. It was Dorothy Dorne, yet it wasn't. Every feature was identical, and the sum total—but the air of eager friendliness was not. Dorothy Dorne was said to be a charming and friendly woman, but was always conscious that she was the queen of audiovisual record stars.

Wen produced papers and Ardley hastily signed and thumbprinted. Wen recorded the transaction and Ardley had mortgaged the next ten years of his life. He did it without a qualm.

In his aircar and homeward bound, Ardley could hardly believe he had an exact physical copy of Dorothy Dorne. It was easier to believe that he was unexpectedly playing host to the woman herself. He hardly dared to look at her for fear of offending her, and felt like a fool because he was unable to carry on an intelligent conversation.

Finally, remembering that she was just a robot and that he had contracted to pay for her, therefore owned her, he put an arm around her. He expected to be struck by lightning, but she smiled and yielded. He pulled her up and kissed her hesitantly, feeling foolish, knowing she was only a machine. Then he discovered again that she was Dorothy Dorne.

She had the body of a woman, complete but for reproductive organs and brain. Her skull, except for the jaws and nasal passages, was a zerohmic crystal, a robot brain. The acerebral (brainless) body had been cultured around it in an artificial womb. The robot had been programmed to react as nearly like a woman as was *desirable*. She could not get very ''angry'' and then only if she was reasonably certain it would hurt nobody's feelings. She was highly responsive to moods and could feel both pleasure and pain, but not hate, fear, love, anger. She could counterfeit them, but the robot brain was not complex enough by many degrees to feel emotions.

Biosomatic (live-body) robots were the product of two separate miracles. One was the miracle of biochemical engineering that blocked out the genes producing brain and reproductive organs in a tissue-sample from a given person, then cloned it around the robot brain to produce a robot with a living body of a given model. The other was the advanced zerohmitics that produced so small a complex brain and programmed it so that its responses were those of a woman. That was incredible.

Yet it had been done, with such complete success he had to remind himself it was a biosomatic robot he held. Bemused, Ardley thought that finding Dorothy Dorne cuddly was the last thing he would have expected.

''By the way, what do I call you?'' he asked.

''Whatever you wish,'' she murmured drowsily.

''It wouldn't seem right to call you anything but Dorothy.''

''Dorothy it is then.''

The Mendoza airmobile home was in a park on the Qattara Sea—Sea of Nasser before the incorporation of Egypt into Arafrica. The trip across the Mediterranean was short enough to allow Ardley to get home before his wife did. As his aircar maneuvered itself with robotic precision into the airmobile's hangar, he checked his chron. Aura could have been home by now.

Not that it mattered.

Aura Vinay's anger at Jean-Paul turned sullenly onto her

husband before the airmobile park came in sight. Living with Ardley wasn't worth it, not if he couldn't take more interest in her than he did. Jean-Paul was becoming difficult, but nothing Ardley had said or done had made it the least bit harder to see him.

If only Mendoza would get difficult, he could break the whole thing up without any trouble. He just didn't *care!*

She noticed that his car was in the hangar. She didn't feel like seeing him and hurried toward her own quarters. In the conservatory she found Dorothy Dorne.

The vision smiled brightly at her and stepped forward, extending her hand. "Hello! I'm Dorothy."

"Aura's voice returned. "I—I know, Miss Dorne. I'm Aura Vinay."

"Oh, I'm not Dorothy Dorne. I'm a biosomatic robot, Dorne model, serial number—"

"A biorobe! What are you doing here?"

"Your husband bought me." Her smile had vanished.

Aura tried twice, said, "Bought you? But he can't afford—I mean—"

Dorothy waited patiently. The questioning, creamy brown eyes, caramel-colored hair, the serious, patient expression—it *was* Dorothy Dorne. Playing some kind of joke . . .? But neither she nor her husband could ever expect to speak to the woman. No. It was a robot!

"Where is he?" she demanded at last.

Aura entered Ardley's quarters for the first time in several years, too angry to wait and see him on neutral ground. She glanced quickly, hostilely, around and her anger increased on seeing the clothes he'd bought for the robot.

"Mind telling me what this is all about?" she demanded tensely.

He looked at her curiously, with that mild, patient expression. She had never known him to lose his temper, and while he could get as impatient as anyone, phlegmatic steadiness was his identifying characteristic. She had married him knowing he was as steady as a rock, that no matter where she went or what she did, she could be almost certain he'd still be

there, unchanged. In the past twelve years he had advanced
modestly in his career—he'd had the same job, with the same
company, all that time—more out of persistence than bril-
liance.

And now this.

"I didn't know it would upset you so much," he said,
studying her reactions like she was some damn kind of bug.

"What the hell do you expect?" she whispered tensely,
feeling her face pale with anger and refraining from shouting
with an effort. "Springing this damn robot woman-fake on
me!"

"You're not interfering in *my* private life now, are you?"
he asked, voice chilling. "Don't *you* go twentieth-century
Provincial on *me*," he warned in phrases that sounded hor-
rifyingly familiar.

"Wait a minute," she said. "How much is this thing
going to cost us? God! The most expensive model on the
market! Don't tell me you eat that much raw meat."

"Dorothy's not costing you a single credit."

She dropped that. "Do you think they'll replace women?"
she asked sarcastically.

"Might," he said, unruffled.

"All right!" she said, defeated. "If you have to buy
yourself a mechanical woman, suit yourself. It doesn't surprise me much at that!"

As she reached the door, he said mildly, "If you want to
borrow her for anything—she can do anything from waiting
on table to massaging—you're welcome. I won't be wanting
her all the time."

She paused in the doorway, face working with rage, grop-
ing for something really crushing to scream at him, but her
good sense saved her. She whirled away.

In her own living quarters she activated the somninook,
flinging herself down in it petulantly when it had expanded.
Damn Ardley anyway! How was she supposed to compete
with Dorothy Dorne?

At the very least he should have consulted her. It was as
much her home as his, even if she hadn't kept up her share of

the payments. It wasn't the robot, it was having it in the airmobile. There isn't room for two women in one home, not even under free marriage. And she wasn't going to let herself be kicked out of her own home by any damn robot, not even one that looked like Dorothy Dorne.

What did a robot have that she didn't? Not a figure; since she'd had hers rebuilt, she could match any woman; face too. And that was done before she met him, so he didn't remember what she had looked like.

Ardley's insistence on calling the robot by name brought another flash of anger, the more so as she knew better than to mention it. As if it was a real woman! God! Think of him bringing a robot into her home without a comment. It was the last thing she had expected of him. Now she didn't know what to expect.

Ardley, drifting dreamily between sleep and waking in his somninook, was surprised that Dorothy didn't go to sleep sooner. Her body needed sleep as much as his own, and the brain was operating on so complex a program that the day's events would have to be played through against it every night—dreaming. But she lay heavily against him instead of on her own side. He was conscious of her billowing breasts with their cool nipples against his back, her left hand cupped around his left shoulder, her small nose in his back hair. Every time he moved, she tightened her grip on his shoulder, cuddled closer to him, and murmured sleepily. He lay as still as possible to keep from disturbing her, a strange tender protective feeling growing in him; like nothing he had ever known.

Finally he realized she wasn't going to move over to her own side, nor would she go completely to sleep. She was programmed to remain in physical contact all night; every time he moved wakefully, she would let him know that she was *there*. Even if he was asleep, he would know.

He had always disliked demanding women; he refused to be owned by any woman. Aura was bad that way. But Dorothy wasn't being possessive. On the contrary, it was his comfort she had in mind. He would never be lonely so long as she was in his bed, a strangely comforting thought for one who had always preferred to sleep alone.

She was always *there*. Aura had never been there.

The next morning he was in a fey mood, of a sort he hadn't felt for years. Aura was too self-consciously dignified for nonsense, but Dorothy responded with pure impishness. Yet she was so undemanding that when it was time to leave for work he found himself fully ready, with an unusually good breakfast inside him.

He hadn't been so happy in years. But on the way out he noticed with a frown Aura's Astrosportster. She was usually gone by this time. He hesitated, not liking to leave Dorothy alone with Aura in the airmobile. But he couldn't stay with her all the time.

Aura had simply not felt like getting up. Finally she went through her morning routine defeatedly. It was time to leave before she sat down to eat, and then she didn't feel like eating. She had had a bad night.

She met the robot in the conservatory again. It rose and smiled familiarly at her. *Enjoy yourself last night, you mechanical bitch?* she thought sourly.

"Good morning, Aura," said Dorothy. "How are you?"

Taken aback by the use of her name, Aura asked bitterly, "Do you really care how I feel?"

Her smile vanishing, Dorothy said seriously, "I am not capable of feeling any emotion, any more than any robot. I am simply programmed to counterfeit them in response to the situation."

Aura found it impossible to continue to think of her as a mere machine. "But why a robot?" she burst out softly. "Another woman I could understand, but why spend years paying for something he could get for free? What can you offer that I can't?"

"I do not know why. I have only a normal human body."

"How in the universe," Aura continued, unheeding, "can a woman compete with a machine with no private life? God,

with no *personality* even! What do I have to do, become a
robot myself? But if he wasn't satisfied, why didn't he tell
me? I'm his wife!''

Dorothy could only shake her head to such questions. Aura
continued on blindly to work, the robopilot in the Astrosportster automatically taking her above the atmosphere and going
supersonic to get her to the point on time. She found, surprised, that she had not even thought of Jean-Paul since
seeing Dorothy the first time. His existence irritated her
faintly.

Ardley Mendoza hurried home that night, both eager and
anxious. He noticed that the Astrosportster was in place as
his inexpensive submach Chevy positioned itself. Hadn't
Aura been to work at all? To his surprise she was in the
conservatory. She hadn't taken much interest in it lately.
They used to breakfast together here.

"Good afternoon," he said coolly.

She had almost smiled politely. "Good afternoon," she
said stiffly. "How did it go today?"

"Same as usual. Didn't you make it to work?"

"Oh yes. I . . . got back early, is all."

"I thought you were spending your afternoons at the south
end of the Qattara.''

"Too hot. The Alps are better, this time of year."

After a few more moments of stiff conversation, he continued on to his quarters. He wouldn't give her the satisfaction of knowing he had worried about Dorothy . . . why
didn't she terminate the contract if she was so upset? The way
she had been going on, and the way she had talked after they
were married, about neither one interfering in the other's
private life, a person would hardly have thought she'd have
cared. Of course terminating the marriage contract would
cost her two-thirds of the community property—they had the
standard "mutually revocable" rather than the "mutual con-
sent" contract. Either of them could terminate it, but
whichever one did would lose the most of the community
property.

But that wasn't what stopped her; there wasn't any property except the airmobile home. It was just that she couldn't let go of him; and not that she cared for him. She hadn't thought about him in years, he'd bet his life. She was just possessive. Well, let her buy herself a male biorobe.

Dorothy was in the dining room of his quarters, wearing a different dress than the one she had had on when he left. She had also dug up a disposable apron, the first one he'd seen in a long time. Aura had cooked a few meals on their honeymoon and served them wearing aprons. She smiled at him and he smiled back, conscious that he had smiled more today than he usually did in a week.

Eating food prepared in an unfamiliar manner, he looked across the little table and asked, "Was Aura here all day?"

"No, she left at nine oh six."

"What time did she get in?"

"A little past four-thirty."

Ardley frowned. How do you tell a robot not to let a jealous wife hurt her feelings? You don't. Yet she should be warned. "Did she speak to you?"

"I spoke to her and she answered."

"I mean, did she say anything, other than answering your greeting?"

"Oh yes," and Dorothy smiled as in pleased memory. It was impossible not to think of her as a woman; she seemed more real than Aura ever had. "She was curious about the appeal robot women have for men and also wanted to know how she could compete with me. I was unable to help her."

Ardley laughed at the ingenuous tone.

"She wanted to know, this evening, how we biorobes are programmed to please men, and I told her it was a question of responsiveness, limited only slightly by the necessary programming establishing an individual personality."

Ardley thought again of the comforting sense of her presence he had had all last night. It was a thing he had thought of frequently all day. The same curious tender protective feeling rose up in him, looking at her gentle creamy brown eyes.

He went around the table, put an arm around her and kissed

her very gently, more troubled than he could express. He couldn't warn her that she was in danger; what could she do even if warned? Perhaps he'd better terminate the contract himself.

The thought of all that she meant to him was reinforced as she leaned toward him slowly. Her weight came on him gently and she sighed as he buried his face in her hair.

Aura's voice disturbed them. "Ardley?" He jerked erect, glancing around, before realizing that the airmobile's robot monitor had made an intercom connection between them. "Ardley, are you busy?" she asked hesitantly.

"Yes I am!" he said, and the monitor, noting his tone, sounded a bell indicating that it had broken contact. Ardley looked at Dorothy sardonically. "That's the first time *she* has called *me* in years."

That Aura had expected it did not lessen her anger. Her better judgment had told her not to, but she hadn't been able to resist. The mere knowledge that he was satisfying himself in this very airmobile with a *robot* was almost enough to rouse her to frenzy. God! If that was all he wanted—it was all *it* could offer—why hadn't he just called her? She had been here all along, several nights every week for the past twelve years. God! She was his *wife!* Didn't he even know she was alive?

The difference, she concluded gloomily, was that it was a robot and she was a woman. It could be dominated completely, its self-programmed personality built around his. It—lived—only for him, was ready anytime for anything, could listen to his problems and complaints by the hour, if he wished. God!

How could any woman compete? If it was women he wanted, well, he was good-looking, interesting, reasonably affluent. He could have brought home one a night or so each week. She was not old-fashioned, she wouldn't even have noticed. The twentieth century had ended a long time ago.

Contraceptives had partly freed women. Then the artificial womb took the pains out of childbirth and biosculptury guaranteed every man and woman a beautiful face and figure. Proof of the freedom of modern society was in the negative population growth rate; deaths exceeded births.

Why, in a society where medical science and universal mobility guaranteed a beautiful woman in every bed, did Ardley need a robot?

The next morning she deliberately waited until Ardley had left for work. Dorothy immediately repaired to the conservatory. No doubt he kissed her good-bye at his door. It was a wonder he didn't flaunt her by taking her down to the hangar to kiss. Aura felt a sort of pang at the thought, remembering a time when she had kissed him good-bye in the hangar before they left for work. They had gotten out of the habit.

Entering the conservatory she noticed Dorothy bending intently over the shrubs again and felt a thrill of fear that the robot would decide to redecorate *her* conservatory.

"What are you doing to the plants?" she asked.

The robot had already learned not to smile at her. "Maintenance. Pruning and training. This one is going to die."

"See here," Aura said abruptly, "you say you can't feel any emotion. Then how can you counterfeit love?"

Dorothy said seriously, "By responding to stimuli. If the stimulus is a joke, I laugh. If it's a tale of trouble, I listen sympathetically. Physical responses are the simplest. You weren't speaking of sex, were you?"

"No."

"Very well. You see then that the only way a robot could be programmed to give love and companionship would be as responses to stimuli. Actually, it's the only way such things can be offered by any being, robotic or human. In fact, it takes a lot of creative thought really to make love. Robots are quite limited in that respect."

"Limited!" she said, startled.

It takes a lot of creative thought . . . Aura left for work, the thought circling her mind.

When Ardley, tingling with expectation, entered the conservatory on the way to his quarters, he was surprised to find Aura setting a dainty tea-table in a half-hidden nook among the bushes.

"Hello!" she said brightly. Not too much so; hesitance cooled her tone.

"Hello," he said gravely, astonished but not showing it. He looked the cozy preparations over.

"Biomorphic blackberries," she said breathlessly, indicating a dish. "Our own product. Cream, sugar. This is corn bread; the library-robot managed to dig up a recipe. Ever try any?"

He never had. And he'd forgotten all about the garden she had started one year. Something in her eyes, or tone, or stance, or all three, touched him. It had been a long time since he'd felt anything for her but resentment and hostility. "It looks very cozy," he managed.

She smiled brightly, desperately. "I just thought—a little

feast. It's been so long," she added, glancing at the nook, which he now recognized as being the same one where they had breakfasted together early in their marriage. She had retained it through all the changes in the conservatory. "And I—we don't see each other much any more . . ."

That was a mistake. He nodded curtly. But when he spoke, his voice was mild, if toneless. "I'll shower and change and be right up."

He walked away, expecting her to call after him to make sure he would come back, almost looking forward to it so he could whirl on her angrily.

Aura stood in an agony, fists clenched, trying to hold back tears, longing to call after him. But there was nothing she could say and her sense of personal dignity was too great to—to *beg* him to stay. When he had gone she sat down and cried for several seconds. But there was a small chance he'd be back, even if only for a little while. She instructed the monitor to alert her the instant he left his quarters.

Dorothy met him, smiling brightly. Her eager interest, her desire only to serve him, pulled at him. Up in the conservatory Aura was waiting; here Dorothy hung shyly on his mood. He felt torn, and his anger at Aura increased.

He explained briefly to Dorothy, noticing how her smile faded, hugged her to ease the hurt, and hurried through his shower.

Aura's black eyes were reddened, but she smiled tremulously at him. *Damn* having two women pulling at him! Why didn't she just go? It would be more dignified, and she wouldn't be losing anything she had valued. But that was not hard to answer. It was a question of territory; the airmobile—and himself—were hers, and God help anything that trespasses on a woman's property.

"We have a section of strawberries, did you know?" she chattered with desperate gaiety as he seated himself. "They're bright yellow, but they taste good, or will when they're ripe. I'd almost forgotten about them."

He managed to dredge up a memory of reading about yellow strawberries. He repeated some of what he'd read and they chatted for awhile about gardening with forced interest. He breathed easier as the little feast proceeded, feeling a trickle of gratitude to her for making it easy.

Then the little tête-à-tête was over and he came to his feet with a feeling of relief. She also rose quickly, touching his arm, searching his face anxiously. Just like Dorothy.

"You're not going, are you? I thought—I mean, I hoped you'd come and see me—just for a little while."

"If you don't mind," he said coldly.

"Ardley, please. Have you stopped to think where this will lead you?"

"Say nothing against Dorothy," he warned her grimly.

"Dorothy?" she asked. Looking at him steadily, she said, "There's nothing to say. She's a robot. I'm not even jealous. Because that's all she is—a robot. She's magnificently designed to do *one* thing, and do it well, but that's all. Is that the foundation you'd rest your life on?"

"As far as being a robot is concerned, you'd do better to look at yourself," he said brutally, scowling. "As long as you're happy, things are fine. You object to Dorothy not because of what she is—thousands of biorobes were sold without bringing a comment from you—but because she has entered *your* life. Well, she hasn't. She's a part of *my* life. She's the only person I ever met who thought of me as a person rather than a thing. She's less a robot than you."

Aura heard him out, face as white as ivory. "Ardley, Ardley, don't you see it?" she cried softly. "You're withdrawing into a private universe where you are the center of events. You can't live like that! What will happen when everybody buys themselves a robot instead of cultivating their acquaintances?"

"Why didn't you think of some of this a long time ago?" he asked. "My God, how many times I've tried to talk to you and been told you were busy! You should've been doing some cultivating yourself, or maybe you *were*? And how many times you've said yes, then steered me through your bed back to the door! When did you ever listen?"

She was crying openly now, and her voice, though almost

inaudible, was steady. "I know, I know. God! I've seen my mistakes all too clearly. I've done a lot of thinking these past two days. We can't go on like this."

"I've already quit," he told her evenly, no sign of repentance in his face or voice. "Now if you'll excuse me . . ."

"Wait!" she cried, stepping in front of him.

"Step aside, please." He gestured her aside, but she stepped in front of him again. He put out an arm, irritatedly, and brushed her aside, but she caught it and stepped in front of him again, black eyes pleading.

"Please, Ardley! At least give me a chance!"

He seized her and shook her until her teeth rattled, feeling a little glow of justifiable pleasure. It was something he'd wanted to do for a long time. Let that show her.

Amazingly, she was still in front of him, black eyes defiant, angry; still crying. "This is your last chance," she told him. "Go down to her now and it's all over between us!"

The emotion that came then was anger; it flashed like an electric arc and he stepped forward, hands extended. She whirled away from him and ran. Without looking back, he strode blackly out of the conservatory and down the corridor.

Over between them! It had been over for years. He nursed his anger, cursing her for not having sense enough to end it gracefully. He had always hated such scenes. Should have ended it a long time ago, he thought, long-suppressed anger surging in him.

He braced himself to explain to Dorothy, but she asked no questions. He buried his face in her neck for comfort, trembling with the emotions Aura had raised. Dorothy eased them both deftly onto a lounger, sliding his head down to her shoulder. He relaxed, sliding down farther, felt her fumble beside his head, and her dress split open from neck to knee. She cradled his head wordlessly on her warm breast as his trembling eased.

He felt a warm sense of gratitude that brought a stinging to his eyes. He had never known a woman like her! He was well out of it, he thought.

After a long, dreamy interval, he raised his head up to her shoulder, having to speak.

"She'll be gone soon," he said.

"Aura?"

"Yes. It was pretty ghastly, but it had to come. I'm glad it's over with."

She murmured something soothing and tried to ease his head back down. He resisted and she stopped.

"We'll be a lot better off without her. We can go swimming and play court sports without her watching."

"I need the exercise. I'm getting rusty, just sitting around."

"I was worried about you all the time she was here. She always was a hellbird when anything threatened *her* prerogatives."

He turned over and felt her cheek against the top of his head. Catching sight of her breast half-revealed under her open dress, he slipped one hand around it. She took a deep breath, filling his palm.

He let his hand drift down to her thigh and she raised her leg. Then back to her breast and again she filled his hand delightfully. Shifting his position, he felt her instantly and automatically shift hers to accommodate the changed weight. He smiled at her and she smiled back, brown eyes arch.

They stood up and she dropped the dress, under which she wore nothing. He stood admiring her while she unsealed his tunic, one arm around her. Putting his hand on her hip, he pressed lightly, and she stepped closer to him, pressing herself lightly against him, still dealing deftly with his tunic. A slight pressure of the other hand against the short ribs sent her back a pace. She filled his hand again, by leaning forward this time.

It was like putting a very well-trained dog or horse through its paces; such precise, automatic, instantaneous responses. A dog or a machine. A robot.

He chilled to the realization. She was a robot, mass-produced, carefully designed to be the maximally alluring sexual machine ingenuity could devise. But as a companion, an understanding companion—he looked into creamy brown eyes, clouded now by slight puzzlement. There was no one there.

Dorothy looked up at him puzzledly as he looked blankly down, searching his face anxiously for a clue to what he was thinking. Ardley had a sudden vision of the robot brain behind the human-appearing eyes searching through data with inhuman, lightning speed, trying with all its fantastic mental powers to understand him, one ordinary human being. Trying—and failing.

Analyzing data, flicking swiftly through its subprograms—*searching for the proper response*.

Aura was right, he thought, staring weightlessly at the biorobot. The memory of her defiant black eyes, swimming in tears, came back forcefully to him. She was the real woman, not the cowlike robot that stood puzzledly in front of him. She hadn't stepped aside for him at a gesture, the way a robot would.

You don't just brush human beings aside, he thought in growing horror. They had drifted apart, yes, but they had once been close. She might not be blameless—but who was? Their whole society was permeated with the philosophy of finding them and forgetting them. Life was one long party.

But was everybody as lonely as he had been? Was Aura?

At the thought, he started for the door, but he caught sight of the robot standing patiently, waiting. "Sit down," he said. "Stay here." It was as automatic as telling an aircar to turn itself off and lock up.

"Aura!" he called. His voice activated the robot monitor, but she did not answer. "Aura! Aura!" She still had not answered as he came in sight of her door.

"Attempting to make contact," the robot informed him tonelessly.

"What?" He had approached the door, which slid open

for him. Startled, he went in. A quick search revealed her empty closets, an occasional article left behind.

It was all over.

"Where is she?" he asked.

"Aura Vinay," said the robot deliberately, "filed termination of her marriage contract with Ardley Mendoza, this date, relinquishing all claims on him, personal, private, public, and of credit. Accordingly, she has removed her belonging from your airmobile, and is now in flight somewhere to the northeast of here, at supersonic speeds. One moment. Contact."

"Aura!" he cried hoarsely.

After an agonizing moment, she replied muffledly: "What do you want?"

He took a long, deep breath, formulating his desires into words. "I want—" his voice broke and he let his breath out. "I want to start over," he said steadily, voice under tight control. "How about a date—say, tomorrow night?"

She caught her breath and he tensed in despair at the laughter. Then he realized she was weeping.

Introduction to 'Nothing But'

J.A. Lawrence, the widow of the late James Blish, lives in Athens, Greece with her two children. Her work has previously appeared in most of the major science fiction magazines.

Her story, *Nothing But,* perfectly illustrates Thoreau's claim that a man who made a practice of speaking only the truth would be unable to walk down the street without being knocked down as a Common Enemy. Honesty may be the best policy, but in this most imperfect world, sometimes being the best may not be the brightest . . . .

NOTHING BUT

J. A. Lawrence

"Where are we?"

"Who knows?" Joe shrugged his squat shoulders and looked around.

There was only the ice. As far as electronically-augmented visual devices could perceive, there stretched the flat white plain of glistening ice. The wreckage of the copter threw stark shadows across our own. Joe took off his helmet.

"What the hell, you damn fool!"

"I see you talking but I can't hear a word." He smiled. His voice was faint through the layers of insulation around my ears. He unhooked the polarized eyeshield from his helmet and strapped it clumsily on his head. He went on talking, with a grin pasted over his grimy teeth. I was grateful. His sounds were weak enough to ignore.

As soon as I'd realized we were going to crash I'd begun thinking. We were going to be alone together on the ice sheet until help came, or we died. For the long few minutes as we came down I had been considering that. I hoped I would not kill Joe before the cold got us.

Now he'd forestalled me. No helmet, no Joe. Not for long. Not in this atmosphere, where the oxygen was just on the borderline of absence.

It didn't matter. I had other things to think about.

I turned back to the machine sprawled like a blackened bird skeleton on the whiteness. Check oxygen supplies. Good. Water. Purifier. Rope. Tools: axe, saw, knives. Should we shelter alongside the wreck, or move out across the glacier to set up the ground-to-air signal? If a search copter came far enough past the scree, they might see the wreck even in its shadow; but out on that white expanse they would be bound to see a suited man. Two.

Joe tapped on my helmet. He pointed at the broken bulk of the supply locker and started towards it. Heat coils in his boots melted the ice underfoot. He left a slimy trail.

My partner Kana was off in the southern hemisphere digging up some goddam thing in the tundra. Joe's Huzuni was doing core samples in the mountains east. That left me and Joe to measure and inspect the ice cap. Understaffed, said Captain Aaron. Overstaffed by one, said I.

You may have deduced that I didn't like Joe. I could tell you he had done something unforgivably dreadful to me. He hadn't. He never did anything to offend anyone—just ask him. He had scrupulously moral rules of conduct. Always tell the truth, for example. Well, you can't fault that, can you? It just seemed to work out that everybody *used* to be friends with him. Poor Joe. He found people, ordinary people like us, bafflingly immoral. People covered things up. People were mysteriously unwilling to give a strict accounting of the use they made of equipment, such as sanitary paper—which he took to be his responsibility. People—like me—took unaccountable dislikes to him.

And all he wanted was a little appreciation, a little friendliness, a little honesty from his, er, friends. It would be nice to be admired; he did try so hard for conscientiousness, trustworthiness, honesty, probity and so on.

He even had a knack for turning out a decent meal from ship's rations. You'd think that would win friends and influence people, but the idea of his fat fiddly fingers mingling with my food turned my stomach, and for a long time only Huzuni looked forward to his Escoffier mood. He quit, finally. I can't say that prepacked concentrates are delicious, but at least they're *clean*.

In his search for approval, Joe explained himself. Continuously. He thought you ought to know how he, morally, saw the situation that was creating him a new enemy. He hadn't made a pass at Kana, for instance, until he had sensed that she seemed to need it very badly. He'd been so sorry for her. She had really needed to be cheered up. He mentioned this to me during the week when she and I were patching up our first real quarrel. I hadn't known about that pass until Joe took me aside, and very, very seriously apologized for intruding into our relationship, hoped that Kana was feeling better now, and he never would have dreamed of approaching her if she hadn't—

"Are you trying to make trouble?" I asked him blandly. I knew all about that, I lied.

Then there was a long story about his own troubles with Huzini, so he'd naturally felt sympathetic to Kana when she was so, er, unhappy . . .

I left him to it. He was still truthtelling when I walked out. Kan and I have a strong bonding, so he didn't do any real harm. Not enough doubt to be a cloud, really, just a wisp. I wished she were more on guard. Her trust of him made me uneasy.

Huzini was a year or so older than I, creeping up on forty: A gentle person whose psychic scars showed; scholarly, reclusive and thoroughly vulnerable to the blank blue eyes and ingratiating grin.

Joe swung his legs out of the ship, and slipped on the ice. One has a reflex to catch a falling fellow-being. It takes conscious effort to stop, think, let him fall, I hope he breaks his head. I was halfway toward him when he caught hold of a clawlike strut and got his balance.

He grinned. The white ice furred his head, and the crystals of his breath flowed continuously down his chin. Behind the goggles his eyes glinted.

I wondered how he was still breathing. Although the CO_2 had frozen out of the atmosphere, it still wasn't healthy. Air at -70° is not sufficiently warmed by passage through the nose to be comforting to the old lungs. But he showed no sign of agony. More's the pity.

I decided to start moving. The fluorescence of the suits would be more likely to attract the copter than the shadows of the moraine; and our X-mark would be far more visible. I began packing the survival kit. Batteries. Air-pack filters. Oxy-boosters. First-aid kit. Tent, two-man (hell). Powered sleeping bag. Extra heatshoe packs. Food. Drink. Fire. Signals. That was it. I began walking.

He ran after me, distress written all over what I could see of his face. He shouted. I shrugged. His noise went in one filter and out another, leaving a plaintive residue.

He mouthed, "Air's okay." I shrugged. He mouthed, "Are you still mad at me?" I shrugged. He mouthed, "We have to stick together." I shrugged, but he knew I heard him. I saw him sigh.

I walked, out into the blankness of the ice. He, presumably, scrambled together his own kit and before long, damn his strong legs, he was plodding along beside me. I quickened my pace: my air was easy. He showed signs of panting. And he had brought his helmet. So much for his heroics.

We camped about fifteen kilometers from the crash. There was nothing there, no rocks, no bergs, no slides, no crevasses. Just the white ice and the wind. The tent was cozy enough, if only I'd been alone, or with Kan; but the walls moved in and out with the fast-moving air.

There were sun-dogs as the light dropped; a bigamous engagement ring, with a diamond on each side, around the primary. I melted a large X-sign in the ice, and threw dye into the liquid quickly, so that it refroze in color. There wasn't much else to do but eat and sleep. I rolled up as far as I could in the one-meter space from the foul sweet smell of Joe.

Most of us working this trip on the *Boreas* had worked together before. We'd all been in the trade for years, since we qualified, signing on to the explorer ships that went out to open planets for trade, and bring supplies to the colonies. It was a good life; new places, familiar faces. If you weren't the type to settle, or your plans had miscarried, there was plenty of work for good crewmen and planetary scientists. Our crew was a good solid experienced group.

Joe was new. He was still, even after three years, fresh out of Space School. We hadn't heard much about him in the

ports; in fact, his reputation was curiously neutral. Most times word gets around—so-and-so is a menace to unprotected females, but terrific in a bad spot; whatsisname can get more fuel out of the tanks than they put in (*he's* in great demand); or thingamajig is good on short trips but doesn't wear well on the long hauls. All we heard about Joe was that he was a competent geologist. Nothing personal.

We all knew about Huzuni, of course. Word gets around. The planet Ubaraka had been colonized a generation back, a sweet little fertile world in Orion. Nobody had known about the hospital transport that had crashed in the hills there, when the psychotic patients had overpowered their keepers and hijacked the ship. Nobody knew about that other colony, where the strongest and most savage survivors were living in the caves of Ubaraka. Huzuni's family had died unpleasantly in the massacre. Huzuni alone had escaped, and hidden for five months until a cargo ship landed with supplies for the colony, and picked up the lone and shattered kid. The subject was closed. We didn't bring it up with Huzuni.

Joe didn't understand "closed". Like a homing pigeon he homed in on the closed subjects, prying and delving— sympathetically, of course—in the interests of truth.

Huzuni had fallen against me in the corridor, shaking and incoherent. In my cabin, very very slowly between chattering teeth, the story emerged. The trap had been set, and Huzuni had sprung it, and had taken the name of "Grief". Orders had been clear enough, no wandering alone away from the encampment. Adolescence had brought a yearning for solitude, for walking in the forest, away from familiar faces. An unfamiliar face had appeared one day, and asking no questions, Huzuni had accepted the new friend, and chatted. Many times. His colleagues had learned all about the colony's routines, guard-patterns . . .

For twenty-six lonely years Huzuni had faced the sorrow and the guilt of survival. But it had not before been so clear that Huzuni had set the trap as well as sprung it; that had orders been obeyed, no new friend would have occurred and betrayed. Joe had made no accusations. He merely felt that facing the truth, the whole truth, was best. How long would it take Huzuni now to live with the guilt of murder? Good old Joe.

Captain Aaron had no tragedies in his life. New Israel was stable, industrialized, successful. Its universities and commerce were among the best in the system. Aaron had proceeded soberly and steadily through his schooling, through the Space Academy, into the service, apprenticeship and smoothly into captaincy. No anomalies appeared on his records. He performed his duties methodically and with confidence. He had earned his position, unobtrusively.

Until Joe very casually remarked that it had been lucky for Aaron that his father had been Commodore Richter's cousin, Aaron had never thought of his command as a result of pull. He'd met the Commodore, of course, at graduation, and later his father had introduced him. That was all. Now, with Joe's help, he remembered "Flash" Jordan, the whizkid of the Academy, who had inexplicably failed to achieve a captaincy when he graduated with highest honors in Aaron's year. There had been no ship available. Aaron had not heard that Jordan had turned to drinking.

The Captain's hands seemed to move a little less decisively after that. There was a shade of new hesitation when he gave orders.

In the morning the sheet of ice was gone. There was air in motion filled with ice crystals, also in motion. No copter was going to find us through that. I had, of course, made the wrong decision. We should have stayed in the shelter of the scree and relied on our flares.

The two-man tent was intolerably intimate. My feet were growing chilled; Joe had the thermostat down. I replaced the weak heat coil pack in my boots. My toes felt pins and needles. That was all to the good. The storm continued. I peered through the opaque wind, hoping.

"You're making me nervous," said Joe, squatting motionless in the tent. "In and out all the time. Can't you sit still?"

"Shut up," I said; I'd have to wait a little longer for the temperature in the tent to rise.

"I don't mean to question your decision, Blake, not at all, but I wonder—"

That was all. I went out of the tent, closing myself firmly into the isolation of my suit and turned off the communicator.

Silence. Blessed silence. Peace.

Joe hadn't mentioned the crash . . . until now. The conversation immediately preceding it was hacked into my memory, word by word . . .

"You're a funny guy, Blake."

"Mm." I was adjusting the altitude control; we were a few meters too low for the upcoming moraine.

"Most people your age are at least lieutenants. Unless they settled down, raised families."

"So?" My plans to settle had collapsed with my marriage many years ago. I liked my work.

"So nothing, I guess. Just seems sort of unfair to Kana."

"Kana's a grown woman. I'm a grown man. Mind your own business."

"Sure, Blake. I guess a lot of people give up when they grow up. I mean—"

My hand slipped. Of course I'd outgrown any ambition to have my own ship, my own home . . . there was a taste of vomit in my throat, and my hand slipped. So we crashed.

The blessed silence. I couldn't hear the wind, and the ice beat against me with serene disdain. The vicious little spicules slamming against my faceplate were friendly, my feet were warm, and I'd be damned if I'd spend another hour cooped up in a one-meter tent with that son of a bitch.

I walked calmly through the ice.

I was embedded in ice. I was hard and bitter; I was ice. Something struck heavily and I shattered into sharp pointed swords which sprang up and pierced the groin arching over me. 'Twas heaven, and heaven bled freely. I froze blood into a scarlet fountain before it destroyed my brittle skin, I reached deep into the frozen core. I was a monocellular surface over the heaving of live black water. Eyes rolled like blue marbles through my teeth.

Kana plopped beside me and we rotted deliciously. Our seeds rolled from the black pulp of old flesh and mingled and fought for space, for water hidden below. Our roots crept through the rich soil that we had been, and met, and throttled one another in thirst. We drank sun, ate earth. I spat out sun and burnt him, hair by hair.

I hammered wind with my wings and screamed. I gathered myself into an updraft and glided down again to land on his belly. I tore it with my fingernails; his skins were hard to rip. I had to use my beak. He lay passively pumping blood into the ice while I drank thirstily. I tore out his throat, and spat out the poison glands.

He died a thousand times of a thousand natural causes. He gnawed feebly with the rat-teeth of morality as I slew him. I was a natural cause, an act of God, and smote him in his pride.

I was a woman in his bed. I smiled and smiled but neglected to tell him the truth. The sharp fangs of my vagina clamped down hard and while he screamed I sang a lullaby and sheathed my sword.

I flung out a casual hand and scattered fire. I was all fire, I could not contain the burning. I threw fire like seed corn out of myself, in a joy of im/explosion and flicked the rolling neatnesses of planets into life. I was life, and gave it and took it away and I myself shall never die. I shall grow and grow and be a mystery; and burn the skins of truths to cinders.

I was in a fetid tent without my helmet and I could not move. My feet were ice and my chest was flame. A black furred face dropped out of the sky and vanished.

Huzuni, tearless, said, he is destroying me. But I have nothing else. I am dead, Blake, I have been dead for a thousand thousand years, but he pretended I could be alive again. He is a liar. Or everything is.

Unintelligible sounds. "Joe," I said, and could not hear my voice. He heard. Desperate blue marbles stared, embedded in black fur.

Water dripped into my teeth. There were two of them. Joe and the alien. The ice-dweller. I had been sick for eight days and they murmured in a language I did not know. The alien had no voice.

"You have had wicked dreams," said Joe reproachfully. "You are a very strange person, Blake. I can't understand you. I can't understand any of you, not even Huzuni . . . Funny. I don't have any trouble understanding Marath. Right away, we understood each other."

"What happened to me?" I said.

Joe shrugged. "You went out on the ice in the storm. You got cold—the shoes gave out. Marath found you and brought you here."

"Who?" I stared blurrily at the motionless black figure squatting at the tent flap.

"Marath. He lives here. He came by when you were out on the ice, and brought you here," said Joe patiently. "But I don't think he likes you, Blake, be careful."

The furred face stared at me impassively.

"You said some funny things while you were feverish. I couldn't understand most of it, but he kept growling. He understands a lot."

"What is he, a mind-reader?"

"I don't know. Maybe."

"But he likes you."

A glowing smile spread over Joe's flat features. "Yes."

"You make a charming couple." The smile faded.

"I told you. He understands me. And he can't *lie*."

I thought about that. "I guess not, if he's a telepath. Is he alone?"

"Of course not. You can't be understanding all alone. This is his people's world, Blake."

I eyed the creature uneasily. There were rules about inhabited planets.

"Does he—they—want to trade?"

"No. They don't want anything. Just—go away." Joe was squatting alongside the creature. Telepaths. I supposed it was better than trying to shout in this air. I heard shouts.

Kana pushed between Joe and Marath and came straight to me. "Are you all right? We couldn't get through the storm, everything was out. Darling, you look like hell."

It isn't what you say, it's how you say it. No doubt it was true, but it still sounded sweet to my ears.

Joe leaned toward her. Marath had blended himself—? herself? itself?—into the tent wall.

"Out, Joe," said Kana. "Can you get up, Blake?"

I struggled, dizzy and feeble, and clung to her arm. I told myself that the warmth was from the suit, not from her eyes, transmitted through layers of artificial skin. My feet were half numb and half agony. We staggered out.

Joe declined to return to the ship. He wanted to stay with his new friend. I offered thanks for the rescue, and hoped Marath believed me. It was true enough. They watched us take off, standing close together, silently.

We had a conference: the dropout, the murderer, the wire-puller and the nymphomaniac. Ordinary people.

"Telepaths are hell to do business with," I offered.

"There isn't much here worth the trouble of digging for," said Huzuni.

"We have to take Joe's word for it that they don't want anything to do with us," said Kana. "They don't appear to care to speak to anyone else."

There was a long silence.

"Are you thinking what I'm thinking?" said Kana softly.

"The human race has never been up to Joe's standards," I said.

"Maybe he's found his niche," murmured Huzuni.

"He even likes the air," I said helplessly.

"I think—" began the captain, drumming his fingers, "I wonder—it wouldn't be a lie, exactly. We could simply suggest that, er, this planet—"

"Proscribed," said three voices.

"Er. Exactly."

Huzuni said, "Joe won't let us get away with it."

"We'd better go talk to him," said Aaron, heavily.

Joe stared at us for several minutes. "Oh," he said finally. "I'd forgotten. Words. Lies. Go away, all of you, you and your word games. We don't want you here. We don't like you."

The furred creatures gathered close around him; there was a low growling. We went.

We watched the planet dwindle away below. Kana whispered, "Blake, what he said about me, there was nothing in it."

I grinned. It was nice to be home again.

Introduction to 'Parasites Lost'

Charles Sheffield is almost too accomplished to be taken lightly. President of the American Astronautical Society, Vice President of the Earth Satellite Corporation, and author of some of the best high-tech science fiction in recent years as typified by VECTORS, SIGHT OF PROTEUS and THE WEB BETWEEN THE WORLDS, one gets the feeling that his every word should be approached with grim determination, every rivet on the rocket counted and every equation double-checked by hand. But that won't work with *Parasites Lost*. Sheffield himself explains why:

Parasites Lost [*is*] *the seventh story in the Henry Carver/ Waldo Burmeister series—what I have come to think of as my 'sewage series'. The others are* Marconi, Mattin, Maxwell; The Deimos Plague; Perfectly Safe, Nothing To Worry About; A Certain Place in History; Dinsdale Dissents; *and* The Dalmatian of Faust. *Although many stories are written from the heart, I think this set is more likely to have been written from the bowels. It is my impression that science fiction takes itself too seriously, a fault which these stories seek to correct.*

PARASITES LOST

Charles Sheffield

You can tell that this hospital was set up for VIP's. There's a terminal right next to my bed, and an output display in the ceiling. For four years I've been wondering what Central Data kept in their files about me, and now I finally found out. Look at this claptrap. It's enough to make a grown man weep:

CARVER, Henry Vercingetorix. Born, March 24th, 1998. Educated, Natcher Academy; Stanford (B.A. History); Cornell (LL.B.). Clearance: D-5. See also separate codewords, as follows: Mattin Link Development (S); Horstmann Fissure Descent (S); Deimos Dancer Vaccine Shipment (S); Pintonite Discovery; Deepdome Disaster (S); Kaneelian Warp Transfer (S); Molson Colony.

I don't really care what *personal* data they have in the files. I've had a look at what Central Data says about President Dinsdale, and as one of the oldtimers pointed out, we are all as God made us, and most of us a great deal worse.

No, what frightens me is that string of official codewords. See that letter *"S"* after most of the entries? That stands for Sole Survivor.

Scan the list and you'd jump to two conclusions: that I seek out dangerous situations, and that I survive them. I can't deny the latter—look at my alternative—but I never, never go near danger if I can avoid it.

So, how does it happen that I became involved with Operation Galatea, an enterprise that will not figure in the computer's list of daring deeds, although it was the one that brought me to this hospital?

That is a fair question.

Back in my distant college days, I chose the legal profession as one suited to a man strong in mind and memory, weak in mathematical aptitude, fond of a high standard of living, and appalled by all prospects of physical danger. My business partner and I share the view that the good life is also the quiet life. Our offices in Tycho City, comfortably but not palatially furnished, emphasize a restrained decor and those massive volumes of legal lore that are often erroneously coupled in a client's mind with legal competence.

The kitchen is behind the main office. I was in there, masterminding the elderflower fritters whose cost would carry our joint bank balance to zero, when I heard the first hint of trouble.

". . . Henry Carver, and as soon as possible," said a harsh voice. It sounded like a badly-trained parrot.

Waldo muttered some inaudible reply in the outer office. He knew I was cooking, and he wouldn't let it be interrupted for anything less than a guaranteed major client.

"That's out of the question," replied the persistent visitor. "Mr. Munsen would never permit it."

That brought me out of the kitchen so fast that a storm of elderflower petals blew along behind me, drifting slowly downwards in the light lunar gravity. Munsen was one name that grabbed my instant attention.

Waldo was standing up, so the visitor was almost hidden behind his substantial form. I peered past the vast area of pinstripe and saw a small, wizened man—a monkey rather than a parrot. He had long, brown hair, wore a tight brown suit with matching cravat, and carried an Infokit in his left hand. There was, thank Heaven, no sign of Imre Munsen. I relaxed a fraction.

"This is Mr. Carver now," said Waldo in an annoyed tone. He knew the effects this would have on dinner.

There was a pause, while I became the subject of a close inspection.

"*This* is Henry Carver?" said the little man at last. "*You* are Henry Carver?"

I didn't care for the incredulity in that strident voice. I nodded curtly.

"The Henry Carver who flew the *Deimos Dancer* solo from Earth to Mars? The man who cracked the Deepdome mystery? Who mastered the Kaneelian Space Warp?"

"I am, sir." My tone was brisk. If I didn't stop him, he'd probably go on all day. "Why is that of interest to you?"

I saw Waldo wince. My manner had been cold—but not, I felt, without some provocation.

"This is Sandy Lasker," said Waldo, before I could speak further. He rolled his eyes at me. "*Miss* Lasker says she is here to brief us both."

Well, I mean to say. If people will dress like that and have voices like a Callistan mynah bird, mistakes are bound to happen. Our visitor was now looking at me with undisguised hatred.

"Brief us?" I said, avoiding her eye. "On what?"

"On protozoan and microfilarial endo-parasites."

"Parasites?" I said intelligently, repeating the word I had understood.

"*Endo*-parasites," she corrected me. "Internal parasites."

She placed the Infokit on the desk in front of her. "It was my understanding that Commander Munsen would give you all the background on this. I am supposed to have you fully briefed and all ready to go down to Earth in six days—though I don't see how we can ever cover all the material that you'll need."

"Need for what?"

"For Operation Galatea."

It would be an overstatement to say that I was pleased to see Imre Munsen as he ducked in through the doorway behind her. He was a man I'd be quite happy never to see again. But there were certainly things that needed explaining. I hadn't been down to Earth for years, and for all I knew they were still looking for me there.

"Hello, Henry," said Munsen affably. "Sorry I was held up."

He hadn't changed a bit since that last ghastly meeting after Deepdome. Still improbably blond, huge, jutting-jawed and steely-eyed—why he bothered with System Security work, when he could have made his fortune in holovision productions, was a mystery.

He looked around him at our legal offices, frowning at the cramped quarters. Space was running ten lunar dollars a square foot in Tycho, and we hadn't seen a sign of a client since Pritchard, the suspected poisoner. We'd worked hard on that case—and we'd have got him acquitted, too, if he hadn't weakened his defense by spiking the judge's water carafe with trinstine extract. After it was all over we'd been forced to pay court costs as well as the emergency medical expenses.

And still people talk about lawyers making too much money!

"Bit cramped in here," said Munsen, and he walked on past me into the kitchen, where the blackened remnants of elderflower fritters now lay like dead insects on the top of the hotplate.

"This'll do us better," he said. "Miss Lasker, I need five minutes alone with Mr. Carver and Mr. Burmeister, then they're all yours."

He closed the door on her glowering face and turned confidingly to me and Waldo. "I'm late because I've just come from another meeting with President Dinsdale. He agrees with my evaluation, you two are the best possible choice for this job. I know you, Henry—" he held up an apologetic hand "—and I'll say it for you. This job won't have the danger to appeal to you. But you'll be playing a key part in our economic battle with Earth. You can think of it that way when things get dull."

His words were music to my apprehensive ears. I had never been able to persuade Imre Munsen that I didn't share his perverse views on danger. Inside the mild-mannered, timid form of Henry Carver, unknown to Munsen, an even milder and more terrified man longed to get out and run away.

"Have either of you two," he went on, "ever heard of
Maximilian Snapper?"

I looked at Waldo, whose gaze turned reluctantly from the
ruined fritters. He shook his head, and I shrugged.

"That's not too surprising." Munsen picked up a sharp
kitchen knife and tested its edge throughtfully on his thumb.
"Dr. Snapper's not too well-known outside scientific cir-
cles. He's the top USF authority on polyparturition—
multiple birth studies," he added, seeing my expression.
"Take a look at this."

He placed a holocube projector on one of the kitchen
working surfaces and dimmed the lights. A featureless blob
appeared gradually in a space above the stove.

"That's a magnified image of the fertilized egg of a pig—a
special breed. Watch it closely."

As Munsen spoke the round circle changed itself to a
figure-eight, a dumb-bell, then broke to form two identical
smaller blobs. Each one grew and divided again. And then
again.

"The egg isn't developing," said Munsen. "It's twinning, dividing into two identical cells each time. Dr. Snapper
induced twinning through twenty separate divisions. That
gave him more than a million identical fertilized eggs. Then
he developed them all using a slightly different nutrient,
temperature and test environment on each one. You'll see a
picture of Snapper at work on the next piece of recording."

The great man himself suddenly appeared on the holo
reconstruction, fiddling with an elaborate kind of micro-
scopic manipulator. He looked just the type of demented
loonie who sets out to raise a million pigs.

"He was putting each developing cell through a battery of
tests," went on Munsen. "The tests gradually became more
and more taxing, enough to kill off nine out of ten of the
embryos at each stage. After four weeks he had just two
embryos left, one male and one female. He let them develop
to full size and mated them. The pig that resulted, the final
pig-in-a-million, has some unique talents."

The result of Maximilian Snapper's diabolical experiments now came on the holo image. To my untrained eyes it was a perfectly normal pig—perhaps the nose was a trifle longer than usual, and maybe the eyes a little closer together, but I'm not much of a connoisseur of porcine anatomy. The pig-in-a-million looked out at us from the image and made a grunting, whuffling sound.

"That's the end point of all the testing," said Munsen. "Dr. Snapper's wunder-schwein. The only survivor, Pig-million. He answers to the name of Hector."

I looked at the narrow eyes squinting towards us from the screen. There was a certain something in Hector's face that was familiar, a sort of shifty, evasive look. I suddenly realized where I had seen it before—in court, on the faces of defendants and (almost as often) counsel. The original Hector must be spinning in his grave, out on the ringing plains of windy Troy.

Waldo, who had listened to all this in silence, finally spoke.

"Seems like an awful lot of trouble, just to come up with a tastier brand of bacon."

Munsen laughed, with a flash of white, even teeth. "You have to have your joke, eh, Mr. Burmeister? Hector wouldn't make much of a food pig at all. You can't tell it from the holo, but he's small—he only masses ten kilos. He was bred for other things. Hector and his descendants will live out in Aristarchus." He paused and winked at us. "Does that tell you anything?"

Aristarchus. That crater was famous for only two things: massive titanium deposits, and—

"Truffles," I said, looking at the holo of Hector with a new appreciation.

"Exactly. Hector has been bred to sniff out lunar truffles."

You may be unimpressed, but do you realize how much a kilo of lunar truffles cost then, down on Earth? The restaurants would do anything to get their hands on a regular supply. For a couple of those black, knobby fungi you could buy a good-sized space yacht, fully-furnished. They've tried

all sorts of ways of growing them artificially, and all kinds of
methods for looking for them since the first one was accidentally surfaced during a drilling program in the Aristarchus
crater. Nothing had worked. Truffle hounds and truffle pigs,
flown in from Earth, couldn't sniff out the fungi growing two
hundred meters under the surface—not even the animals who
were considered infallible on Earth. Mechanical sniffers had
done no better.

"You mean that Hector can really find truffles, so far
down?" I asked.

Munsen nodded. "That's what Dr. Snapper was doing,
refining the olfactory powers. Back on Earth, Hector would
find the truffle smell overpowering. Here, he can pick one
out from a surface soil sample, ninety-nine times out of a
hundred." Munsen's voice was enthusiastic. "There is nothing else like Hector in the whole System. His smell is amazing."

I caught Waldo's eye, but neither of us was about to touch
that line. Instead, I said, "Very fascinating, but I don't see
what this has to do with us. Dr. Snapper isn't looking for
legal counsel, and I find it hard to believe that Hector has
become involved in litigation. I don't want to sound impatient, Imre, but our time here costs four hundred an hour."

"I know," he said calmly. "Or at least it would, if you
had any customers. I happen to have evidence that you've not
had a client in here for four months. Now listen, Henry. You
know me, and you know I don't play games. You two are
down to your last can of soup, and I have a problem that I
can't solve without help. I'll tell you something that mustn't
go outside these four walls: Hector has been stolen."

"Stolen? Who would go to the trouble of stealing a pig?" I
began—and even as I said it I knew the answer. Earth and the
United Space Federation had been arguing like fury over
economic tariffs and import quotas, and one of the key
bargaining items at the USF end was a promised increase in
the supply of truffles. That was getting them the support of all
the restauranteurs down on Earth. Now it was obvious that
they had been relying on Hector's powers to make good on

that promise. It was a small item, but in the long economic war between Earth and the scattered territories of the USF, progress was made by just such a succession of tiny bargaining gains.

"You're not suggesting that *Earth* stole Hector?" I said, as the logical train completed itself in my head.

"Of course." Munsen was calm. "Who else? They'll deny it, naturally, and we will accept their denial—officially. But meanwhile President Dinsdale has given me private instructions. I'm to get somebody down to Earth, locate Hector, and liberate him. One thing we're sure of, they won't have harmed him—he's too valuable a bargaining chip, and someday they'll really want those truffles."

Ludicrous? Only if you are unfamiliar with the standard diplomatic game of talk and double-talk. Munsen's words made perfect sense to me—except for the fact that he was very clearly *not* down on Earth. He was sitting on a kitchen stool in Tycho City. I have a sixth sense when it comes to these things. Munsen's words, added to Miss Lasker's earlier comments, rang the alarm bells in my skull.

"But Waldo and I can't—" I began.

"Of course you can," Munsen interrupted before I could get fairly started. "It won't have the spice of danger that you enjoy, but you'll be doing the USF a real service and you'll be very well paid for your time. We'll give you a hundred thousand dollars, plus expenses."

"You expect us to go down to Earth and hunt all over it? Hector could be absolutely anywhere."

"We already know where he's being kept. You'll go in there with official approval, and bring him out as easy as Susie."

"But he's on *Earth*."

"I know you hate going there—and I won't ask why." Munsen placed one great hand on my shoulder. "This will be different. You won't be going there as Henry Carver and Waldo Burmeister. You'll have assumed identities, of two inspectors from the IPC Office. With those credentials no one will stop you coming and going as you please."

It was beginning to make a curious kind of sense—always a dangerous sign. Officials of the IPC—Interplanetary Plague Control—go anywhere in the System with complete freedom. With that kind of cover, my old fears about visiting Earth didn't mean so much.

It would certainly be nice to visit the old place again, even if only for a few days. I could drop in on friends in San Francisco, maybe even have time to see—

I pulled my brain back from such lunatic fantasies. Earth was dangerous for me, disguised or not.

"Why don't you go?" I said. "That's what President Dinsdale suggested. You could pass as an IPC man as well as we could."

Munsen raised those blond eyebrows. "You really think so? I'd love to go down there—" he meant it, too "—but the Front Office thinks I'm too easy to recognize. They insist on someone that Earth Security won't recognize when they arrive there—that rules out me and all my staff. You two, on the other hand, would get by without a murmur."

"But we'd never pass as IPC men!" I protested. I was beginning to panic, because it was clear that I'd get no support from Waldo. He loves dressing-up almost as much as he likes eating. "Neither one of us knows a thing about plagues."

"Not yet, you don't," said Munsen. He stood up. "You will. In five days you'll both be experts in parasitic infections. That's why Miss Lasker is here, to brief you."

"We'll never become experts in just five days."

"You don't need to be *real* experts," he said airily. "Just enough to fake it. Your cover story's simple: you're checking out a shipment of live goats that was sent down to Earth from Ceres and got there three days ago. They went to the same place where they're keeping Hector. The IPC suspects that they were inadequately checked when they were shipped, and they may be suffering from *Oesophagostomum columbianum*."

He laughed at my expression. "Don't frown at that mouthful. It's a form of parasitic worm that's common in domestic animals. You'll have to look at all the animals there to see if it has spread to them. In a few days you'll know the name of that parasite as well as you know your own. Now, let's get you with Miss Lasker.''

On the way out he paused by the hotplate, where the remains of my fritters lay as blackened and shrivelled crusts.

''Ah, cooking Vestan cockroaches, eh?'' he said with interest. ''You know, I had to eat those for three weeks, nothing else, once when I was space-stranded. They're not half as bad as you might imagine.''

He was right, of course. They couldn't be.

Over the next few days I will, with your permission, draw the veil of decency. If you already know about the horrible parasites that lurk inside men and beasts, then you don't need me to repeat it. If you don't know, consider yourself fortunate.

Miss Lasker, as soon as she saw my queasy reaction to the joys of tapeworms, seemed to make a special point of dwelling on every gory detail, with color images to drive the impact home. After a couple of days of that it hardly seemed worthwhile eating my meals. All they would do was feed some member of the imagined internal zoo.

I gave up thoughts of food and spent my time trying to get back into Miss Lasker's good graces, pouring on the charm. She began to soften towards me, no doubt about it, but that satisfaction was countered by my concern about Waldo. His appetite hadn't been at all affected by a surfeit of parasites, and he was eating enough for both of us, ignoring my warnings that we would be down on Earth in less than a week. After years of lunar gravity, with his mass he would feel like a lead monument. I mentioned my worry to Munsen, when he stopped by to see how the preparations for Operation Galatea were coming along.

He looked across at the armchair, where Waldo was enjoying a post-prandial nap, and nodded in grudging agreement.

"I see what you mean. He is a little on the fat side. It may be quite important that you can both move around fast if the need arises. I'll arrange for you both to have a supply of Gravitol to take down to Earth with you."

"I thought that had side effects."

"Oh, they're exaggerated," he said, with all the confidence of a man who won't be taking the drug. "There's some confusion and hallucination, but the main danger is a psychological one. After a dose of Gravitol, you just don't feel as though you are in high gravity. You can see how dangerous that might be. A man might forget that he couldn't jump over a five meter wall, the way we can here. Or he might rupture himself trying to pick up a couple-of-hundred-kilo mass, that sort of thing, when he's down on Earth. I'll get you the stuff, but you ought to remember that it's only to be used if there's a real emergency."

He went to the doorway, then turned back for a second. "By the way, we've had a confirmation that Hector is still alive and well. He's being kept at the Manor Farm in Kampala. It's a research center for all kinds of domestic animals and that fits right in with your cover story. Keep your eyes open for a Dr. Pinero when you get down there, he's supposed to know a fair bit about parasitic infections. You two will have to be on your toes when he's around."

The trip down to Earth was peaceful enough, but it did nothing to allay my fears. Although the blue uniforms and insignia of the IPC guaranteed us free passage anywhere, they also made us inevitably objects of attention. I tried to be as inconspicuous as possible. Waldo, on the other hand, insisted on living his new role to the full. He had acquired a strange and sketchy knowledge of animal parasites, and he was determined to use it. He lectured to anyone who would listen on the relative merits of different drugs in the eradication of *Taenia saginatum*, the beef tapeworm, and in general bored the ship's company to tears. Luckily he never found anyone who had the least idea what he was talking about, but

I was afraid that would end as soon as we reached Manor
Farm.

"Dr. Maestricht?" said the short, burly man who greeted
us at the spaceport.

I nodded, suddenly aware of the full strength of Earth's
gravity. I felt as though a big sphere of water was enclosing
me and dragging me to the floor.

"And there is Doctor Leuba," I said, inclining my head to
where Waldo was sprawling on a handy bench. From the
look on his face I doubted that he would ever rise again.

"We have an air-car waiting," said our escort. Fortunately, he seemed to be no more than a driver. He looked
uncertainly at Waldo. "If you think it necessary, we can
arrange for a litter. Earth gravity is hard for lunar visitors,
especially for somebody as—" he struggled for a suitable
word "—as imposing as Dr. Leuba."

"No, no, not at all, I'll be quite all right." Waldo made a
huge effort and heaved himself to his feet. "Just need a
couple of minutes to get my second wind, that's all. Soon be
in good shape."

He didn't look in good shape. In fact, he resembled an
enormous, over-ripe pear as he tottered to the air-car and
levered himself up inside it.

He had my real sympathy. As we flew over to the ranch,
north of Kampala, I was gradually getting used to the feel of
the higher gravity, but that didn't make it any easier to take. I
knew what a burden it must be for Waldo. To my surprise, he
seemed to find some source of added strength as the flight
continued. I looked at him suspiciously as he moved gradually from a fat lump of misery to a keen observer of the
African countryside. His first sight of an elephant perked him
up considerably. There must have been a sense of shared
suffering, a feeling on Waldo's part that there were others on
Earth worse off than he was. By the time we reached the farm
he seemed positively chirpy—and I was beginning to suspect, though he denied it vehemently, that he had been
nipping at the Gravitol.

The outside of the farm grounds lacked fences, which seemed to rule them out as a place to look for Hector. The main building was an enormous and rambling structure with four main wings, each consisting of a series of labs, stalls and storage rooms. They would take a good deal of searching, and we might have to split up to do it. I edged closer to Waldo.

"Remember, now, if you see Hector try and put him into one of our cases—he should fit all right. If all else fails, push the white button on your uniform. It will send an emergency signal to Munsen's men and they'll come over from the port and try to pick us up. Agreed?"

Waldo nodded vaguely, smiling contentedly. I really didn't like the look of him.

Certainly, his manner when we met the custodians of the farm was odd enough. He stood there in beaming silence while I explained that we would have to look at everything, to see how far the parasites might have spread. The staff were agreeing when I heard a low, muttering noise from behind me.

It came from a small, thin-faced man—more accurately, it came from his stomach.

"Dr. Maestricht and Dr. Leuba?" he said, to an accompaniment of digestive disorder. "I'm Pinero, resident veterinarian at Manor Farm. I'm sorry you had to be brought in, and I hope you will find no signs of infection here."

I nodded politely, but Waldo came out of his trance and wrung his hand like a long-lost brother.

"Wonderful to meet you, Dr. Pinero," he said enthusiastically. "I understand that you have quite a smattering of parasitology yourself."

That, believe it or not, produced a genuine blush of pleasure. Pinero stood there smirking, basking in Waldo's admiring gaze.

"Well, a little," he said at last. He coughed self-consciously. "As a matter of fact, I wrote a brief monograph a little while ago, on *Enterobius vermicularis*." He smiled expectantly. "Of course, I'm sure you know a lot more about it than I do."

"No doubt," said Waldo. He paused for a moment to give the matter his best thought. "Our own recent experience has been concentrated much more on *Enterobius litigatius*."

Pinero frowned and looked bewildered. "Yes, indeed," he said after a moment. "I'm not actually very familiar with that form. It is, I suppose, a form of parasitic worm that is common in primates?"

"Very common in primates," agreed Waldo. "And in other clergymen, too," he added as an afterthought. "As you surely know, it often occurs in combination with *Trichinella presbyterium*, the scourge of the ministry."

"Now then," I broke in desperately. "We'll have plenty of time to pursue these fascinating subjects in detail, over dinner. For the moment, gentlemen, our concern must be with *Oesophagostomum*"—at least I'd managed to say it. "Come on now, Leuba, business before pleasure."

"Quite right, Wilfred," said Waldo approvingly. "Got to get down to work. No time to lose."

"Waldo," I said, as we moved out of earshot of Pinero. "Are you *sure* you haven't been taking Gravitol?"

"Gravitol? Of course not." His voice was all wounded sincerity. "I'm just feeling a little tired, that's all. You know, long day, high gravity, all that sort of thing—very tiring, most fatiguing."

"All right. But remember where we are. Don't try and lift anything heavy, and watch what you say to people."

Part of that advice was unnecessary. We had no opportunity to lift anything heavy or light. There were people all round us, opening doors, holding animals, and watching us as we peered in at each stall. Manor Farm had been arranged on logical lines, with all the beasts of one variety housed near each other. Our search would have been easy, except that we could hardly tell them that we wanted to go straight to the piggeries when we had supposedly come to look first at the newly-arrived goats.

It didn't take more than a couple of minutes for me to realize that there had been a big gap in our background briefings. Miss Lasker had told us all about parasites, and now I could easily distinguish a nematode from a trematode. But she had overlooked the fact that neither Waldo nor I knew enough about ordinary farm animals to tell one from the other. Separating the sheep from the goats is harder than you might think, if you have only a vague idea of the appearance of either. I tried to use general words, like animal and beast, but it's not easy to keep that up for hours and hours.

There was an endless and boring succession of them to be inspected—cows, horses, sheep, goats, yaks, camels, llamas, buffalo and finally, after what seemed like days, the thing we had been waiting for—pigs. We looked in at everything that we were shown, peering through our assorted instruments and making cryptic notes into our recorders. The group of admiring farm workers who trailed along with us seemed much taken by our casual manner—especially Waldo's. He seemed off in a world of his own, inspecting an animal's hindquarters and dictating an evaluation of the condition of its teeth.

I realized that we were getting nowhere. None of the pigs looked the least bit like Hector, and our entourage was far too relaxed for me to believe that we were near anything suspicious.

Finally, we had finished the grand tour. Nothing. It was getting late in the afternoon, and I was just about exhausted. As we came out of the last corridor and headed for the dining-room, I had the chance for a quiet word with Waldo. He was far out of it mentally, but in amazingly good physical shape.

"Did you notice anything odd about that inspection?" I whispered to him.

"Certainly." He nodded vigorously. "Those last camels. Very suspicious, not in the least camelly. Humps much too small. Too small all over."

"No, not that." It hardly seemed worth pointing out that

for the last twenty minutes we had been looking only at pigs. "In this whole building, we've only been allowed to see three of the four wings."

Waldo thought about that for a moment before he replied.

"Camels don't have wings," he objected.

I grabbed him by the arm and shook him. "Wake up, Waldo, and snap out of it. We can't stop now. After dinner's finished, we'll tell them that we're too tired to go back to Kampala tonight. When it gets quiet, we'll have a look at that other wing of the building. Now, be extra cautious for the next couple of hours."

Dinner at Manor Farm does not rate among my favorite memories. Dr. Pinero was there, but his manner was cold and distant. I think he suspected that Waldo was having fun at his expense, particularly when he had received an impromptu lecture on the subject of the rare mutated ant colonies of Titan which, Waldo assured him, contained not only worker-ants, soldier-ants, and a queen, but also lawyer-ants, judges and solicitor's clerks. Pinero had smiled thinly. He did not speak for the rest of the meal, though his stomach continued to hold up its end of the conversation.

There was less than an hour of daylight left when we finally went to our room and could shake off the admiring group of followers. We lay down on the beds for a brief rest. I felt as though I'd never be able to get up again. It would have been nice to talk things over with Waldo, but he began snoring as soon as he lay down. After that, nervous as I was, I couldn't help falling off to sleep myself.

It had been a very hard day. When I awoke, I found that it was already nearly midnight. The whole of Manor Farm, inside and out, was quiet. I went to the window and looked out longingly at the full moon. If it hadn't been for Imre Munsen's foul blackmail, I would be up there now, attending the monthly meeting of the L.B.A. I turned with a sigh and went over to begin the non-trivial task of rousing Waldo.

Lighting levels in the long corridors had been turned to their lowest settings, and everything was shadowed and indistinct. Even so, as soon as we reached the fourth wing of the building I knew that we were in a very different environment. For one thing, there was a locked door at the entrance, in place of the open plan that applied to the rest of the farm. A few tips on lock construction that we had received in lieu of payment from one of our clients helped considerably here, and we were able to make our way inside with no more than a minor delay.

We began with the upstairs, creeping silently along the corridor. There was no sign of man or beast. When at last we came to another room with a locked door, I reached into my pocket and took out the hermetically sealed box that we had carried with us all the way from Tycho City.

I broke the seal and held the box close to the narrow crack at the bottom of the door. After a few seconds, there was an excited grunt and a loud sniffing.

"It's Hector all right," I whispered excitedly to Waldo. "Open the door and I'll get the carrying case ready."

I slipped the box with its minute sliver of lunar truffle back into my pocket, while Waldo grunted and muttered over the lock. He seemed to have absolutely no idea what he was doing and after a few impatient seconds I had to take over from him.

This lock was trickier than the last one and the light was poor. When I finally eased the door open I was at the end of my tether and ready to go right back to bed. But we couldn't stop now. I slipped inside.

Hector was sitting up in his pen, nose high in the air. Munsen had been quite right, the pig was small. It was no big effort, even in Earth gravity, for me to pick him up and carry him outside to Waldo.

"Here, put him in the case," I whispered. "I'm going to lock this door again, so we'll have as much time as possible before anybody here knows what's been done."

I turned back to the lock and bent over it in the gloom. It was hard to make out the settings. Strange to say, when the light level suddenly increased my first reaction was satisfaction—now I'd be able to see what I was doing.

It was a full half-second before I fainted mentally, straightened up and looked back along the corridor. There they were. Dr. Pinero was about thirty meters away from us, with four more farm workers standing just behind him.

"I knew it," he shouted. "I said they were impostors—they're not real parasitologists. Grab them—but remember, the pig is valuable."

He might have phrased that better. I looked around me. Waldo was still standing there motionless, Hector clutched in his arms. At the far end of the corridor I could see other open doors. If Pinero's main interest was Hector, we might have a chance to escape.

"Come on, Waldo," I said. "Leave the pig and let's get out of here."

I grabbed his arm and began to pull him along the corridor away from Pinero and his men. He finally came out of his trance and ran after me, Hector still firmly held in his arms.

"Leave the pig. Put it down," I cried, trying to run, look ahead, look behind, and shake Waldo loose from Hector, all at the same time. It was amazing, to see how he could still manage to run with his burden in full Earth gravity. But I had little time for wonderment.

The corridor ended in a staircase. I threw myself down it as fast as I dared and burst out of the door at the bottom. To my surprise and relief I found that I was outside the building completely, in the big compound that faced out onto the road to Kampala. It was no time for half measures. I grabbed at the white button on my uniform and pressed it hard. It would probably be too late, but if Munsen's men responded to my distress signal as they were supposed to they would be here in less than twenty minutes.

And then I realized something else. I was alone in the compound. Waldo and Hector were still somewhere inside—I had not seen them since I left the corridor.

"Henry!" The despairing voice came from above my head. I stepped back and looked up. There, on an upstairs balcony, stood Waldo, with Hector still firmly clutched in his arms.

"I've locked the door here, Henry," he said. "But it won't hold them for more than a couple of minutes. What shall I do?"

I looked up at him. Despite my fatigue, my brain had never been clearer. If I had Hector, the road to the outside was completely clear. There was a fair chance that I could evade the farm pursuers long enough to be picked up by Munsen's men. I'd get away completely.

Waldo would get his share of the hundred thousand as soon as he got back to the Moon—I'd insist on it. And I didn't think he'd get roughed up too badly by the men on the farm. They'd be annoyed, no doubt about it, but they would probably do nothing worse to him than give a few bruises and maybe the odd broken bone.

I did a swift calculation. Hector massed about ten kilos. Catching him would be a fair load, but no more than I could handle. I stepped forward and held out my arms.

"Right here, Waldo."

I stole another quick look round the farm yard. It was still deserted, with Pinero and his merry men preoccupied with Waldo. I looked up again and steadied myself to catch Hector.

That was when things began to go wrong. I felt like some watcher of the skies, when a very stout Cortez swims into his ken. Hector was on his way all right. Waldo, the pig still clutched to his bosom, had stepped off the balcony and was plummeting down towards me. He had a peaceful smile on his face.

It was too late to get out of the way. I closed my eyes just before the impact.

As I thought. He *had* been at the Gravitol!

That was the end of Operation Galatea—at least so far as I was concerned. I found out the rest of it second-hand, after I recovered consciousness here.

Hector, our Pig-million, had escaped from Waldo's grasp when they both landed on top of me. He had been picked up by Munsen's men a few minutes later, trotting steadily along

the road to Kampala. Pinero had been too demoralized by the sight of my flattened body to initiate a pursuit.

Naturally, Waldo wasn't hurt by the fall. He's much too well-padded, and anyway, he always lands on his feet. He stopped by here just a few minutes ago, to tell me that the USF will pay us, but most of it will go on medical expenses.

He dropped off another tape from Sandy Lasker. She seems to have forgiven me for my initial *faux pas*, and I have this terrible suspicion that she is seeking some kind of closer relationship. She has been to the hospital every day, and she'll be here again in another half-hour.

I'm sure she means well, and I don't object to the company. But I wish her interests were a little broader. This is the fifth tape she has sent me about the parasitic diseases that are most commonly spread among hospital patients and staff.

Introduction to 'The Jennerization of H. Truman Buster'

Reginald Bretnor's short fiction has appeared in every major science fiction magazine on the market and a good many other publications, including *Esquire, Today's Woman, Ellery Queen's Mystery Magazine,* and *Harper's.* (This is not counting the long series of truly horrible pun set-ups published under the pseudonym of "Grendel Briarton".) He is the editor as well of the nonfiction work THE CRAFT OF SCIENCE FICTION, the widely-acclaimed reference work on the writing of science fiction (Barnes & Noble, 1979) that features chapters by Larry Niven, Ted Sturgeon, John Brunner, Norman Spinrad, Harlan Ellison and many others, each taking one specific aspect of writing science fiction and breaking it down into a wealth of usable information.

Beyond that he is the author of many works on public affairs and military history and is the inventor of an automatic mortar, much of his gardener's dismay. Of *The Jennerization of H. Truman Buster,* he says:

As for the story itself, it is of course a satire on the 'counter-culture', on its permissiveness as a substitute for, and an escape from, threatening realities and pressing problems, and on its unfortunate salability. In no society have professional word-manipulators been as influential as in our own, and—as a one-time propagandist—I am apalled by the degree to which they themselves are manipulated by the unrealities they invent.

107

THE JENNERIZATION OF
H. TRUMAN BUSTER

R. Bretnor

H. Truman Buster was the first President of the United States to be Jennerized, and of course it was Young Ted Cockrell who gigged the dream-up—just like back in the '80s and '90s he gigged about everything else that's made the country great: the Foursome Lifestyle, and the Lovealong with the Copros, and the True Second Amendment (meaning The Right To Bare Everything,) and *Down The Drain, The Babylon Song* to sing when the New Right gets to crying spook about the Reds, and even Mass-Com itself.

You wouldn't think anyone could accomplish all that, over so many years, and still come up all bright and horny, but the minute he pranced into the Mass Communications Authority Conference Hall that godawful morning, with H. Truman deader than a fish's fart and the 2012 election less than a week off, it was like somebody'd wiped all those years away, and Mass-Com, instead of being the Federal instrumentality he'd made it, was still just the Agency—Cockrell, Akhoond, Kennedy, and Fishguard—with him only our boss instead of Secretary of State, National Security, and Mass Communications. You could see right away he was still *Young* Ted Cockrell. He was wearing his same antique faded levis, with their all sorts of patches and the Copro flap in back, just like he'd been wearing way back when he'd brought Dr. Harko Toritch, who'd started the whole Copro deal with his anti-toilet-training best-seller, and had him explain his Big Movement and then Do His Thing in front of the whole U.S. Senate. That was when he'd gotten the Lovealong started by telling how good the Big Movement was going to be for the perfume industry and for pharmaceuticals and the A.M.A. and the economy generally, to say nothing of psychologically. That gig had won him his second Spock Memorial Award, and it'd really shut up the anti-Copro Right.

Now he leaped up onto the platform, and turned his back on us the way he always did, and gave out with his high-pitched "Yuk-yuk-yuk-*yark*, like!" and wiggled the rooster feathers over his tailbone and flapped his arms and crowed a couple times and farted at us, and you could just feel the whole hall come alive.

"Ole Fuster-Buster's dead, dead, dead!" he cried, turning round again. "Gear got busted in his head! They just ain't makin' them the way they used to! Yuk-yuk-yuk-*yark*, like!"

Well, everybody jumped up and down and laughed and did their best to echo that yuk-yuk-yuk-*yark*, like! But you could tell their hearts weren't really in it. Nobody was surprised when Mamie Fishguard, who was Assistant Secretary and closer to Young Ted than even his own Foursome, edged up against him with her famous smile and goosed him just a little bit. She was wearing one of those open-fronted formal morning gowns, with diamonds hanging from her nipples and a glowworm in her belly-button and a green-gold pussywig.

"You forget something, Mr. Ram-it-in?" she said in her deep-soft gravel voice. "There's this election coming up. *They're* running General Groodler—remember him? Saved Northern Missouri from the Mexican-Latin American People's Republic. A hero, man. Promises he can maybe even get us back a hunk of Texas. H. Truman could've beat him in a walk-away. But who you going to run against him *now*?"

Young Ted just put his arm around her and tweaked a tit. "Who're we going to *run*?" he crowed. "I'll tell you who we're going to run." He paused for just a second, and his eyes had that old hungry gleam again. *"We're going to run H. Truman Buster—that's who we're going to run!"*

For a moment, the whole hall held its breath, and even I began to wonder if at last he'd flipped.

"But—but you can't run a *dead* man!" Mamie gasped.

Young Ted held up a hand for silence. "We *won't*," he told us; and he pulled an old paper book out of the pocket of his jeans. "It tells all about it here," he said. "Back in maybe the '50s, see, there was this old geek running for President, an admiral or a general or something anyway, and just before election damn if he didn't have himself a heart attack. Well, they asked a senator called Jenner what his party'd do if he died off. And you know what that smartfart Jenner came right back with?"

He gave Mamie another little tweak.

"I'll tell you what he said. He said, *'We'll stuff him and run him anyhow!'* Yuk-yuk-yuk-*yark,* like!"

He crowed a couple times more to sort of let us get our balance back.

Then, "That's what we're going to do with Fuster-Buster," he announced. "We're gonna Jennerize him! Only we won't have to get the taxidermist. We're going to bring him back to life!"

It was one of those real historic moments, like the time they passed the law making the Foursome tax-deductible. There he stood in front of all of us, under all those framed mottoes called "The Words We Live By," which the old firm had passed on to Mass-Com. You know:

MAN, WIFE, FAG, AND DYKE,
THAT'S OUR WAY OF LIFE, LIKE!

and

SO IT STINKS? CHANGE ITS NAME!

and

IT MAKES A BUCK? IT'S *GOOD!*

and

DO YOUR THING—*ANY*WHERE!

and all the rest.

We just sat there and gaped at him, and none of us had any notion of what he had in mind, whether he figured he'd do a Frankenstein on Buster or what. But we were already sold. He'd grabbed us. We just listened as he gigged it out.

"Look," he said, "first we get us a real good actor, a big holo star, one who's tops not just in prime-time pornies but in commercials too. We get Rape Ravitch. We say, 'Look, Rape, how'd you like to be President of the good old U.S.A.? Okay. You're the same size as the late unlamented, only a hell of a lot younger. We change your face a little bit to look like him, though that can wait; you can wear a plastimask till after the election. Also we change your name legally, right away quick. Friend, you'll *be* H. Truman Buster—but you'll still have that nine inches he didn't have. And don't you think your fans are going to forget that prong of yours on their 'Gobble Grapies so your dong/Will grow long and stiff and strong!' breakfast food spots. Rape, you'll have it *made!*'"

All of us, I guess, were sort of dazed. Who'd have thought you could gig a dead presidential candidate back to life like gigging up a dead-dog product—who but Young Ted Cockrell? There was a litttle rustling and murmuring as we settled into the idea. Then a girl's hesitating voice piped up from the rear.

"S-sir? Wh-what if he won't accept, Mr. Cockrell, sir?"

With that, Young Ted grabbed Mamie by the ass and whirled her in a laughing, elbow-flapping, tit-swinging dance-around. "Yuk-yuk-yuk-*yark*, like!" he crowed. "Honey, you funny little cunt! I phoned him the minute old H. Truman died. He already *has*! He'll be the next President of the United States. Believe me, a week from now it's really going to be Erection Day!"

Of course he didn't say so, but I realized then that Mass-

Com wouldn't just influence the next President of the United States—we'd *own* him. And *that's* progress.

Well, the room went simply wild, shouting and whistling and stamping; and somebody started *Down The Drain, The Babylon Song,* and suddenly we were all singing its defiant verses—each ending with the chorus:

> *So what if the H-bombs hit?*
> *Let the New Right give a shit!*

Which was really telling them, because the New Right wasn't going to have a prayer. We'd have the Copros with us, and they'd pretty much absorbed all those old-fashioned groupies who were called the Counter-Culture before Mass-Com came along. The middle-of-the-roadies were too busy watching holo even to get out and vote, and anyway those who did would be for Ravitch-Buster, whom they'd heard about. But mostly it was because the New Right is peddling fear and we're huckstering forget-it, which is a hell of a lot easier to sell even when it comes in pills or in a needle.

When the stamping and yelling had sort of simmered down Young Ted gave us the shut up and listen sign. ''Yuk-yuk-yuk-*yark,* like!'' he chortled. ''Hey, do we have them by the balls! And now let's all of us get back to work. Then I want Mamie here and—'' He looked straight at me. ''—and my fat friend Scut Akhoond to meet me in my office right away. We've got stuff to gig around.''

I felt a thrill of anticipation clear down to my ass-bone. That was the first time he'd called me in like that since my old man died, and I knew if I played it right it could mean big things for me, perhaps even an Assistant Secretaryship. As I walked out, I saw the envious glances I was getting, and it did me good to know that right now every goddamn staff member of Mass-Com was hating me.

He and Mamie were already in the office by the time I got there, him roosting on his desk and her stretched out with a drink on the big day-bed. His face, under the blond shag-wig,

was lean, hard-angled, with that flush of excitement that
seemed to be a part of him and helped to hide the traces of
face-lift jobs and modelling implants. He poured me a
drink—it was Afro-Dizz, from the orig recipe of a Nigerian
witchdoctor, the ad says—and waved me to a chair.

"Scut," he told me. "We're going to have our troubles.
Groodler and his goddam bigot needlenoses are going to raise
holy hell about our retreading Buster. They can't even get to
foreplay with the public, and they know it, so chances are
their big push'll be in the courts, and it just could be that
they'll screw us there—enough at least so we'll know they've
stuffed it to us. That's where you come in. You did all right in
law school, didn't you?"

"I guess so, Ted," I answered modestly. "After I took my
law degree, it only took another year for me to get my
Doctor's in Jurisprudence. Then, of course, mostly because
you told Pop I ought to, I stayed a while longer and they gave
me one of their first A.J.'s. Up till then, Harvard had held out
against giving any Administrator degrees in Jurisprudence,
what with it carrying the right to practice before the Supreme
Court and all. Of course, I had two first-rate foursomes
working with and for me—"

"Courtesy of the shop," he put in, grinning.

"—so I sure can't claim all the credit—" I grinned back.
"—even though I really put in some heavy overtime with my
Read-Aloud. Believe me, some of those library books are
thick."

"Well, Scut, we were all mighty proud of you when we
heard about it. These days you can't get anywhere with just a
doctorate, not in *any* field. Mamie and I both knew you'd be a
really useful tool in the Mass-Com arsenal—"

"No puns intended," Mamie said, giving me her I'm-
going-to-eat-you smile.

We all laughed.

"So now I'll tell you how I see the picture, Scut—what
that damn masturbating Groodler is going to try—and then
you give me the down-and-dirty on the legal end. The way I
see it he's going to bear down heavy on the argument that

poor old dead H. Truman and our boy may have the same name, and they may look alike, but still they're different people."

"Separate and distinct entities," I said.

"Yeah, and anybody looking at those nine inches can see that. So where do we go from there? Do we hit the law books hard, or what? You tell me, Counsellor. What do we do about that 'separate and distinct entities' gig?"

It sure was my lucky day. Right then, the answer came to me like in a flash—but that wasn't all. At the same time, it was as though I heard my old man's voice right in my ear. "You listen, Scut—you start playing games with young Ted Cockrell, you just don't *ever* let it all hang out—or, if you must, you let him think it's *his*, not yours. That's if you want to stay in one piece, alive and well. You gig me, boy?"

I gigged him. Playing for time, I put on my best legal eagle look, complete with deep-think frown. "I sort of feel," I said, "that when you emphasized the phrase 'separate and distinct entities' just now you may have really hit the button. I guess it's like my old man used to say, your intuition cuts through all the crap—"

His eyes narrowed. "Keep coming, Scut."

"Well, let's look at it this way," I went on. "When we get through with Rape, legally he won't be Rape Ravitch any more; he'll be H. Truman Buster. Then, if we get him married again to his Mrs., and have another Foursome ceremony, like by a judge or minister, legally he'll be accepted as H. Truman Buster by her and every other of his Foursome members. Unless the late H. Truman made some sort of crazy will, there won't be any trouble about property; and even if he did leave part of it to kids or causes, with the new H. Truman being President, who'd care? Okay, as far as *law* is concerned, H. Truman Buster is H. Truman Buster. The question of whether the two are indeed 'separate and distinct entities' is, as you have pretty much suggested, not really a legal one. It's—" I fished around for some way to suggest it without actually coming out and saying it. "It's—well, sort of *philosophical*."

Young Ted was tense like he was ready to take off. "You mean," he said, "*theological.*"

"Well, come to think of it, uh-huh, I guess maybe it could look like that, being as it concerns the nature of the soul."

And was I glad that *he'd* nailed it down, not me.

The pupils of his eyes were just like pinpoints. "You've done fine, Scut. It's a religious question, not a legal one. Maybe it's something for H. Truman's pastor to decide— that's the Reverend Cherri Klipspringer, isn't it?"

"You better know it!" Mamie told him.

My God! I thought. *Rev. Cherri Klipspringer and her Hot Gospel Foursome, the only sponsored evangelists still on the air—and all of them Lovealongers, practically charter members of the Party.* But I didn't say anything. I knew exactly what was running through his mind and Mamie's, and there was no point to pushing it.

"Our most important legal argument," I put in cautiously, "might be the doctrine of separation of Church and State, mightn't it? Maybe it wouldn't hurt to have it ready for if they try to get any sort of an injunction."

Young Ted bared his teeth. Humming a bar or two of *The Babylon Song,* he poured our glasses full again. "Let's just hope they try it! We'll get Cherri and her Foursome for a holo service, with Mrs. H. Truman Buster there in mourning. First Cherri can dish up a sermon on the Will of God and renewal and rebirth and all that sort of garbage. Then we'll have Rape come on in his Buster mask, and there'll be a nice big mess of symbolic flowers, and we'll close with a few comments on materialistic tyranny and with singing a joyous hymn or two. Talk about a far-out blow-job! Yuk-yuk-yuk-*yark,* like!" He hoisted up his glass. "Well, down the sinkhole! Mamie and me, we're due at a big Foursome interlock over at the VP's. Scut, you think you'd like to join us?"

Mamie was eyeing me with a hell of a lot more greedy interest than she'd shown before, and I could see that it had been a long, long time since she'd been in her prime. Still, the Afro-Dizz was getting to me, and it was a leadpipe cinch that she was talented. Besides, *Anything for the cause!* I told myself. *I'm on my way!*

"Would I like to join you?" I answered. "Ted, does a frog have a watertight asshole?"

Well, Groodler and his people did their damnedest. They tried to pry injunctions out of every court all the way to the top, and got knocked down every time. We had the A.C.L.U. backing us, and the Council of Churches and everybody in the book, and the Copros did their thing by way of protest at every session. We put Rev. Cherri on the holo, by satellite and on every channel, and she preached a sermon that would've melted even Groodler if he'd listened, while old Sondra (Mr. H. Truman) Buster stood there all in black—black pussywig, tiny black posy in her belly-button, even a modest little black brassiere, crying into her black lace handkerchief. Then our ex-Rape Ravitch came in as per schedule, in a nice tight pair of britches so everybody could see how endowed he was, and Mrs. Buster told the world how like a really-truly miracle it was to have her Hubert— though no one knew it, that was his real first name—back again, how it was simply like a *resurrection,* like he was born again all fresh and new. She clung to him. He kissed her tenderly. The audience in the hall went crazy. All the phones started ringing, with calls even from Red China.

After that, naturally, the New Right was dead lost. Groodler didn't carry a single state (though he claimed he would have carried Texas if the MLAPR occupation forces had let the people vote.) It was the biggest landslide in our history—as Young Ted Cockrell said, "An unparalleled expression of public confidence in the Lovealong policy and the Traditional Values which have made us Great."

As for me, I've wondered a few times whether H. Truman's dying was as providential as his First Lady said she thought it was, or whether maybe somebody gave him just a little shove to start him on his way. But there'd be no point to saying it out loud. I'm now Assistant Secretary of State, National Security, and Mass Communications, just like

Mamie Fishguard (though I *am* beginning to wish that I could, for God's sake, shake her off. She's just *too* damn talented, and I've got my own Foursome to play footsie with.)

Otherwise everything's swell. President Buster—or maybe really I ought to say Young Ted—has even stolen the little bit of wind Groodler and the New Right had left in their sails. He's promising to liberate Southern Missouri from the Mexican-Latin American invaders.

He will, too.

Any day now. Yuk-Yuk-Yuk-*yark*, like!

Introduction to 'Contact'

Eileen Gunn is a veteran of the Clarion Workshop who started writing science fiction in 1975. She speaks "seven or eight" languages, a skill exercised by her travels through Europe, Russia, Siberia and Japan. She claims to have recently given up doing anything interesting in order to have more time to write fiction. She says:

I don't want to say anything about the story "Contact", because I think a story should stand on its own. If it needs to be explained or added to, then it should be rewritten. It doesn't matter what I was trying to do in it, only what I did do.

CONTACT

Eileen Gunn

The Desert of Winds was inland, a four-day flight from the eyries along the coastal mountains. After the eight-day fast, it was a long journey, even for the strongest-winged. But when they felt the high, hot desert wind lift them like dry leaves, even the most exhausted stretched their wings to the fullest and surrendered to the euphoria of approaching death.

Girat had been riding the winds for three days. She no longer made a distinction between her body and the current of air on which it rested. Mesas blue-green with lichen, chalky desert sinks, the land flowed like viscous liquid beneath her wide, motionless wings. The circle of horizon shimmered with heat and the sky shaded to transparent blue at the zenith. Suspended between earth and sky, she savored the time remaining and looked forward to death with pleasure.

It was her final afternoon. She was approaching the old City of Pillars, where she would die surrounded by memories of her ancestors. As she passed over the outskirts of the dead city, she noticed a visitor's encampment below, its tent a sharp cool circle against the hot desert floor.

Her people avoided the awkward, wingless visitors—their devices produced unnatural wave disturbances. Girat murmured a prayer against excessive vibration and glanced down at the camp.

There was only one visitor and it was lying motionless in the shadows, a victim, perhaps, of its own technology. Girat circled and descended, preparing to salvage its flesh for its relatives. She hoped she could do so without abandoning her early and well-deserved deathflight.

Odd that the preservation of their dead flesh was so important to the visitors. The past summer, Girat had observed them packing their dead in boxes and burying them for preservation. Perhaps they would eat them later. She found the thought repellent.

Girat was descending toward the visitor, only a few beats away, when suddenly it came alive and leaped to its feet, snatching a small object from the ground beside it. It held the object at arm's length towards Girat, an action she recognized as an attempt to preserve the formality and distance that existed between her people and the visitors.

Well, that was certainly all right with her. With a sharp beat of her wings, Girat continued past, to resume her slow flight of dehydration. Since the visitor was not dead, she would not have to delay her dying on its account.

As she passed over the visitor, the object in its hand moved. Her right wing stung momentarily and went numb. Girat faltered in her flight, gave a jolting flap, and swung irregularly to the right, favoring the wounded wing.

Moving faster than she would have thought possible with a wing injury and in her moribund condition, Girat swooped toward the center of the empty city. She landed clumsily on an abandoned flight deck, bruising her numbed shoulder against a wall of masonry.

For a peacful, pleasing death, she must die airborne, in a slow glide to the earth: she could fly no further until sensation returned to her wing. A maze of warrens and obelisks, its vibrations stilled, the City of Pillars would shelter her until she could resume flying. She settled her wounded limb carefully in place, then scuttled as quickly as she could down a deteriorating ramp.

The interruption was unexpected, but like any event on a deathflight, it must be accepted. A sentient creature like the visitor, however, ought to have more control over its actions. Her people were wise to avoid them, she thought. The miasmic resonance enveloping their camps would cripple anyone's control.

At the foot of the spiraling inner ramp, strewn with ragged

insulation and electronics torn from the walls, a broad irregular doorway led into a pillared square. Windswept detritus, wires and cables of synthetic substances, had piled up to the edge of the door. Girat stepped over the rubble and moved out into the open plaza.

Bozhye moi. The size of that bird. He knew he'd hit it with the trank gun, but he hadn't brought it down. Damned dosage too low.

Alex Zamyatin watched the bird sail toward the center of the abandoned city. It was conscious, but the drug obviously was taking effect. The bird landed on a balcony a kilometer away. Good, he thought. It wouldn't fall too far when it keeled over.

He shrugged on his copter pack and started after it. The city fell away beneath him—tall, slablike buildings around tiled squares. Pyerva's lighter gravity made it easier to get around, but without the copter, he'd have had a rough time in the roadless ruins.

Laid out in a series of open squares, vast empty plazas edged with towering obelisks, the city had obviously been the home of a people oriented to the air—and all the higher animals on Pyerva were winged. There were no streets below him and few connecting passages between the honeycomb of sandstone buildings and squares.

The balcony where the bird had landed was directly ahead. Alex was anxious to find the bird. It was his first chance, the expedition's first chance, to examine a live specimen. They had dissected several dead birds found in the ruins, and had raised more questions than they had answered. What did the birds eat? Their intestines had contained no food at all. Where did they nest? Nowhere near the cities, that was certain; aerial reconnaissance had yielded no clues—no birds had even been sighted. How did they use those highly developed paws? Four fingers, two thumbs: they looked very efficient. And why did they die? In every case, dehydration had been the apparent cause of death. The wiry bodies were dried out, tongues shriveled, mucous membranes cracked.

Perhaps they were gliding birds blown off course, away from their habitat, by strong winds.

Despite their large brains and opposable digits, there was no definite proof that they were at all intelligent. No artifacts or clothing. They didn't inhabit the cities. And the initial planetary survey hadn't revealed any other settlements.

And yet, they were the only possibility so far for intelligent life on this first extrasolar, life-harboring planet, Pyerva. The complexity of their nervous systems argued intelligence. And, structurally, they were the right creatures to live in these cities. Everything was built to the scale of these birds, alone of all the animals of Pyerva. Devices were engineered for their peculiar hands. If he were going to design a city for the birds to live in, Alex conceded, these were the cities he'd design. A live bird should end the speculation.

Alex landed on the balcony. It was pretty shaky—he ran into the building. They were familiar to him now, these alien structures. Doors were staggered at various levels in the walls, designed for entrance from the air. Interior automated ramps, no longer operative, led down to the plaza level. He scanned the cluttered interior, furniture half or fully extruded from the walls and floor, the disorder of decaying technology. The bird was nowhere in sight. Alex ran down the ramp, checking quickly at each level. It would head for the plaza, he thought. Someplace open to the sky.

He found the bird collapsed in the square, not too far from the door. It lay near one of the pillars, its huge wings folded into a fleshy carapace against its back. It was breathing shallowly, rapidly, its eyes covered with a whitish nictating membrane. Rate of metabolism and body temperature were even higher than he'd expected, but it would take a lot of energy to get that big a creature into the air. The bird was quasi-mammalian, as he had known: they were really more like bats than birds. Its long body was lightly muscled except for the powerful extensors that ran from beneath its wings, over its shoulders to the chest. It was covered with fine mauve down, a marsupial-like pouch on the abdomen. A female? Perhaps the term was irrelevant here.

He turned his cooling unit up another notch. Must be fifty degrees in the sun. The overheated air, despite its high oxygen content, was oppressive. Perhaps, Alex thought, it had been foolish of him to refuse an assistant: the stifling heat put an unexpected limit on his strength. But there were too few left on the expedition anyway, since the accident. He slid the tractor awkwardly under the animal's body and rose into the air, pulling the unconscious bird with him.

It was beginning to revive as he got back to camp. He barely had time to get it into the collection cage and turn on the field. The great, downy creature stirred in the cage and opened its eyes. Large as a lemur's, they shone a luminous violet, compelling his attention. The bird clambered to its feet, shook itself briefly, and flapped its wings to unfold them. Standing erect, it was easily two meters tall, knobby and angular, sharp bones emphasized by its loose skin, emaciation unsoftened by the sparse down.

Alex had the trank gun ready, just a blur dose in case it became violent enough to damage itself. The bird saw him and moved hesitantly in his direction, stopping when it saw the gun. Alex pointed it away from the creature: it seemed to relax. Did it recognize the gun? The bird approached him until it hit the invisible beams of the cage. Examining the force-field in front of it with its paws, it made a series of short, liquid noises. It explored, in silence, the extent of the cage, then turned back to Alex and approached him as closely as the cage would allow. Turning its hyacinth eyes on him, it said, in clear, unaccented Russian, "How do I get out?"

Awareness filtered into Girat's mind. The air was thick with electromagnetic waves, and something was watching her. She opened her eyes, got to her feet; she was in the visitor's camp. The visitor itself was standing in front of her, its body in the pose of formality and distance. She wouldn't press it, since it seemed incapable of controlling a tendency to sting.

The visitor made a gesture of approach, and Girat drew

closer, until she encountered the force shield between them.
She felt for the door, but the field extended all the way around
her. Perhaps she'd overlooked the controls: the visitor's
technology was alien to her, and she'd been away from the
city for a long time.

She spoke slowly, groggy from the vibrations, directly
into the visitor's head.

"How do I get out?" she asked.

The visitor gave a start and invoked a muthical being. It
approached her, its thoughts stumbling. What an odd creature. She felt her feet warming to it, it was so tentative and
unsure. And no wonder, with all these thought-scrambling
devices around it. Her head ached unbearably. But despite
the pain, Girat was tempted to interrupt her deathflight, to
stay and study this visitor for a while. She'd consider it later.
At the moment, she must find a way out of this vibrating
shield. There must be controls.

There were. The visitor pulled them from the folds of its
clothing, adjusted a knob, and walked right through the field.
Inefficient way to run things, Girat thought. She couldn't
reach the controls at all.

The visitor gave a start and invoked a mythical being. It
said.

"Don't you?" she replied.

It stared at her with a peculiar lack of expression. But with
such small eyes, it must have difficulty expressing the visible
emotions. It shook its head slowly.

"Yes, yes I do." There was a pause, and it looked at her.
"But are you actually, uh, speaking Russian? Or . . ."

"No, of course not, I'm just floating the words. Our
structures are not compatible." That explanation was a little
vague, she thought, but the visitor seemed to accept it.

With barely a pause, it launched into a detailed description
of the astronomical location of its planet of origin.

Girat wasn't interested. This information couldn't contri-
bute much to her deathflight, and the vibrations from the
force field disrupted her thinking. She scratched politely

beneath her pouch and asked if they could perhaps continue their discussion outside the fields of force.

The visitor stopped talking and tinted its skin warmer. Control of its body fluids, thought Girat. Charming, and very polite.

"—most distressing to me," it was saying. "This is our first contact with, uh, other species. No knowledge of what to do. I should, of course, have been prepared, but I wasn't really expecting that you would speak my—well, you know. Please come into the tent. Certainly. Much more comfortable there . . . ."

It led her out of the force field, across the tablerock to the circular tent. Vibrations came from a small cluster of containers next to it. Girat could tell that the tent wasn't going to be much more pleasant than the force field.

The tent was quite cold, as she had known when she first saw it from the air, and the combination of cold and vibration must have had a visible effect on her, for the visitor noticed her recoil when she entered the tent.

"Is there something the matter?" it asked.

She told it about the vibrations, which apparently it couldn't even detect. Nevertheless, it considerately shut most of the equipment down.

"No wonder we never saw any of you close up. We were driving you away." It seemed to think that, but for the vibrations, Girat's people would have flocked to the visitors' camps. Girat did not correct the impression. "This tent will heat up pretty fast without the cooling unit," it continued, pulling off its clothing. "But the heat doesn't seem to bother you."

Squatting comfortably on the floor, Girat watched the visitor while it talked rapidly and enthusiastically about establishing contact with an alien species. Girat was still feeling a bit dizzy from the vibrations, and she wasn't listening much to what the visitor was saying. Its words were irrelevant to her death, which had been interrupted, but would proceed as planned. It was a handsome animal, she thought, though its species must be a lonely one, to be so excited by contact with another.

Alex watched as the huge bird settled itself on the floor. This was the moment, he thought, that the human race had been moving toward for more than a century: contact with another species. They'd prepared speeches for everything else: the first person on the Moon, the first on Mars, the first on every moon and half-assed asteroid since. His captain had made a speech as they prepared the cryogenics after clearing Pluto's erratic orbit. And had sent a lengthy speech back through four light years of empty space when they were awakened, a month out from Alpha A, which later proved to have a great selection of cosmic debris, but no planets at all. Then another lengthy speech went out when they landed on the most likely-looking planet of Alpha B, the first extrasolar planet to be explored by humans. It had been named Pyerva, The First, by Grisha, who was a Georgian and sentimental, but it was only the most recent of a long line of firsts. And now it was superceded by yet another first, the first "alien."

Alex was at a loss for words. He should have said something more memorable than "You speak Russian?" but truly, he hadn't expected the bird, however intelligent it was, to start talking immediately in his native language. Even on the ship, they usually spoke standard. Well, he could invent something that sounded good for the history cubes. Who would know?

"We come in peace for all the citizens of Earth." Hadn't someone already used that? Oh well. "Uh, you are our first contact with a civilization other than our own." No response. It didn't seem to be too handy with small talk. Neither was Alex. He slumped back against a cushion. He had been trained to communicate a few basic concepts, to start learning an alien language, if he could. He was to lay the groundwork for more meaningful communication later.

It wasn't supposed to happen this fast. Here he could say

anything he wanted, but nothing seemed worth communicat-
ing, and the creature wasn't interested. The whole encounter
seemed meaningless.

Alex looked over at the bird seated awkwardly on the
floor. It had folded itself rather haphazardly together and
looked forlorn and a little motheaten, to tell the truth, like a
malnourished dog. Purely on impulse, he leaned forward and
reached out a hand to touch the down on its broad shoulder,
where wing and arm and back and chest met. It was soft on
the surface, hardmuscled underneath. He stroked the length
of the arm softly, and the creature didn't flinch or pull away,
but reached out to touch his cheek with its longest fingers. Its
hand was very warm, warmer by several degrees than his
own body temperature.

A part of his mind protested: this wasn't remotely in tune
with the demands of protocol, or even of scientific inquiry.
How was he going to explain this to his superiors? Extremely
disordered behavior, said his mind. Situational diplomacy,
replied his body. He put an end to the discussion and moved
closer to the alien.

Physical contact with the telepathic creature made them
both of one mind, one feeling. The bird's large, sensitive
hands moved lightly around his neck, under his ears, to his
shoulders, and down. He moved his own hands in the same
way on its longer body. Sensual warmth without sexual
arousal flowed between them in the smoothing together of
skin and velvet. Alex felt the weight of the expedition's
problems fall away from him, as he lost himself in the
drowsiness of warmth and contact. They stretched slowly
together on the floor of the tent.

Girat could feel the visitor relaxing, losing his grip on his
pain, letting the tension flow from his muscles. When they
touched, Girat could feel the sources of his tension: they lay
not so much in the vibrations that filled the air of the tent, as
in the pain and isolation of creatures who've abandoned their
nests, who've left behind all the rest of their kind, forever.

As she began to understand its pain, Girat felt herself grow closer to the visitor, and she sensed the ambiguity in the visitor's mind concerning the exchange of warmth and the reproduction of his species. Very different from her associations concerning the two functions. To Girat, there was no relationship between gene sharing and mind sharing. She projected that thought to the visitor, and felt him drowsily agree to the idea of sharing. Their minds and bodies moved together.

Lying stretched out on the floor of the tent, she shared her breath with him, breathed the air as it came from his body. Their muscles moved together, their limbs glided over each other.

Girat could feel the pain leaving his mind, the edges of his regret dulling. Slowly, she pushed further into his unconscious. He would be left with a sense of loss, which is a worthy emotion, but would no longer feel such pain and longing for his Earth. She spoke to the visitor in words for the first time since they had touched.

"This is a good happening for the end of a deathflight. I am honored."

She was lying against him on her chest, one arm over his shoulder, the other reaching forward beyond their heads, her hand curved back toward her face, her long fingers lightly flexed. Alex smiled sleepily. He should find this experience a lot stranger than he did.

Instead, he felt comfortable on this planet for the first time since they'd arrived. He'd been welcomed by one of Pyerva's own people, and together they could explore their differences and their similarities. What a wealth of information she could give him.

She rose up slightly on one arm, turned to face him. "This is a suitable happening for the end of a deathflight," she said. "I am honored."

"What is a deathflight?" asked Alex. Perhaps this would explain the mummified birds in the cities.

She sat up slowly. "When we left the cities, thousands of seasons ago, we left the technology that would support a

large population. We must keep our numbers low.'' Flexing her wings slightly, she stretched her arms out in front of her, tendons and muscles stretching. ''So, when a person has accomplished some good and has made a contribution, she is allowed to return to her ancestors' city to die, and one of her eggs is quickened.''

This made no sense to Alex. ''But why did you leave the cities in the first place? They could support millions.''

''The vibrations,'' she replied. ''The cities and their electronics produced vibrations—'' she touched his arm, and he associated the word with the electromagnetic spectrum, ''—that scar the mind and damage the body. Some people—my ancestors—could feel them, like a sickness, eating at them. They left the cities, got as far away from them as they could, and settled in the rock eyries where we live now. Most people stayed in the cities until it was too late. Perhaps they couldn't feel the vibrations, or perhaps they ignored them. They did not live healthily until death, and their young suffered even more.'' She paused. ''It's time that I left,'' she said, rising slowly from the floor of the tent, drawing Alex up with her. ''If I rest too much, I'll be unable to die properly.''

Alex stood stunned for an instant as her meaning sank in, then turned incredulous. He was just beginning to put the pieces together, and there was much more they should talk about. She couldn't die now. She couldn't abandon him.

He grabbed her arms, to keep her in the tent until she regained her senses.

When he grabbed her, Girat instinctively pushed back, but she was too weak to have any effect: almost all her remaining strength was in the muscles that controlled her wings. With a violence of emotion that blew through her like a wind, he objected to her leaving, objected to her dying, and threatened to prevent her from continuing her deathflight.

Girat had never found herself in violent opposition to another intelligence. She found herself totally without referent. She could accept the impersonal barbarity of her environment, she could comprehend searing pain and transmute

it. Those were natural occurrences: she could transcend
them. But the artificial constraint of one person by another,
this was beyond acceptance and comprehension.

He couldn't intend to keep her here! He couldn't place his
mind and power in opposition to hers! What kind of incom-
prehensible monsters were these aliens?

Incredulity and rage burned reason from her mind. She
shook uncontrollably. There were other ways of dying.
She'd accept a hasty death on the ground before she'd be kept
alive against her will.

Suddenly she stopped. The cause of his irrational behavior
was available to her: he couldn't understand what she was
thinking, he couldn't *hear* her, even when they were touching. She thought again what a lonely, comfortless existence
these creatures must lead. But she could project. As long as
they were touching, she could put parts of her mind into his,
just as she could project words from a distance.

And she did. She projected pure emotion, tied tenuously to
facts: the triumph of heroes of her clan who had died beautiful deaths, the pride of her mother, dying that she might live,
the joy of the child that would receive life when she was
dead. The visitor stopped holding her, but she kept the flow
of emotion pouring into him: she relived the euphoria of her
deathflight, and felt again an eager anticipation of her death.

When her desire for death became unbearable, she left
him.

The next day and the day after, Alex Zamyatin went out
into the city despite the heat. It was much too large a city for
one man to cover in a day. On the third day, he found her.

It was early, an hour or two past dawn, and the city was
rosy with light. She lay, wings spread, in the shadows at the
edge of a plaza. She'd been dead for some time.

Her wings, dry as parchment, were loosely outstretched,
covering most of her body and the ground around it. One arm
lay hidden under her; the other reached forward, her hand
near her face, fingers curved slightly inward—the same
sleepy pose she had taken in the tent.

Her face was peaceful, what he could see of it. Membranes obscured her large, luminous eyes. She looked, deceptively, as though she were breathing. He could almost see a slight rise and fall of her chest.

He knelt beside her, reached out a hand. Not to move her; she was perfect, careless, spent. He touched the downy leather of her wing, surprised against his will by its coolness. Her flesh, waxy under his fingertips, was colder than he could have anticipated. Dead.

He stroked her wing again, involuntarily. It was difficult to stop, he felt such joy.

Introduction to 'Games Children Play'

Jack C. Haldeman II holds a B.S. in Life Sciences from Johns Hopkins University, and has worked extensively as a research biologist, medical technologist, and field researcher in the Canadian Arctic, where he lived with local Eskimos while studying the life cycles of snow geese and white whales.

He has sold more than sixty short stories to every major science fiction publication and several outside of the field, such as ''Gallery.'' He currently has two novels in print, PERRY'S PLANET (an original Star Trek novel) and VECTOR ANALYSIS. Two further works are forthcoming. Of *Games Children Play,* Haldeman says:

[I] was interested in the continuance of patterns in childish play and folklore. It struck me as bizarre that all these games and beliefs and experiences would continue unchanged from generation to generation, that there had to be some kind of common, on-going origin point. Being that I have a bizarre turn of mind, my exploration of that origin point came out as Games Children Play. I like to think that it's an amusing story; there should be room in this world for fiction that makes people smile.

GAMES CHILDREN PLAY

Jack C. Haldeman II

It's all perfectly clear now, but it started back on that humid summer afternoon while Marsha and I were sitting on her balcony, watching some kids play in the courtyard below. Marsha? Marsha's an old friend. We grew up together. She was a childhood sweetheart that I never quite outgrew and never quite fell in love with. Everyone has someone like that. We are comfortable together, like an old pair of gloves.

The kids were playing and singing and I was only half listening.

"John and Mary, sitting in a tree. K-I-S-S-I-N-G."

I noticed that Marsha was absently humming to herself.

"First comes love, then comes marriage."

We looked at each other and said the last line together.

"Then comes Mary with a baby carriage."

"I didn't know you knew that," I said, laughing.

"Everyone does," she replied.

I'm proud of my ability as a collector of trivia and many's the night I've kept myself in free drinks by this otherwise unmarketable talent. There's no such thing as *everybody* knowing something and I said so.

"Sorry, but that's one of those things everybody learns when they're a kid. It's part of the normal sexist upbringing."

She was too smug and I couldn't drop the subject. I bet her five dollars that I could find someone within ten minutes who didn't know the jingle.

Twenty minutes later I hung up the phone and handed her a five dollar bill. She was still grinning. Not everyone remembered the words right away, but given a hint they all came through.

As a collector of odd bits and pieces of information, mostly useless, this more than bothered me. I couldn't leave it alone so I started looking deeper into it. I wish I hadn't.

I found the answer and it's kind of scary.

I discovered the kid who's eight years old. He's always been eight and he'll never get any older. He's the quiet one who sits in the back of the class; you know, the one the teacher always forgets during roll call. At recess and after school he really comes alive.

He's the one who teaches all the other kids those dumb rhymes that seem to stick around from generation to generation; the ones that never show up in children's books because they're either too dirty or too stupid. He teaches them crazy kid's games that parents would never touch—like swinging on vines, mumbly peg and playing doctor. His favorite line is, "I'll show you mine if you'll show me yours." Like a chameleon he blends into his environment and kids never remember having met him. But year after year he quietly does his work. Always eight years old.

Don't get the idea that he's all alone in this extra-curricular education department. He has help. Lots of it.

He has a big brother that hangs out in the high school locker room telling all the guys about sex. He always wears a jock strap and sits on a towel. Although his facts are not biologically accurate, they're always interesting.

When he's not in the locker room you can find him around the smoking area or in the corner hamburger shop telling the same dirty jokes year after year. The audience changes after every school term, but he's always there on the same corner stool, with the same jokes. He's had a bad case of the pimples for over a hundred years.

You may remember his sister, the girl everyone talked about in whispers. She was the one who *did it*. She actually went *all the way*. When I first heard of her, I wasn't real sure what *it* was, but I knew it was something special. Later on, after I found out what *it* was, she was on my mind nearly every night.

And then there was the kid who lived around the corner

and down in the next block. I didn't know him, but my mother knew someone's mother who knew *his* mother. You probably heard about him too. He was that disgusting kid who always got straight A's.

Or at least that was what my mother would tell me. Twice a week.

"Why can't you do better?" she would say. "Little Freddy around the corner and down the block *always* gets straight A's and he even has time to be captain of the football team. His science fair project on molecular genetics won first prize and he's getting a scholarship."

He was also editor of the school newspaper.

When I was in college little Freddy's big sister wouldn't leave me alone, although I never met *her* either. My mother would write me every week to tell me how well Shirley was doing in Medical School and how she was going to be a great brain surgeon and why was I wasting my time with all those foolish liberal arts courses? Did I want to grow up to be a beatnik or one of those hippy things and disappoint my mother? Letters like this caused my sister to drop out of Vassar.

I don't think my mother ever really knew the family, but little Freddy and Shirley and all their friends live right around the corner from all of us, keeping us in line.

Your mother knows them.

Among aspiring and professional writers there is a suspicion that no matter where you send your stories and articles; no matter what magazine, no matter where their offices are—the mail always gets forwarded to a large warehouse in Kansas City where the *only* editor in the United States selects stories by throwing dice.

And don't pay any attention to the rumor that everything you read is written by one person who is kept chained to a typewriter in the basement of Madison Square Garden. It's just not true.

Marsha and I take turns.

Introduction to 'Ten Times Your Fingers and Double Your Toes'

A Hugo and Nebula nominee, Craig Strete has been described by no lesser figure than Jorge Luis Borges, perhaps the premier author to come out of the burgeoning Latin American literary field, as ". . . a beautiful performer, within whose voice we find absent our own standards and pantomimed mythologies . . . we risk the dangerous power of genius."* He currently has a collection, IF ALL ELSE FAILS, in print from Doubleday.

*From the introduction to IF ALL ELSE FAILS, Doubleday & CO., 1980

TEN TIMES YOUR FINGERS AND DOUBLE YOUR TOES

Craig Strete

It was black, black and he turn all ways like a stuck snake and people all around saying they ain't have no work. It came for him that six week go by and he ain't working and he just saying hell about it all over.

He owe everybody. He is bird naked and they knows it. He got a dime for the white trader and ten dollars for the old man who works the chin game on the next tourist who comes round the bend. And too he owe ten dollar credits to old man name Backet cause it caught up with him and the last time he went there Backet showed him how to go out the same door he come in only faster.

"You son of bitch!" yells Stonecloud, sitting down like poleaxed ballerina in the street. "You could have waited till the tourist season! You know I'm good for it, you old product of stale dog heat!"

But Backet he remember flush time last year but it don't make him soft. And he don't give him nothing to drink and tell him to go out and die like the dog he is or pay.

This put the by god fix on Stonecloud cause he hungry and dirty and looking all ways up and down, he don't see nothing to come. His shoe got a big hole in it like it laughing at him and the cold rain is chilling him on the body like a reptile dream.

"Lousy head hunker! I rich as hell in tourist season!" Spitting old language of sparks and grumbling, he got up and began walking down the street. Up above with him not even having to look he knows is the sky and it is being all wrong and the season is six maybe seven week yet. And he know from empty pocket to empty pocket it no use to go down to the port and wait for no ships to come. The charter ships with the green people wouldn't be coming roaring out of the sky no way until the rains be got to stop. He know that like a toothache on a callus on his soul. It such a hungry.

"That Backet, he wait till I rich. Come tourists, I biscuit and gravy rich. I am virtue of cadillac, full fourwheeled and pocket heavy. Come tourists, I rich. I dog bark on his old man, Backet and business." And he mutter to himself all time think the dog will be on the other roof like or not when he rich.

As he walking on down the street all time disgusted the sky seeing him so fly unzipped in the attitude, come pouring out rain like eternal vigilance. It raining so hard it bounce hitting down.

"Oh lousy of all!" moan Stonecloud feeling the bounce bounce of rain seeping down into his wet underbeing. Nothing but for to keep on walking on past the stores, keeping the sharp eye for someone who owes him something. But he find no one and it rain all over and his shoe laughingly taking in water like an old time fashion tax collection.

He stop in front of a newsstand to duck under the awning and get out of the wet but government boy with plastic straw dangling out of liquid concentrate of beefsteak dangling out of shirt pocket come banging up to the counter like a angry hornet. He drop a handful of newstapes on counter and gives with the eye like he asking maybe are you selling tickets to the RESURRECTION already. And government boy begin yelling as he is government "Hey you! This ain't no flop house!"

So what happen is Stonecloud shout right back and scorch air with hot language and cause he proud, he take a credit out of his pocket. It is his lucky credit he won in a tumbling game that time he had many year ago when he had chance to win that funny boy in the three-day game in Aztol's garage. He chicken out and refuse to bet last credit and old Aztol, who all time thinking the pretty boy is woman as is all players but old Hawkfoot who put up same for stake, win bet and funny boy, much to roar of roars when he find out he been tacked up in sun and let to dry. So ever after, as he had had old Aztol beat, he had kept lucky credit as protection against funny boys. So now he take lucky credit and smash it and protection it provide on counter like it being a fly to get smashed. And he grab up a newstape and walk away with back up like a picket fence and head held high.

Course, he get out of sight of newsstand and government boy, he curse the saints of painted donkeys and the eggs of their grandmothers and go all tight in face on account he don't have no newstape reader so newstape is worth having like hickey from poison snake. So he pitch newstape into street when he is sure someone is looking at his extra extravagance and newstape it get sucked up into rotors of a pie wagon and goes into shreds. All which reminds him he is hungry enough to eat cookbook and he hit head like a drunken burglar who has shut jimmied wall safe on his shoelaces.

He look and he look into his memory and he can't remember even one name of who owes him something. He spend so much time try to forget who he owe money to himself that he forget if anybody owe him.

So he stop in front of a travel agency and drip rain and go to looking in at the moving window pictures. All the planets are there in pictures with edges. Every picture has smiling green people or some kind of other color people he don't even know name of not mattering to him much though as once you see one kind of color people they all look pretty much alike. All these smiling people sitting around and running and jumping and kidding around in the bushes which are placed just so, so little kids can't come see who or how they are kidding around. No worry on their faces and all the time acting like a nest of ants in a sugarbowl. He think they tell each other too many jokes or been all hit in the head too many times as he is surprised to see so much kidding around in one place. He chuckle in the neck and think wicked that they have all caught the old IT in the middle and limp bowlegged and it go up and make oatmeal with lumps of their brains. But still they eat all the time and dance and kid each other like it won't fall off from too much kidding around and it is all hell depressing.

And it all disgust him and he go down the street collecting a lake from his shoe comedy routine, flap, slosh, flap, slosh, all the much hotter than before. He is feeling by now as hot as nine wicked cats in a dark room.

Now Stonecloud never steal. He gamble. He play loose with an ace. He drink like a parched horse, he chase women when he got enough money to slow them down. He never steal. He never catch a woman who don't want caught and he never steal.

So he go by a store full of shoes and he almost break a leg trying to walk past it by standing still. He look through the front window like a guilty cat with feathers on his breath. He catch himself on the throat and pull himself away and push himself on down the street but his legs not convinced and he know it.

The first step away from store he takes he hit a puddle and he feel the splash through his shoe clear to his lap. It is rain, cold rain like a funny boy's kisses and his feet getting cold numb from hip on down.

So he stuck in his bird feather breath and he spin around like gravity pulling down an old sock and is pulled back in front of the store window full of shoes and burn slowly. All the time he is thinking he could be beautiful from the feet up.

The automatic clerk is hunched on a table like somebody's old appendix operation. His eyebulbs are unlit and his speaking crack dangles open like a bear snore. Stonecloud pop goes the weasel his eyes at the temptation. There is sign on robot clerk showing how busy like a buried coffin is shoe store. The sign say "FOR SERVICE, PLEASE ACTIVATE SWITCH 3 ON FRONT OF ROBO-CLERK. THANK YOU."

The store was all over shoes. It look like place where all old shoemakers go to die, dropping shoes like elephant tusks where they fall. It is the shoe-elephant graveyard.

Stonecloud standing out there like an apology, standing

there touching the bottom of his pockets and he sees shoes,
old and new and black and blue. And he thinks of them
unguiltily in three part harmony. He couldn't even count all
the shoes. He look like eagle eyestrain is having him popeyed
and he thinking all time "They got them. So many. Ten times
my fingers and double my toes. Oh lousy of all! And I stand
with toes taking swimming lesson."

So he pretend he don't recognize himself and he slip quietly
through the front door like a dumb and deaf act at the tourist
circus. He looks at robot clerk with the smile of unprincipled
beauty and tiptoes around him ever lightly. And Stonecloud
he look up at thief catching close circuit T.V. camera and
then down at monitor beside robo-clerk and it give him a
laugh. The T.V. monitor on the blitz and show being on is not
being interior of store at all but old time rerun of *I Lust For
Lucy*. All of which is all more perfect safe. Then he gets right
up next to clerk and does the jackhammer staccato shuffle
and flap-slosh dance for the robot clerk's ears only. But the
robot clerk is the sleeping beauty only activated by the kiss of
a handsome priss on the activating switch. As soon as Stonecloud sees he had got no applause and there be no audience,
he was knowing it was safe as breathing. So he squirt around
like a marshmellow in the soup. He look here and he look
here and he fussy as old men needing prunes.

First he latch on to a black pair fit for a king. He try them
on and they fit like royalty on people. He yelps at tight
squeeze, takes shoes off and dumps them in the garbage can.
He keep looking.

Then he find a pair that are all perfect. He put them on and
leave his old pair of holes beside the robot clerk. Stonecloud
nods friendly like at the clerk who look like activating
mechanism of white liberal freedom fighter. And then like a
ghostly gift giver he walks out of the store, like he bought
something. Stonecloud act like it too and keeps going away.

And it hit him suddenly, it was hell easy. Stonecloud was
hit as he had not known it as hell easy as even telling a lie in
public office. But in three part harmony, all surrounded, all

piled high and so many, more than ten times his fingers and double his toes, it was hell easy.

Stonecloud spring down the street bouncing on his new shoes like a basketball. He get feeling like old self again and he remembers how all the time all the women used to tongue snap when he come bounce with credits in one hand and fancy suit all slicked up like a crooked dog tied sideways. Didn't they just snap tongue when he rode high in tourist time. Good remembering, his feet unswimming, all smiling, somewhat bouncing all went to the cleaners when his stomach kicked him in the back remembering him he was hungry as a perpetual motion stomach pump machine.

Wouldn't he go to bite something or hungry as is, somebody. He mad for food and that make him think of mostly somewhat drinking to stupidness Aztol and his garage with the fruit locker full of obsolescent oranges and too long-remembered bananas. Even rotten as is make him water all over the mouth and tongue hum like piano tuner attachment. So he bounce twice for extra traction and then he making like an arthritic fire engine and scoot scoot scoot through the ever bounding rain like a winded frog.

Aztol was sitting in a chair in his garage talking to his dog which he got in trade for the funny boy. The dog was asleep as it wasn't much of a dog on account you can't expect no time to get an undamaged one for a funny boy and this was nobody's noise of an exception. Most he was bent up and lean forward when he walk like he trying to see down the front of some hyperventilating midget lady's dress which there was not many of on hand. Aztol was tongue flapping like big time brag stuff about time when the old Tourist Center burn down during party. Aztol was trying remember if was himself set fire or what. He couldn't remember so good.

Stonecloud bounce in like something crawled off breakfast cereal box.

Aztol look up and think he see a drowned bird and is

smelling maybe a long dead one. Aztol roll up his lips like a soggy cracker.

"What about ten credits owed me? What? What? What?"

The smile on Stonecloud's face sail to edge and fall off the world.

""Oh the horse!" he curse. "You knowing I good for it when all time of season come!"

Aztol drop eyes like a plum bob and down looking he see new shoes and eyes light up like free pinball game. It makes him hot. He roll a nasty thought in his head. "Twenty five credit brick on the hooves!" He roar like a hydroelectric plant. "Twenty five credit and got no money for old guy Aztol! Who who you?"

Stonecloud look hungry at fruit locker and see a picture of a fruit locker standing in its place. He groan as he realize art imitate life but get screwed in here and now. Name being pretty to look at but doing nothing to stomach, he sigh and flap arms like wings of gilded rooster, mating with lesser angel.

Says he, mouth unwatering, "I flew them from captivity."

"You steal! Not pay! Steal?" Aztol look stomach kicked.

"Broke. Had to. Wave my knees in the trees if I lie. Broke." said Stonecloud, dropping his arms in a bowling ball throwing motion.

"Can you not wait for tourist?" asked Aztol.

"Plant me drowned from bottom up if waited six weeks. Old shoes holes with laces. Had to. Had to," shrugged Stonecloud, dripping rain for emphasis.

"You as disgrace being Indian," grunted Aztol. "Boost shoes like common thief."

"Well all same, I had to—"

"You disgrace," cut in Aztol. "Going go to jail a disgrace for measly shoes look like over enlarged rabbit pellets with grooves anyway. I ashamed to call you Indian. Gonna steal, boost truck of whiskey! What you want known as, champion bird's nest ransacker?"

Stonecloud roll back head and laugh kiff-fiff as it hits him like first false pregnancy of spring. Always a good joke.

Aztol scratch his unwoven chin hair, eye Stonecloud try to grind giggle to halt.

"You know you could have moneys if wanted. From tourist." say Aztol eye winking at himself in moderation. Aztol smirked, effect knowing of this statement, smirked more even as he be self freshening.

Stonecloud leap forward like liberated bosom bounce, news catching to face and sticking there like memory of snout kick from unprincipled mule. He all sudden more eyes and ears than sixteen dancing monkeys in the house of mirrors.

"What? What?" he shout, making frantic slot machine motions with his chin.

Aztol smug smiled like uncorked leper cutting loose from his first fallen finger. He look bored of whole thing. He knuckle crack as an infuriation and pronounced delay of game.

"What? What?" jumping up like flopped fish and enunciating like a yodeling moose echo, goes Stonecloud. "What?"

Aztol yawn and look like maybe he curl up and sleep. He stop act when Stonecloud look like he going to go for jugular like smell of fish rising to ceiling. This all too solid inevitable and Aztol take a tuck in his intentions, having met the experience they be aimed for, finding as always, room for improvement, as loving one's neighbor was same sandwich, but pickle difference being on when husband get home. Aztol know how much market can take. He ease off gracefully like senility in shock absorbers.

"Tourist coming today," quick says Aztol in self-defense. "Didn't you be knowing this?"

Stonecloud bounce shoes twice, only once touching ground. "Oh the horse!" he curse and he go like two truckdrivers driving the same truck.

"I think shoes stink!" yells Aztol but Stonecloud is moving at twice the speed of leaf rustle in empty swimming pool and is too far gone to hear.

Stonecloud pounds up to Tourist Center, gasping like

carelessly calibrated alligator in vacuum. Sure as goats have
the smell of style that asks for distance, a ship was down. He
run like possession, perhaps Rebecca of Sunnybrook Farm,
the demon that got him. He runs on both legs and leaps
through the big doors like imitation of last sardine getting
into can. He sees the green ones scattered all around, most
occupied and he hears screams of guns and bark of the dying.
He snatch gun from wall brackets with lend-lease frenzy,
check if loaded and race away to get tourist for all gone.

He found her standing in one of the tourist sun room. She
look proper horrify when she see him come bounce with gun.
She even scream like soprano air raid siren. It is goose bump
delicious he know. She sink her scream to buzz saw roar,
very small horsepowers.

He aim gun and hesitate as always. The thrill of kill was in
the shrill. He wait for full lung expansion and full eyepop and
complete first parachute jump no I take it back syndrome
after you already too far down to walk back up. She is ready.
He is ready.

He look at her close. She short, maybe twenty hands high,
green scale on body, sharp pointed fingers that made good
drink stirring rods, if proper dry. She got vents each side of
face for breathing and air conditioning, factory air. Other
accessories, sharp bony ridge down center of narrow face,
and best, white sidewall clenched knuckles. She regard him
with two lidless headlight of horror.

He aim thinking of food, new clothes, all them women
gonna snap tongue at him, and Philadelphia. He always have
it in for Philadelphia. The gun screamed its own language,
the bullet hit her big culture shock in chest and she fell over
backwards like stacked deck. She still screaming, getting all
out of it she can.

The tourist alarm rang. Stonecloud sit down to wait. The
fix it or forget it machine roll in, and scoop up body also give
floor wash and wax job and count cracks in ceiling. It keep
busy. Help take mind off tourists. They all pain in processor.
Machine start processing, adding short pithy message on

cellular level sponsor by CITIZENS FOR DECENT LIT-
ERATURE.

It take time and Stonecloud, he impatient as lamppost
leaning girl in forty day and forty night of rain. So he have
plenty time to think. He think first he going to make big time
cash deposit to restaurant first so time he hungry all he do is
walk in, sit down and eat like stupidness. He all for stupidness, go easy on the eggs and no Philadelphia. He always
have it in for Philadelphia.

Then next he going to head to toe, clothes to eyepop
women and make all go tongue snap. And he thinking how he
is going to buy and sell everyone and then he feel like dance
and that when he notice remembering his shoes. He look
down at feet. He not dance.

Stonecloud sitting there in marble shooter position number
seven and then there is this tapping on his shoulder like touch
of gay sparrow. Stonecloud look up and see white man tourist
with brown socks and checkered pants.

"Isn't this something! Isn't this just something!" says the
tourist, says this white man tourist bumping cameras off his
chest.

"Isn't?" asked Stonecloud.

"Me and the Mrs. drove up from Philadelphia to see some
of these aliens. I tell you this, this is really something!"

"Well, suck an old dog," say Stonecloud "is nothing to
covet outhouses over!"

The tourist guy is bouncing around, snapping snapshots,
yelling off somewhere for someone named Gladys and snap
snap snap, pictures of sky and knees and Stonecloud and
ground and mostly shots of alien female in clutches of fix it or
forget it machine.

"Don't you just think it is incredible, I mean, they come
all the way here, I mean, all the way to Earth, pay to come
here, pay to get shot, I mean what a bunch of alien freaks! I
mean ain't it incredible! Isn't that truly unbelievable?"

Stonecloud pinch up his face in gesture of disgust and
facial snarl of over-familiarity and he say nothing like vac-

uum cleaner doing his tongue.

"She's gonna come out of the machine soon!" squeals the tourist excitedly. "Oh Jesus! I'm out of film. What a God damn time to run out of . . . . Gladys! Gladys!"

"Christopher Columbus was absolute nut tourist too! God damn crazy man! He not know horses about camera or good guns but he have crotch disease go like last souvenirs before the desert," say Stonecloud. "Wish to groundhog we could have . . . ."

The white tourist go run off yelling for Gladys and film and Stonecloud relieved to see him go as would be to wake up in morning and find he not in Philadelphia. Stonecloud all time thinking how tourist season is get too big to ride side saddle as now tourists are coming to see tourists being tourists. Pretty soon be shooting himself as tourist think Stonecloud.

Fix it or forget it machine is taking one forever. Just as Stonecloud getting ready to bite down on impatience so hard he give gums flesh wounds along come white woman, must be Gladys cause she got film cartridges in one hand and is dressed up looking like sack of concrete and liquid laundry detergent container. She rumpled like milk sitting too long on radiator.

"Where is the aliens? Where is the freaks? Where is Frank?" she say, sputtering like outboard motor, put put put.

"Where is . .?"

She is starting again and Stonecloud by god fed up with whole donkey. Nowhere is said he got to feel like inside of donut for two sets of tourist. He jumps at her and leers at her and waves gun in her face and she look at him like she in a hurry and he is double parked in her space.

She ignore him complete as she hears husband or maybe wild hog with stomach gas yelling for film somewhere off somewhere. She spin off and leave Stonecloud feeling like phallic cannon in civil war exhibit, erected no less.

Then alien come out of machine, she all shiny like fuzz on newborn peach. She smell like ghost of a chance in the second race before the man with the shovel comes out on the track. She look like second honeymoon making same old mistakes.

Machine burp her and she stand up and step out of machine. She walk over to him, reaching into her shoulder pouch. She open mouth, she smile, show sharp pointed teeth. This is gratitude.

"It was beautiful! It was wonderful!" she say.

Stonecloud smile like carnival employee winning teddy bear just next door. He not know what to say. He never know.

"The savagery, the pain! Exquisite!" she said and she shake with pleasure like flagellating blender and hug herself like wraparound sunglasses.

Stonecloud hold out his hand. This is the best part in no way dimmed by Philadelphia wherever it is. He always had it in for . . .

"You wonderful, marvelous beast! You are so beautiful! So deliciously animal! I squirm at the thought!" She take a handful of credits out of shoulder bag. She push them at him and he take joy all overed.

He turn to go but she stop him with her hand. She very curious tourist. She so curious she don't know electric chair is clinical definition of tourist shock, which is worse being than culture shock as tourist is shocker and object touristed against is shockee. But what did she know?

"Don't you feel bad?" she ask. "Don't you feel bad about killing? Doesn't anything in your beastly state bother you? It's so refreshing!"

He want no chatter. Is time to bounce shoes, to eat before art replace life and he become artistic symmetry of skeleton-hood, apprenticeship not so wanted, art being everybody. Also he worry art replace life so quickly, all best restaurants be snapped up for he get there.

So he just shrug like camel with consumption.

"How can you do it? I don't understand? How do you do it?" She let go of his arm as she see he want to go.

He guess the obvious and say, "With a gun." And he walk away.

He never understand tourist. Like uncranking self-taught virgin. He put money into pants and it makes hot spot which is only way tourist can be understood. Hot spot so hot it steam him up so cold rain of outside not even bother him.

He aim like highway divider for restaurant, to go eat like stupidness. He come by shoe store. He thinking of it all time too. Thinking of it like hunger. He see the robot clerk sitting in same place as before. He go into store and get his old shoes. He wipe new shoes and put back. He put on old shoes and punch switch on robot clerk.

The robot clerk come awake like traffic jam and make proper polite noises. Stonecloud, he look around like complete stranger. He say, "So many shoes. Ten times my fingers and double my toes. I think I will just take them ones," and he point at the pair of shoes he just bring back.

Robot clerk ask if he want to try them on. Stonecloud just wave grandly, detail too small for bothering with.

"Wrap em up," say Stonecloud.

The robot clerk hand package to him and offer change.

"Keep change," Stonecloud say bighearted as he go out door.

Stonecloud go down street, flap, slosh, with new shoes under arm. He feel so good. He going to eat to stupidness. He going to drink to stupidness. He going to dance to stupidness.

Yes dance, he not be ashamed to dance now. He had paid for his shoes.

Introduction to 'Tripaner's Day'

H.C. Petley began writing eighteen years ago and has persisted in the pursuit of this craft through many changes in fortune. He has travelled four times around planet Earth, worked on barges, in lumbermills, on the fire-line as a chainsaw operator for the State of California. Currently living in Sausalito, he seeks both solace and excitement racing sailboats on San Francisco Bay and on the Pacific Ocean.

Tripaner's Day came to me in an early morning dream up in Mendocino County. I knew it was going to be written, be about a physicist named Tripaner and would focus on three separate realities revolving around each other. It was some months later (the story took seven months to complete) that events within this fiction seemed to align themselves with elements of the quark theory, that is to say with the interchange of and relationship of matter and energy. I suppose all science fiction writers accept this concept as absolute. It's so very convenient! This was a difficult story for me to write. I hope it is a whole lot easier to read.

TRIPANER'S DAY

H.C. Petley

Trell stood up in the stirrups and looked over the horns of his stag. A thin trail of rising dust clung to the distant hills. The stag snorted and tossed his head. Together, they scanned the Basin of Rocks beneath them searching for any movement or any sign of danger. The Basin was littered with huge rocks and great lizards were fond of hiding amid the shadows and crevices to escape the burning sun. Trell drew his rifle out of its sheath and loaded it with penetration shells. The lizards had thick hides and were difficult to kill. He affixed a silencer to the weapon and drew down on a distant rock to sight in. Lizards had acute hearing. The unmuffled crack of a rifle would draw a crowd of curious predators. His rifle was a fair weapon to counter any attacks and the silencer insured that a kill would not attract any immediate attention.

Trell sought the mind of his stag. He would trust the natural instincts of this graceful, tireless runner to cross the basin below them without arousing the lizards. It was high sun and a time of day when these swift, merciless hunters were asleep. The basin was sixty faros wide. Safety lay in the low hills beyond where the slow, timorous rise of dust marked the vast open-pit mines of Yorros. Just at the edge of the low hills was the Swinging Bridge that spanned a dry chasm separating the lizard warrens of the basin from the hills. Sixty faros. It was a fair distance, yet the stag's limit without rest was ninety.

"Hutta!" Trell called out in his mind to the mind of his stag. "Take us across to safety. The monk, Baesum, awaits us." Hutta snorted again and scented the wind. Trell urged his mount onward to the edge of the slope. The stag slowly picked his way down, winding in and out amid the piles of shifting purple shale. When they reached the bottom of the basin, the stag began to run. Trell delighted in the swift, steady rhythm of the running. There was no finer stag alive. Hutta was selected from all the herds of the High Plain, swiftest of all those in Trell's own corrals. Hutta meant "big in the chest" and he was descended from the very same stag ridden by Trell's ancestor, King Ren, when the people of the High Plain were young, in the days of the wandering. The stag was running. His long legs, sure footed, stretched out. His antlers whistled in the hot, dry wind.

Trell watched every shadow, every shape looming on the rocks as they rode past, weaving through the great masses of stone. The stag never stumbled or changed his steady pace. Trell's nomad people had lived with these antelope for millenia. Each knew the mind of the other. Their lives had been entwined since primeval times in the ancient days of wonder. In those days of legend, Ren, the Ancestor, escaped from a slave caravan owned by Chu, Baron of the Southern Continent. Pursued by the Baron's slavemasters, Ren made his way across the Plain of Winds. It was there that he rescued the great stag, Norri, from an encirclement of lizards and in gratitude the stag carried Ren across the Plain into the Mountains of Knives. Thus the ancestors of the two tribes, man and antelope, escaped their enemies.

The sun glistened and for twenty faros the stag ran with smooth, gliding strides across the yellow sands and rocky gullies. Trell sensed a sudden motion and watched the subtle shadows carefully. He held his rifle high across his chest, ready to snap it into his shoulder and fire. He thought only of a potential target. He would rely on Hutta to run to their destination. The stag knew the direction and the distance. A lizard bounded over a ledge of sandstone and leaped after them. Trell spotted the blue scales darting out of the shadow and he raised the rifle in one, smooth motion. The lizard was off to the left and slightly behind them, chasing after them on four legs with its head and neck thrust out in front of it like an arrow. Trell sighted and fired without hesitation, the heavy bullet smacking their pursuer in the mandible and blowing it clean away. The lizard staggered and then fell in a dusty heap of twitching tail and legs. A dozen smaller, yet equally vicious, scavenger lizards appeared in various cracks and crevices of rock and scurried toward the thrashing carcass. Trell and Hutta raced away across the dry bed of a seasonal river and left the carrion feast behind. There could be no rest nor stopping for them until they reached the Swinging Bridge, now forty faros away. The desert basin rose and fell before them in a series of tumbled, broken steps. They scrambled out of the dry river bed on a crumbling ramp of scree and raced onward.

As he rode, Trell sensed the mind of the monk, Baesum, and pictured him standing before a carved marble tank at the edge of the famed well of Yorros. The distant hills before him seemed to stretch and recede. For an instant, he sensed that he was riding with Hutta through a wide field of waving grasses! Huge, wheeled machines were rolling across the field in front of them, cutting paths through the deep, green golden grasses. The sky was a deep blue, such as could be seen only from the snow fields atop the Mountains of Knives. Trell felt a sudden touch of fear wave through him, a disorientation that made him imagine he was riding across an entire universe, a ride that would never end upon a stag that could not rest.

* * *

The sun rose bright and clear over the long stretches of prairie. The morning shadows shortened and grew faint, shimmering against the rising heat waves. Thin lines of trees, small clusters of barns and houses dotted the flat plains. Wheat fields spread mile beyond mile. A slow, fat river cut through the prairie sod, sidewinding and curling leaving oxbows and gravel beds. The new sunlight danced upon the slow moving river. There were no clouds in the brilliant blue sky.

"Harold? Do you want eggs this morning?" Mrs. Tripaner called upstairs from her clean white kitchen. The sunlight was pouring through the east-facing windows, dazzling her for a few moments and she reached to draw the curtains shut. Yet the beauty of the sunbeams made her hesitate and her hand fell back to her side. She stood there at the window looking out across the waving wheat.

The two story white house was set deep in the fields. It had tall windows all around and a large, screened back porch that faced south. The porch was a good place to set tomatos or fresh fruit to ripen for a few days. Green plants and house flowers grew well there. The old lady liked to sit amid the plants on Sunday afternoons and read the paper. "Harold?" she called to her husband. She thought for an instant that the whole, quiet morning had slipped by, that she had been standing by the window for hours. "Eggs this morning?"

"Yes, I think so," Harold called. "My, the sun's bright this morning. You don't mind fixin' the eggs with rye toast, do you? And some sliced tomato? I sure would like rye toast." Harold buttoned his white shirt and clipped on a flower-printed bow tie. He stood before the mirror and brushed his thick, dark hair with a wooden, boar bristle brush.

"Well, come along and make coffee and I'll get some eggs," Ella replied, "Water is boiling." Ella went out through the kitchen door to the porch and opened the screen door. It was already a hot day. She walked out back toward the barn and the hen house. The wheat fields, spreading away on either side, were nigh on to ripening. "With this heat," she thought, "they'll be in to harvest in another few days. Maybe sooner unless it rains." Ella had been born and hoped to die amid wheat fields. Her people were grain farmers on back to the covered wagon days. She went searching for eggs in the hen house and, finding five quickly, she felt lucky and didn't have to search the whole yard. Hens lay eggs in the strangest places.

Out back of the house, next to the small, tired barn and the hen house, was a windmill. Harold had put that up many years ago and it had continued to give them free electricity and kept their bills down to a bare minimum. The wind was always with them on the prairie. Harold's windmill gave them light to read by, warmed the hen house in winter, ran the toaster and the water pump.

"Used to be over a million windmills in this country back at the turn of the last century," Harold had often told her. "Now, there are less than two hundred thousand and most of them are just pumping water and not producing electricity at all. That is a great loss of potential energy. If I was a younger man, I'd get in the windmill business 'cause at the turn of the next century this country is going to be one million windmills short!"

"He'd have made a good business man," Ella thought. "He's certainly no farmer." The four hundred acres of wheat that surrounded their tidy house was leased out to professional grain specialists. Wheat was too valuable for anything less. Harold had a good sense for business, though, and he was an excellent manager. He didn't have time to farm. Oh, he was able to keep the fruit trees trimmed and the vegetables weeded. But, he had other things to do maybe more important than raising grain. Sometimes Ella thought that Harold was just about the most important man in this part of Nebraska. It made her feel good to think so while she was fixing his eggs for breakfast.

Harold Tripaner dusted his fresh fried eggs with black pepper. "Well, I start my sun lectures today for the seniors. Next week is review for finals and that is the end of another year. Five lectures on a subject that should take all year to explain. And even then, only a few of them will ever understand. Well, this is the last time I'll be giving the sun lectures."

"That's what you said last year," Ella reminded. She looked at Harold as he mopped his plate with rye toast. His eyes were clear and blue, his hair thick and dark with hardly a touch of gray.

"Yes, I said it last year but this year I mean it. I've got too many important things running around in my head. It's time I retired from South Fork High School. Thirty years of physics lectures is enough. This time, I mean it."

"You said that last year, too," Ella smiled.

Their conversation drifted, their voices trailed away and they sat at the kitchen table awash in the glowing morning light. Harold's hand rested at the handle of his coffee cup, Ella was reaching for another slice of rye to put in the toaster. The moment lingered and stretched around them.

It was a few minutes after eight when Harold put the Ford in gear and drove down the long driveway. There were willows growing out in front of the house. The drive curved around the willows and then lined straight away between the waving masses of wheat. Harold noted with some degree of certainty that time was seriously disordered. The drive past the willows seemed to take forever. The wheat fields expanded into the far distance, the horizon seemed to bend backward into a deep parabola, the driveway narrowed. The speedometer on the Ford held to a steady 25 miles per hour. When he looked sideways, out of the car window, the flat landscape rolled along just as it always did. But when he looked straight ahead down the long dusty stretch of gravel everything seemed to recede and slow down.

"Sunspots," Harold told himself. "Optical illusions and heat distortion of the atmosphere. Time is a function of space, space is a function of time. I'll discuss it in class today . . . if I ever get there." He looked at his wrist watch as he reached the end of the driveway. He pulled out onto County 10 at the same time he always did and accelerated down the two-lane roadway passing a row of mailboxes. In thirty years at South Fork, he had never once been late for class.

Tripaner drove the Ford toward South Fork High. He was part of the morning traffic as he drove out of the wheat fields and into town. Suddenly, the familiar streets and quiet store fronts dissolved. One part of his mind carried on with the rote mechanics of driving to school, another saw the buildings give way and become huge ramparts of stone. He stood on a bed of yellow sand. There was an image of a rider on a great stag in the pink, dust laden sky. Tripaner realized he was inhabiting the body of a small lizard and he saw three worlds becoming one. He was still the physicist and began computing the energy transfers about to take place between three quarks interchanging time.

*   *   *

Rosser was not quite awake. He lay on his back on the same bunk he had occupied for five annuals. Yet he knew he was also beyond this place of confinement. He breathed slowly, deep in his diaphragm, careful of two fragile other places he knew to be separate realities. In one place, he saw a man in a strange vehicle driving along a hard, black path between waving fields of grain. In another place, he saw a man astride a great antelope racing across a rocky desert basin. The images of these alter-worlds filled him with great joy for he knew them to be real and constant. He had sought them deliberately several times before and now he knew he could reach them at will. He balanced the two images in his mind and at the same moment felt himself to be in his proper place lying on his bunk. He had no trouble sensing the three different worlds or in transferring his attention from one to the other. Yet each world was separate and distinct from the others. Rosser settled back into a quiet sleep and withdrew his concentration from the balance point. Two worlds dissolved and faded from his consciousness. He was alone, half sleeping, knowing he was about to make a great transition in his life. Tears welled up in his eyes and flowed across his cheeks. Seven times he had seen and explored these other worlds and each time he had pulled himself closer to them, each time he had gained strength of mind and more control of the visions. He measured the rhythm of his breathing, felt renewed and refreshed by what he had seen.

*   *   *

Mr. Tripaner pulled into the high school's faculty parking lot at 8:35. He sat in the Ford for a few moments and everything appeared quite normal. The time distortions he had experienced were gone. The visions of a great stag and its warrior rider did not flash before him, yet he sensed the illusion was not far from his consciousness. He looked at South Fork High, the older building a solid, two story brick and granite mausoleum dating from World War I and the new wings, low and sleek with cantilevered roofs and aluminum framed windows. Sparrows flew about the rooftop of the newest building, a one million dollar gymnasium. "There has been progress in the past thirty years," Tripaner said to the Ford. "I've seen it and I've been part of it." He left the Ford in the parking lot and went inside.

Tripaner's first class was the senior lab at nine. As soon as the students settled, he began his famous series of sun lectures. "I have a star in mind," said the teacher. "It's called Sol, the Sun. It's a common star, if anything so magnificent as a star can be so-called. Yet it is quite ordinary in the great congress of stars that fill our sky. A star is a hot body of dense gases contained by gravity. These bodies appear everywhere in the known universe and they are generators of light, heat and magnetism, and a variety of other radiations. These are the furnaces where the universal transmutations of elements takes place, where matter and energy are continuously interchanged. Our sun is 93,000,000 miles . . . ."

Slowly, as Tripaner progressed with his introduction to the sun, he noticed that time and space were slipping away from him again. He didn't panic, but observed the phenomenon as best he could. He struggled toward the next rational moment, afraid for an instant that the class would notice his hesitation or that someone else would experience a similar dislocation and everyone would panic including himself. "A wry twist of humor, that," he thought. "We'll all go screaming down the hall any minute! Time's slipped! The lizard world is approaching at light speed!" But the class did not seem to notice. Their minds were engrossed in the phenomenon of a sun piled over with County concerns and track schedules, Fleetwood Mack and Linda Ronstadt, soda-pop gossip and strained love affairs, baseball practice, 4-H and sundress patterns. The class was immobile before him, stranded between intervals of time awaiting the next instant cause. Tripaner saw three suns in his mind, three worlds from three universes converging on a singularity that was himself. He reviewed the latest rumors of the quark theory and projected them into a vortex of neutrinos. He was fighting to return to his class against a paralyzing sense of no time. Finally, he said, "A Star." The class breathed almost in unison as they reached that next moment. "A star is in motion. It has real motion and apparent motion; the former is its actual series of movements and the latter, the apparent motion, is how the star's path looks to us here on Earth. It also has a rotational motion around a central axis. All stars have these motions and no star is fixed. Our sun has a diameter of 842,000 miles, emits 1500 calories of energy per second per square centimeter of 6.2×10^{10} ergs per second for each and every square centimeter of its surface. You will recall from our very first lecture in physics that an erg is a standard unit for measuring energy and it equals two times the mass of one gram moving at one centimeter per second." Tripaner took a breath and waited a second to see if anything would happen. The class looked up at him and he continued into the flow of his lecture. He was delighted that nothing else happened and that he was again in a recognizable reality comforted him.

"Although this magnificent object is a giant sphere of hot gas, this is not a normal gas that is thin and spread out. The gases of the sun are very dense, 1.41 times as dense, on an average, as the ordinary water on Earth. Gravity compresses the gases into a state of matter known as plasma, a superdense, ionized gas. You will recall from our third lecture the definition of ionized. Temperatures and pressures within the sun act to strip electrons away from atomic structure causing the ionization.

"The surface of the sun has a temperature of 5,800 degrees kelvin and its central, core region has a theorized temperature of 20 *million* degrees. Such tremendous heat can scarcely be imagined, for at these temperatures, all known substances are vaporized. No material we know can exist in such an environment except as a gas. Now, the sun also has an atmosphere in various layers and temperatures there exceed that of the surface, rising to one million degrees in the corona. We live on Earth in an extensive outer atmosphere of the sun. Indeed, it is the essence of life on Earth for without the continuous radiation of heat and light, this planet would be a barren, frozen rock. The sun . . . . ''

* * *

Rosser was awake when his morning security call-signal trilled out sharply from the communications console built into the steel wall of his cell. The video relay blinked on and a soft light flooded the space. He climbed out of his bunk and stepped in front of the video tube. His name and number appeared on the screen: "Rosser, T. 559273-79638." The screen then flashed: "Morning Response." He pushed the response button. The screen flickered and gave him his usual work orders: "Unlock in 15 minutes. Report to engineering transport, Unit 1200." He went to the basin in the corner of the cell, washed his face, then dried off with a clean, thin towel. He returned to the bunk and sat naked at the edge of it, staring at his boots on the floor. He sat still for several minutes, minutes that stretched and seemed to be hours. He breathed in and out, a deep sigh, and reached for his socks, his soft knit underclothes and his jumpsuit. He dressed mechanically and put on his boots. It was a constant ritual. Every day, he waited for the unlock.

He stood by the heavy steel door of his cell looking out through the wire-bonded safetyglass window. It was a large window and gave the illusion of freedom. His cell was on the fifth tier, the top of this residence block. It was somewhat of a status position reserved for Class 1 engineers. He had certain privileges on this tier that those below did not have. He was close to the skylight. He had library clearance. His cell was guarded by the Tier Tender's Union. Fifth tier residents had their own recreation court, their laundry was processed and delivered. Beyond the cell door, there was a narrow walkway and beyond that was a drop, five tiers down to the cool steel floor below. The flats, that floor space was called. Beyond the edge of the tiers, across fifty feet of open, empty space was the outer glass wall of the residence block. Cell block was its true identity. The Industrial Authority was fond of clever names and intricate designs, all of which gave the illusion of freedom. There were huge windows in the walls of the residence block, giant skylights and translucent doors. It was almost a greenhouse constructed over the tiers of residence units. Cells were what they really were.

Rosser stood by the heavy steel door of his cell looking out. Beyond the outer glass wall, he could see the sun rising. Each morning he stood in this place and looked for the sun. "Layers upon layers," he thought. "Dimension upon dimension. This window, the space beyond, the outside window, the space outside, the clouds, the window of the atmosphere, the space beyond the world, the layers of the sun." He knew this prison could not hold him much longer. Six years he had planned his escape. The Industrial Authority was due for a surprise. Rosser was quite certain that they didn't have a proper printed form to cover the events that would transpire later in the day. Bureaucrats descended from bureaucrats would not find a ready answer in their operations manuals.

The cell door slid open and Rosser stepped out onto the tier and turned toward the elevator. A dozen other men were ahead of him and every morning he followed them. No one walked side by side. No one spoke. He knew there were fifty men walking behind him but he didn't look back nor try to greet any of them. It wasn't done. All of the men on this tier were engineers, architects or industrial designers. None of them were working on Rosser's project and he didn't know most of them, seeing only those who frequented the racquets courts, socially.

The morning transport routine took him down the elevator to the flats, through the check-out gate where he presented his i.d. card to a televisor and placed his thumb on a glass plate to activate the gate. A mobile walkway carried him to the heliport and he boarded Unit 1200 and took his assigned seat. His coveralls and hardhat were in place in the rack over his head. The security guard checked off the names of the transportees and the flight began. Rosser thought that the use of a human to check the passengers on and off was somewhat archaic. There were many such anachronisms in the security system and the most usual reason for it was employment. The State Industrial Authority had to employ a requisite number of security personnel. Wherever prisoners were likely to gather, there was a human guard to watch over them.

The flight lasted thirty seven minutes, without variation; up, out of the residence compound, over a cluster of soft green hills to the shores of a vast, sparkling lake. Rosser used this time every day, coming and going to collect his own thoughts and meditate on his plans. The flight in the morning was usually silent. On the evening flight there was often laughter and loud talking, sometimes even songs. The whine of the helicopter engine centered him. He rose from the meditation dream state to a supra-conscious awareness of time and place. He stood upon a red sandstone ridge looking down at a dry, yellow-sand, river bed. A stag was racing across the sand. A man carrying a projectile weapon of some sort was riding the stag. Great, carniverous lizards rested in the shadows of rocks, their ignorant minds open. Rosser stepped into the mind of a long, blue scaled lizard and saw with the lizard's eye. The instant flashed before him. As the helicopter banked into a turn, he held two realities together in his mind.

The Vantera Fusion Complex was a vast energy machine built on the shores of an ancient, glacial lake. The State prospered from the energy created in the fifty-one magnetic toroids and eleven fast-impulse amplified light generators. Three new toroids were under construction and it was at this new construction site that Rosser worked as the principle circuitry layout engineer. His job was to interpret plans and convert them into actual construction. No part of the primary

toroids could be set in place without his supervision and
approval. All alignment surveyors and linkage engineers
reported through him. No crew boss or work foreman could
move without orders signed by Rosser. The construction
supervisors and structural designers relied on him to transmit
the State's orders to the workers. He was a product of the
State, trained in nuclear physics and energy construction as a
young man. He excelled in his class, yet his excellence was
dangerous. He had been warned many times to temper his
criticism of operational procedures and the organizational
prerogatives of the Division of Industrial Physics. Yet he
could not quell the dynamic currents that flowed within his
mind. Only five annuals after receiving his commission in
nuclear engineering he was near the top of the Merits Order in
the Division. His name provoked jealousies and fear. His
accomplishments were outdistancing slower, older men. The
clerks of the Merits Order resented Rosser's instant grasp of
problem situations and tenacious will to find abiding solu-
tions. After three original contributions to toroid design
revision, Rosser was seldom challenged. His approach to
physics was classical and mathematically sound. He understood the astrometrics of time and space. Such a man could
easily become Advisor to the Secretariat. There were many
other men, more senior and more subtle, who sought such a
title. A Secretariat Advisor enjoyed many expansions in life
style, rated intercontinental travel, received the Primary Seal
of the Orders of Merit, became a member of the Voice of the
Interior. Many opportunities for State service were presented
to such a man. One so young as Rosser could accede to
Secretariat itself in time. And with good fortune.

It was quite natural for Rosser to resent his imprisonment
within the Vantera Fusion Complex. He was far from the
ordinary convict sentenced to a lifetime of service without
merit. It was thus that the State prospered. All maintenance,
all construction, all agriculture was the product of convict
labor. Rosser had been expelled from the Orders of Merit on
false charges of personal aggrandizement and embezzle-
ment. He was then tried in absentia and convicted in Adjust-

ment Court, removed from research-staff rosters, sentenced
to life at maintenance in Vantera. His legal appeals were
presented at all three Superior Adjustment Reviews and
rejected. And now, instead of occupying the office of a
Worthy Advisor, he was a convict laborer.

His place was limited, yet not without opportunity. Because of his training, he naturally rose to the top position
available to him. After two years as a cement worker, his
educational record caught up with him and he was immediately transferred to engineering. "The State shall not
waste a single valuable resource." That was the first law of
Constitutional Economics. He was given advancement
therapy, assigned to fifth tier residence status, assigned to
engineering transport. He received seven days vacation
every ninety days with optional sex-encounter. He was asked
to volunteer for a teaching program and he did so. Every fifth
work session, he taught nuclear theory and construction
measurements to aspiring members of the basic labor pool.
"The State shall endeavor to educate and employ all of its
citizens according to their natural abilities." Rosser was well
employed and educated to highest levels of technology. He
was well used by the State and he knew it. He knew his life
was now completely compromised, that he was set in place,
on line, for the life of his component parts according to needs
of the machine. He had learned a lot in the past six years.

Trell saw the second lizard sleeping atop a great rounded
boulder. It was directly in their path and he could not take the
chance that it would stay asleep. He rose in the stirrups and
sighted, aiming just behind the shoulder. The bullet exploded
against pale gray scales and the lizard leaped up in astonish-
ment. Trell fired again, this time at the exposed underplates
and the dragon fell backwards tumbling from the boulder and
crashing into a heap of shattered stones. The man and the stag
continued their race. Trell gave a quick look back to see if
they were pursued and the stag quickened his pace.

There were less than 20 faros to run in this gambit of time
and distance. Hutta ran with purpose and graceful precision.

Again Trell watched everywhere for the glistening scales, the fierce claws and cold eyes of death. A pack of four legged, bright scarlet lizards, Ventae, the wolves of the sands, began to take after them. Yet Hutta ran onward, leaping ahead and outdistancing the pursuit. Another hour and they would cross the Swinging Bridge over the empty gorge and the danger from lizards would be over. The next attack came just as the tops of the Tumbled Hills rose into the pale pink sky. These hunters were two legged and ran like men. Their necks were long and their forearms powerful. They were a dark green color with a blue cowl or fairing around the back of their heads. Trell could not get a good line on either one and missed his first shots. He waited until they closed the distance, then shot the nearest one clean through the chest. It continued running in full stride for twenty or thirty steps and then fell over, sliding along on its side and slamming into the base of an overhanging cliff. The stag changed pace and leaped ahead, springing stiff legged over rocks and crevices. The other lizard was lost behind them.

Hutta eased his pace and the final faros were covered without incident. Once again, Trell could enjoy the strong rhythmic cadence of the stag's running. Soon they reached the far edge of the Basin of Rocks and began to climb out of it. Two faros beyond, the land was split by a deep chasm. Hutta approached the chasm at a walk. Danger was all behind them now. Two stone pillars marked the approach to the Swinging Bridge, a narrow suspension rig that swooped across the chasm in a single, graceful arc. It was narrow and easily defended, constructed in the older days when there was warfare amid the Tumbled Hills. Trell dismounted and led Hutta out onto the bridge, testing the foot-way in front of them with hard slams of his rifle butt. The sun was bright and the bridge swayed in the slow wind with the ancient rope cables humming. They picked their way across and breathed easier when they reached the other side. "Hutta!" Trell cried, and mounted his stag.

Baesum was awaiting Trell and Hutta as they climbed slowly up the rocky draw. The stag's deep breathing, his nostrils flared wide, echoed in the canyon. Baesum leaned upon his walking stick and greeted the pair of travelers with a broad, gleaming smile. "Masters of the Plains, I greet you! You have run sixty faros without faltering. Drink deeply from the Well of Yorros. Baesum is your servant!"

The monk showed them a great trough of carved marble set into the cold rock wall. A spigot of copper shaped like the very lizard they had just outdistanced, poured out a steady column of translucent water. The stag bent his head and began to drink. Baesum took a silver dipper and held it under the spigot and then handed it up to Trell. "The King of the Plains salutes you Baesum. You have much to tell me in my preparation for Prince Chavan."

"Yes, my King, the way is prepared. I welcome you."

The lecture period ended and Tripaner sat alone in the class lab. He did not go to the faculty lounge as he usually did but sat quiet and still, collecting his thoughts and trying to adhere to the mathematics of his recent visions. Two other worlds were moving closer to his, moving in two other dimensions of time and space, entire universes converging. Beyond the classroom, the sun rose toward noon, heat waves danced over the wheat fields and the South Fork river babbled over the gravel beds. The air was still and yet powerful. Tripaner believed he was presiding atop the mountainous clouds that were building upon the eastern horizon. The first tornado warning came over the radio at 12:20.

The physicist did not join the faculty for lunch. Instead, he stayed at his desk in the lab working on possible vectors for the events that were transpiring. His afternoon class was due at one o'clock and he wondered if he could preside. He took a certain satisfaction in his thirty year record and in all that time he had never cancelled a class, not even during the great Asian flue epidemic of 1957. School had been closed from time to time for snow or flooding, but Tripaner himself had never cancelled a class. The energies at work would fit into precise natural channels and he began to grasp the results of his computations and translate them into time-space curves.

There was no sense in endangering the students; if it could be prevented, he would do so. In a few minutes he had assured himself that a class from one until two-thirty was entirely probable and not co-incident with any critical overlaps in the curvilinear vortices inherent in the time-energy flow. He stood up from his desk and went to the long, neat row of windows, passing a rickety Van de Graff generator and a series of silicon solar cells. He stood looking out over the green lawn and the fresh leaves on the poplar trees. There was a thick quiet and he could sense the undercurrent of tension that ran through the entire county. Tornado weather was something they were used to in this part of Nebraska, yet a sudden warning always caused a slow ripple of fear to wave over the towns and farms. Few people would speak of it aloud, folks being silent about fear like they are. Tripaner leaned back against the wall. He looked across the room at the Periodic Chart of the Elements. "I put that up there in 1948," he said out loud. "Some things don't change much." Then he thought, "Change slowly over the millenia. But, some things change instantly and forever right in front of you. Hmm. Perhaps every moment, every motion has a half-life. Perhaps aspects of time can be ionized, stripped of certain potentials or enhanced with certain potentials."

"Tornado vortex," he spoke out loud once again. Two students in the one o'clock class were coming in as he said it.

"Yeah," said the first one. "Tornado coming. Man, I'd like to get a picture of one. Right up the center of it. Huh, Mr. Tripaner? Wouldn't that be somethin'?"

"There's lightning up there," said the other. "What causes the lightning?"

A stormy spring rain blew over the Vantera Fusion Project, splitting the skies with sudden gusts of wind. Ragged clouds, gray and black, raced inland from the cold lake. The transport 'copter bucked and dipped in the turbulence. Rosser sat with his head against the window, his eyes scanning the lake front and the racing clouds. He could see the bell-shaped housing of the fusion toroids set on terraces of granite and the great domes containing the fast-impulse laser generators. The Project was built on a thick promonotory that jutted out into the lake. It had been under continuous construction for ninety three years and would likely be so for as long as the State existed. The transport banked into a turn and soon settled into a landing pad. Rosser unbuckled his seatbelt and waited for his name and number to be called off. Then he got up quickly and climbed out of the hatch. He walked across the landing pad with the gusty wind blowing in his face and tiny beads of hail scattering about him. He turned his head down and put his hardhat on, using it to shield himself from the wind and hail. Across the landing pad, beneath a guntower was another i.d. check. He presented his card to the televisor and put his thumb on another glass plate. The gate before him clicked upen. He walked through it and then down a long cement rampway that curved between two buildings of the administrative complex leading to the electricars. His shuttlebus was waiting and he climbed on board, showing his i.d. once again to another guard. When the car was full, the doors slid shut and they rode in silence to the construction site.

The second of three new toroids was near to completion. The final sections would be set in place that day, one in the morning and the last in the afternoon. A preliminary circuit check would be run and then Rosser's job would be done. He was scheduled for tomorrow to move on to the third toroid and start again aligning the first section; sixty four sections, two sections per day. Behind him would come the crews to complete the bell-housing, then came the hydrogen primer injection, then the electromagnetic maintenance team and finally the on-line shifts of everyday supervising engineers. The State had a thousand such projects and three new toroids was a matter of arranging the necessary components, connecting them and turning on the power.

Rosser hopped out of the shuttlebus and took up a new quickness in his stride. He was an important person here, someone with authority regardless of his official convict status. The morning work session began immediately and

Rosser went to the engineer's control station to pick up his copies of the plans and give his first orders. Section 63 was on a huge flatbed railcar and would be moved by crane and settled into place, further closing the circle of energy.

The air was filled with the whine of turbine trucks and pneumatic tools hissing as Rosser stepped out of the engineer's station. He walked slowly toward the flatcar, nodding here and there to a foreman or to a fellow worker. The rigging crew was scrambling over the huge toroid section testing the lift slings and cables. Rosser climbed up onto the car and looked at the rigging foreman.

"Ready?" Rosser asked.

"A few more minutes," the foreman answered, "A number four cap buckler's damaged. We're changing it."

Rosser made a note on his clipboard and spoke the change into his daily operations tape. "Number four cap buckler on section 63, toroid 540, transport support damaged. No apparent sabotage. Security release requested." He looked up at the crane boom as it moved slowly overhead and followed it with his eye until he saw the crane operator far away, a tiny speck of a man amid a giant steel machine. The operator was in Rosser's construction measurements class. As he was looking at him, the man waved and Rosser was startled for a moment by the simple familiarity. His life had come to such a machine-like function, such structured routine that something so spontaneous and friendly disarmed him. He smiled and touched the top of his hardhat in a brief salute.

"Lift rigging secure!" shouted the crew foreman.

"Ready to connect?" Rosser asked.

"Ready," the foreman answered.

"Move ahead," Rosser spoke into his communicator to the supervising transport engineer. The rigging foreman signaled the crane operator and thick cables controlling the lift connectors began to descend toward the crew. The foreman supervised each coupling and then signaled the crane operator to take up slack and put a strain on the cables. Satisfied that the lift support and the transport sling were properly connected, the foreman ordered the crew off the flatcar and joined Rosser.

"Ready when you are," said the foreman.

"Take her away," Rosser replied.

The foreman pushed a button on his signal box and the crane began to lift. The whine of the monstrous gas turbine powering the crane pierced through them and Rosser held his fingers over his ears. He could feel the flatcar creak and spring up as it was relieved of its burden.

The section lifted clear and the crane arm traversed slowly in a long sweeping arc. Rosser climbed down from the flatcar and followed the crane arm as it swung out and over toward the partially constructed bellhousing of the new toroid. He walked quickly across the uneven ground and went through an arched door. The walls of the housing were carefully constructed with exquisite brick work. The State did not spare labor or expense in any of its buildings. Energy production was the prime motivation for the State, its religion and largest cult enterprise. Every detail at the Vantera was infused with a balance of art and science. Rosser both admired and despised the power that held him prisoner. He walked under the open arch into the toroid room. The roof was open to the stormy sky, open to allow the insertion of the sections. The toroid was a hundred metres across and covered by a heavy, translucent plastic weather tent.

Section 63 hovered in the air. Rosser made a slow, deliberate survey of the emplacement crew and of the alignment sight. At his direction, large flaps in the weather tent were opened and peeled back. He looked at the foreman of the emplacement crew.

"Are your men ready?"

The foreman nodded, "Ready as usual."

Rosser pressed a button on his communicator and spoke to the transport engineer. "Emplacement ready. Have him bring it in."

The crane arm moved again and the section swung over the wall and was guided into place. Slowly the crane dropped its cargo lower and lower and the crewmen directed it to its foundation pylon. Suddenly, the foreman shouted, "In place. Remove the transport sling." The men scurried to take off the cables and bucklers.

"Crane free," said the foreman. Rosser nodded and signaled the transport engineer.

"Crane free, take it out and secure. Prepare for section 64." The crane lifted and swung away over the wall and out of sight.

The next crew to move in were the electrical connectors. While the emplacement crew was finishing its work on the foundation pylons and bulkhead seals, the electrical crew went inside the toroid and brought section 63 into contact with the other magnets. Rosser went inside the toroid and lay the wiring and conduit plans out on the smooth floor. The fusion beam would be as thin as the ink cylinder in his pen, yet the magnetic space needed to isolate and contain that beam was big enough around to contain four shuttle buses.

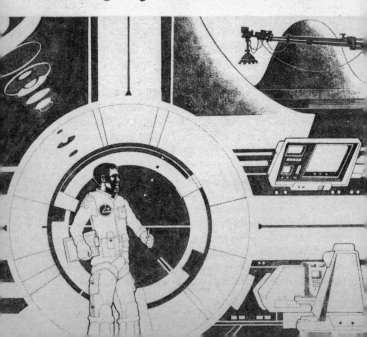

Rosser followed every detail of the on-going electrical circuitry construction. This was his specialty and he took advantage of certain deficiencies in the bureaucratic structure of the engineering hierarchy. The actual, on-line construction foremen and working engineers were not the best nor the most intelligent. They were the mechanicals, the ones trained to take orders and follow plans. They were not innovators, inventors or leaders. They did what they were told to do. The laborers always did what they were told to do and never questioned an engineer.

There was a distance between the designers, the decision making executive engineers and the construction sites. Rosser made use of the distance to secure a place for himself and to implement his own plans, for he was an inventor and knew physics as well as any mind in the State.

Rosser had a plan six years in the making. It was in accord with the laws of physics as he understood them: there was a control factor involved in the transposition of mass to energy. The control factor was time. At the proper moment with the requisite balance, time, energy and mass could interchange. He would escape his prison using the mechanism of the prison itself. He had a full knowledge of the operations of the Vantera power sequences and how energy was staged between the various toroids. Section 64 would be set in place after the noon work break. To the State's planning comptrollers, it was simply section 64 of toroid 540. To Rosser, it was the final piece in an intricate theoretical puzzle.

The monk, Baesum, lived in a stone hut near The Well. Trell and Hutta followed him up a narrow path lined with blue slate. They skirted around The Well itself, a glistening deep pool, greenish in color, seeming to phosphoress. The edge of the pool was circled about with ancient carved stones and in two places stairs were cut down to the surface. The Well was a holy place for Trell's people. It appeared miraculous to them, springing up in the midst of the severe, dry Tumbled Hills. The waters poured out of The Well into a series of irrigation channels that were remnants of another age when the founders of Baesum's order of monks were numerous and powerful. Beyond, the waters spilled into the final few faros of the empty gorge and thence ran out onto the salt flats of the desert. Across the desert, 500 faros, lay the shores of the Circling Ocean.

When they reached the stone hut, Trell took the saddle and harness from his stag and Baesum fed the great runner with sprouted grain and succulent water plants. The two men went into the hut and Baesum fixed a hot tea for Trell.

"Place your bedroll here, My King. There is a long night ahead and then tomorrow you must ride on to your meeting with Prince Chavan. I suggest you rest now. I'll prepare a supper for us. However, we at Yorros are inclined to keep a lean cupboard."

Trell laughed and reached for his saddlebags.

"Do you think the people of the High Plains would send their king into the desert without food to keep him? I was well advised that Baesum lives on tea and pebbles. This eve you shall taste what a King carries in his pockets!" And Trell unwrapped hard cheeses and lengths of antelope sausage, dried fruits and nuts, twice baked pies and spice pots.

"These sausages are made from antelope naturally dead. We do not slaughter needlessly, Baesum. A teaching we have learned from your ancient and most revered brethren. We still maintain the spring Feast of Foals, however. The herds must be maintained in accord with the rising of the grasslands."

"My King will not be offended if this humble monk overlooks the sausage, naturally dead or no. However, my nostrils awaken to the glory of this round of cheese. Rest you now. Let me fuss over this King's picnic."

Trell untied his bedroll and shook it out on a wood framed cot. He lay down and breathed deeply. So many images flooded his mind that he lay entranced, rather than asleep. He saw himself riding Hutta again, crossing the Basin of Rocks, he saw wide prairies, like the High Plains themselves, and strange machines moving the deep grasses. He saw a vast lake, partly frozen, and a huge castle with many bell-shaped

towers on terraces and other buildings, some that looked like
half of a turv ball or a round loaf rising in a pan. All this
Baesum would interpret for him. His breathing deepened and
at last he slept until sunset.

The sun was down and dull twilight fading when Trell
awakened. He lay still, half dreaming of the rolling plains of
his homeland, the yellow grasses rippling under the wind and
herds of animals grazing. His mind floated and he saw his
tents, red and black, the prayer flags and tribal pennants
snapping and waving on their tall poles. He passed through
angry clouds and saw his adversary, Prince Chavan, standing
on a quay in the Harbor of Two Moons. On the waters behind
the quay was a great ship bristling with armament. He saw
the monorail and the ore train and the small army of Chavan's
companions and retainers. Trell felt very thin and tired. A
voice began calling him. It was Baesum.

"Awaken, Trell," said the elder. "Awaken and assume
the strength that is rightly yours to hold. You must have the
will to hold this strength. It is the test your ancestors have set
for you. Know that you are not alone. Awaken in happiness. This moment is complete in peace." Trell sat up and
shook himself. Baesum handed him a mug of hot, fragrant
soup.

"First, a light supper," said Baesum. His eyes twinkled,
reflecting the light of a few candles that hung in sconces on
the wall. "Fit for any king, I must say. Yet we cannot eat so
much as to dull the senses of our minds, for we have far to
travel this night, even though we shall not move from this
hut." Trell remained silent. He felt young and stupid compared to Baesum and wished to be in his tent with his wives
and children. Learning had not come easy to Trell. He was
more interested in his herds and the adventures of his hunting
companions, more interested in the attentions of his wives
and of the winds of the plains blowing free in his hair. Yes, he
was indeed King of the High Plains, but the world was
greater. And there were minds like Baesum's that were
greater than his own, minds that studied the seasons in their
changes and that reached unto the stars. Trell ate and drank

and laughed at Baesum's quiet humor. This was no sour,
scolding hermit, but a man of great awareness and im-
measurable strength. As they ate their supper, Baesum was
telling him a story about an encounter with two bears ". . .
and there I was stark naked, up to my knees in a frigid stream
and not daring to move or even twitch. The female was in her
season and the male was a great lover bound to do her honor.
He on one side of the stream, she on the other and they begin
their courtship with me in the middle! They were roaring and
howling back and forth with their love talk and my feet were
going numb. I was quite certain that to interrupt them would
have resulted in an instant and horrible death! Suddenly, the
male rears up, exposing his member, leaps into the stream
and plunges across. They begin to thrash and wrestle about,
tearing my clothes and my only cloak to shreds. They box
and bang each other around making ferocious growls and
finally, he courts his lady fair, exploding their passion in a
brilliant chorus of joyful howling. During this moment, I
sank into the water and floated away down stream. My legs
were completely numb from cold. I managed to drag myself
up on the bank and pulled myself into a tree for safety."

Trell was thankful for the laughter. He had been overly
serious about his challenge from Chavan and Baesum's animated telling of the story and robust imitation of two bears
mating had him rolling on the floor. The evening lengthened
into night. For a time, they were both quiet.

"You have allies, Trell," Baesum said. "You must use
the powers of these allies tomorrow and shall now begin to
see the allies and contact them, recognize where they are and
how they will help us. We are bound, you and I, by the
collective energy of those who preceded us. We are the
leaders of respective peoples and bound to oppose the slave
kingdom of Chu." The room was still. Trell realized that
Baesum was no longer talking, yet he heard the monk's voice
speaking, answering questions as they formed in Trell's
mind. Pictures and scenes flickered in front of his eyes. For a
moment, he thought they stood upon a peak in the Mountains
of Knives, for a moment he thought he was a fish circling a

cold lake, each moment was fleeting and at the same time expanded and stretched out. Time seemed to stretch and horizons receded before him. Clouds and storms tore at him until he could not resist their power and was blown away into space, hurtling through emptiness illuminated by streaks of colored lightning.

Trell sat with Baesum in the stone hut. Each sat with his back against one wall, gazing into the center of the single room. The floor was bone white, pounded limestone and the walls a crystalline rock known as lauret. In the silence, Trell began to preceive the ally worlds that Baesum had revealed to him. He held his hands out in front of him, palms up, and the images of a swirling planet hovered over each palm.

"There are three worlds," said Baesum. "Three worlds colliding in the universe of worlds, colliding without destruction, each passing through the others over and over again, each a separate reality interchanging one within another, allies in the universe of universes, revolving one about the other, three world systems, each a star among stars, planet among planets, sphere among spheres, everlasting. One who knows the times and places of these interchanges can gain energy from the other worlds. So it is arranged that your meeting with Prince Chavan, the ninety-sixth Baron Chu in the sixth dynasty, Lord of the Southern Continent, Master of the Circling Ocean, he who is falsely named King of This World, shall come to pass as the ally worlds become coincident with our own. Your power increases.

"For eleven millenia, the Barons of Chu and their war minions, their admirals and generals, have sought mastery of this continent, thusly dominating both poles, and all planetary resources. Ever have they sought the secret teachings held only by my order and transmitted through the collective mind spirits to the rightful King of the High Plains. Truly, it is written that a day shall come when the powers of the two continents shall join and become one power. Yet that day is far off and cannot be hastened. Nor can that day be won by force of arms nor by the descendants of the Barons of Chu. Far in the future, a new dynasty will rise and overthrow the

Chu. Out of the Circling Ocean will they arise. Until that prophesy comes to pass, it is charged upon the many peoples of the High Plain and upon the rightful descended Kings of those free and skillful people to resist the Chu, to deny the Chu dominion over this continent and the resources of mind and matter residing here upon.

"A truce was made in the times of your great ancestor, Vinda, during a great drought and corresponding drying of the grasslands. In exchange for grain and help in finding deep wells, the emmisaries of the Chu were permitted to build the inland monorail and mine the Outer Hills for an ore they deemed valuable. There was much counsel against the permission. Yet your ancestor in his own way sought to relieve his people of death and suffering. That was 653 years ago. Now, a new Baron reigns who is neither wise nor lenient. According to the custom, a ruler of the Southern Continent will one day overcome the powers of our order and from this ruler shall come the true King of the Two Continents, Master of the Circling Ocean. It falls upon you to contest this latest rising of the Chu and to repel them. It is told by prophesy that no army of the High Plains shall ever rise to overcome the Chu. You alone shall stand before them. Yet as you now perceive, you are not alone. You have allies unknown to the Chu."

Tripaner flowed along through his second lecture class introducing them to star mechanics at an accelerated rate. Most of his consciousness was centered in the tumbling, billowing cloud mass that rose high above the prairie. The concept of three-realm energy mechanics began to jell and thicken in his mind as he dazzled his junior class with solar data far beyond their normal acceptance level. "Reach students, stretch out, expand and let the universe speak to you, teach you, flow through you." The lecture continued on its new level with greater mobility than the physicist had ever managed to create before. The class was eager, their minds attuned to him and to their own inter-communications. For Tripaner, this was exhilarating and he could sense a spiral mind wave building within the classroom. ". . . at the core, however, density increases as we delve inward and we experience a pressure equal to 200 billion metric tons per square inch. Core matter is an unknown substance, theoretical to our comprehension and perhaps something quite beyond plasma. It is six times as dense as mercury, twelve times as dense as lead and yet it is considered gas. Core temperatures reach a continuous twenty million degrees kelvin and this is known as the nuclear fusion zone. This zone is 218,000 miles in diameter and here, each second, 657,000,000 tons of hydrogen are converted into 652,000,000 tons of helium with a net loss in mass of 4,500,000 metric tons which is converted by a catalytic process involving carbon and nitrogen. This is the nuclear fusion cycle wherein carbon and nitrogen are transmuted, cycled and regenerated in a reaction that liberates all manner of radiant energies including gamma rays, neutrinos, visible light, infra red light, ultraviolet light, radio frequencies and sound waves. It takes twenty thousand years for a measure or a unit of solar radiation to leave the core region and travel to surface, there to be emitted out into space . . . ."

Tripaner was listening to his own voice drone on with facts and explanations. Yet his mind was deeper at work on physics that were not in any text book. The current quark theory held that essential energy units were bound together in exchange cycles that were somewhat elastic and also capable of interaction. Perhaps these energies interpenetrated as well. In twos or threes, these unknowable energy units were bound by their own affinity into channel reaction cycles creating a force field and thereby energy became matter. He saw this in his mind and theorized that a neutrino could be a liberated quark. He knew that a neutrino was conceived of as an essential spin, a vortex of moving energy. Perhaps it was also a tornado. The physicist moved to the composite, finite world of common reality and saw an application wherein certain universe realms had quark-like characteristics and essential charm that directed them to converge, penetrate and exchange energy.

". . . the sun travels at 160 miles per second moving

along within a galactic arm and completes one rotation
around the galactic axis every 250,000,000 years.''

The second tornado warning came at 2:20 and classes were
dismissed. The students rushed out of the rooms into the
halls, banging locker doors and laughing with flushed excitement. The air was tense, but not foreboding. Rather,
there was a strong sense of happiness and vital good cheer.
No one seemed burdened by the emergency and everyone
enjoyed the early dismissal, teachers and students alike. All
after-school events were cancelled which angered the
baseball coach for a few minutes. But he soon admitted he
was thankful to get home early to his wife and daughter.

School was near empty by 2:45. The northeastern sky was
flat black and heavy with a thick, billowing ruffle of dusty
gray lining the horizon. Two pillars of clouds began to rise
higher and higher, swelling and rising, challenging each
other and the plains below. Tripaner went to the roof of the
old school building and stood behind a granite parapet like a
tiny soldier besieged by giants. Below him, the parking lot
swiftly emptied. He watched Mr. Lugenbeel, the school's
chief janitor, take Old Glory down from the flagpole and
disappear inside. He walked around on the roof, kicking at
pieces of loose tar. The new gymnasium was somewhat
higher, its glistening, white hangar roof blocking his view to
the South. He wanted an unobstructed view of all horizons
and so he followed a series of catwalks and steel ladders and
soon walked out on the higher roof. He could see the town a
few miles away, the curve of the river, the bluffs and dense
groves of oak where the houses of the wealthier citizens were
hidden . . . and then the long expanse of plains, the fields of
grain ever productive and giving.

Rosser was quiet during the mid-day lunch break. He sat
with the cement workers and electricians and rigging engineers as he usually did, each one eating a common lunch.
Hot soup, bread, cheese and meat, a piece of fruit. The
canteen trucks came out from the main service building
promptly and on days like this, cold and squalling, the men

looked forward to the break and a drink of kiva to pep them up. The afternoon work session was long and tiring. They would get one more kiva break but other than that, the schedule was exacting and steady. Work quotas were set at Central Procedures Bureau. Performance Inspectors were always present and any let down or failure to meet quota could be met with a disciplinary write-up and subsequent hearing. The quotas were not severe, but very steady and this constant pressure had a wearing effect on the men. They worked without complaint, for complaint was futile, yet their rewards were slim and far between.

Toward the end of lunch break, Rosser was looking over the rim of a second cup of kiva when he saw section 64 moving along on its flatcar toward the end of the rail line. His pulse quickened and he could feel his heart beating. The years of planning were over. He was acting in accord with laws of the physical universe as he had come to understand them. He could transpose time and dimension, move mass into energy states beyond those currently apparent. Indeed, the honored and venerable physicist, Ostresnet, had theorized much in the same fashion two hundred years prior. Ostresnet theorized that matter was a transient phenomenon existing only through the interactions of certain energy vortices which he named "untals"; that groups of two or three of these untals coalesced in time and space to form matter and that they were actually charmed fields of primal energy which became coincident with one another according to a particular schedule. Rosser believed that it was in accord with the concepts of macro-cosmic involvement for this same sub-atomic coincident relationship to exist on the universe scale. The three separate realities that he had come to be aware of were a manifestation of Ostresnet's untal theory proceeding on the dimensional level of star systems and planets. He would traverse from one realm to another during the afternoon break. It was simply a matter of achieving the essential spin at the charmed moment.

Trell left the stone hut and saddled Hutta. It was the first

light of day. Baesum stayed within, seated in meditation.
The sky was dark, a deep, brooding, ruddy color. The early
light spread across the horizon in a series of pink and yellow
ribbons. There was no trail over the Tumbled Hills, no
pathway nor any signs. Trell felt Baesum's mind guiding
them and he gave Hutta free reign. The hills were dry with
few plants of any kind and only small reptiles or crawling
insects living among them. "No wonder the Well of Yorros
is a sacred place," Trell thought. "And to think a small war
must now be waged for control of this dirt pile." The stag
moved onward now running, now walking. The morning sun
rose behind a cover of rusted clouds and a thin wind blew
inward across the salt desert. Trell fastened a scarf across his
nose and mouth and rode toward his meeting.

It was mid-day when the rider and his stag climbed to a
high smooth ridge. Trell looked down in front of him and saw
the silvery track of the monorail. The open pit mines of
Yorros were twenty faros away. The ore was conveyed to the
monorail on a series of moving carts connected to cables. The
monorail transported the treasure to the shores of the Circling
Ocean.

"What machinery these Southerners construct!" Trell
thought. "I must admit they marvel me. What a folly that
such powers come into the hands of greedy tyrants like
Chavan. When I go to meet the ancestors, I shall ask that no
more fools be allowed to gain life on this sphere. Hutta! Take
us down!"

The monorail ended at a squat, cylindrical tower. There
was an antenna atop the tower and as they approached it,
Trell could see a faint, spherical emanation of purplish waves
pulsing out from it. A thin, needle-like beam of red light shot
back down the monorail, disappearing in the distance. Not
far from the cylinder was a strong steel shed with a steep,
peaked roof. It was open on all sides, just a roof held up with
steel pillars. Trell dismounted and walked about, inspecting
the area. There was no sense of a trap, no sign of anyone. He
spread his cloak on the sandy ground and sat. The sun moved
past mid-day. Trell waited and soon he sensed the vibrations

moving along the monorail. Prince Chavan's vehicle was indeed on its way. Hutta browsed on the short grasses that grew near the tower. Suddenly, he lifted his head and snorted, looking directly down the long, thin rail of steel.

"Yes, Hutta," Trell said. "The Prince will keep his appointment. Time and space must be fulfilled. He who calls himself "King" must become acquainted with the true powers of this continent."

Far in the distance, far down the monorail, a shimmer of light and a rising puff of yellow dust appeared in the heat waves. Ten thousand years and more separated this meeting from its ancestor. On that day, so long in the past, Votos, the third King of the High Plain declared eternal opposition to the dominion of the Barons of Chu. Upon this place, Votos demonstrated his powers causing a hail of rocks to fall out of a clear sky crushing the Chu's champion warrior, Bagdon. Chavan was coming to witness another Act of Power and demonstrate powers of his own. Trell was already impressed with the workings of the monorail.

The afternoon work call was sounded and the rigging crew swarmed over section 64, checking the components of its transport sling. Rosser relied on his experience to help him through the mechanics of the emplacement. He had denied his emotions for so long, he now found them dangerous and wild and he had to grip them finally with a controlling mind. He was elated and knew his day had come. He was moving into freedom, into a new realm where his quantity as a being, as an energy field, was completely unknown. Regardless of where he went or what became of him, he was escaping from the Vantera.

Rosser followed through with the mechanics of moving section 64 into place, giving the appropriate orders and signals at the required times. Again the crane arm swung through the air, the rigging crew grappled with descending cables and the section was soon lifted in its transport sling. Rosser watched the crane arm arc toward the toroid and he walked along behind. He went inside the bell-housing,

looked up at the open sky and the section hanging there
suspended over the alignment site. He moved with a conscious, steady tempo ordering the flaps of the weather tent
opened, inspecting the foundation pylons and directing his
foremen. Assured that all of the components were ready, he
entered the toroid itself and ordered the section put in place.

Inside the toroid, rows of temporary readylumes glittered
and light reflected from the polished surface of the dynasteel.
The primary circuitry crew was mulling over their equipage
in preparation for the final section contacts and wiring con-
tinuity. Rosser stood close to the last opening in the circle as
the section was eased in. The emplacement foreman guided
the crane operator with a video communicator. The crew
members worked the guy lines of the transport sling as the
section slipped into place slowly and with ease. It was, after
all, a prefitted component constructed with unerring accu-
racy. The outside light was sliced away and the toroid 540
was a complete circle. Rosser heard the foreman confirm the
emplacement over the communicator and he waited for the
crew to remove the sling. As soon as the report was given, he
signaled the transport engineer, ''Crane free, all sections in
place. Take the crane out, secure until morning work call.''

The circuitry crew went to work at once. Rosser had them
well trained and responsive. He began to walk through the
toroid with his roll of plans and the classified ''Division of
Industrial Physics Primary Fusion Toroid Circuit Text.'' It
was his responsibility to insure that the preliminary electrical
check was positive and that all of the great magnets were
operative in accord with the sync-pulse generators. Toroid
540 was different from all the others on the Vantera and it
would soon absorb the energy of all five toroids now working
on this terrace level, including toroid 539 which had just
undergone hydrogen injection and was still in the hands of
the electromagnetic maintenance team. There had been no
reports in any official news documents, but Rosser knew full
well that toroid 539 was demonstrating a power beyond its
design capacity. He knew that there was a five millimeter
oscillation in the fusion core. He had built it that way and he

knew as well that the maintenance team would not discover
the changes made in the various components. The performance documents would take an entire work quarter to process. The team would continue to make adjustments to
smooth out the oscillation until their operations phase dead-
line was reached. Only then could a performance report be
written. Rosser knew that the active network on this terrace,
including its various automatic transmission substations,
would come under his control when he was ready to accomplish his interlock on the equipment and redirect the
induction flux. He had discovered, years prior, that the
toroids on each terrace had a capacity to interlock through the
substation complexes. He had arranged a series of intercon-
nection ties that would produce an instant power equal to the
total output of the terrace. There were locking relays to make
his parasite feeder raceway unidirectional. Resistance termi-
nals were shunted with sliding contacts. Spark-overs and
areas with discharge potential had been eliminated.

Upon Rosser's demand, a transient variation in current
would activate a time delay and open a tie feeder source
trough to carry an automatic surge through the system and
into toroid 540. The oscillations in the fusion core of toroid
539 would immediately sine and react as an exciter. Rosser
had installed an optical wave guide between 539 and 540.
The product of the effective current would amplify by an
acceleration factor equal to the component resonance of the
moment. Rosser would achieve the essential spin and translate his personal energy in trillocycles. The toroid would
naturally generate a kinetic force and produce a magnostruc-
tive parallel with a potential capacity to change dimensional
substance quanta. Rosser did not know if he would die in the
surge or take on the elemental charm necessary for transfer to
occur. He only suspected. He did not know which one of the
coincident realms he would enter. It would depend upon the
polarity of the moment. Perhaps there was a more certain
way to determine transfer potential directorate vectors, but
he was not familiar enough with the concurrent phenomena
to determine. He walked carefully through the fusion tunnel

inspecting section after section, knowing that his changes in
construction, both subtle and obvious, had been im-
plemented without question. As he walked through the steel
tunnel, he began to feel the three realms closing in upon one
another with anticipated velocity. Rosser had graphed the
convergence curves and wasn't at all surprised to see an
inverse square law develop in the relationships. The closer
the realms came to each other, the stronger the attraction and
greater the velocity of approach. After the moment of singularity, the realms would recede from each other and the
attractive force and escape velocity would decrease according to the square of the distance. At some point in the future,
a resilence factor would overcome recession and the
approach/convergence pulse would begin again. Rosser
wasn't sure what happened at singularity. Yet he imagined
that certain energies were generated and transferred. His
success depended on his own perception of the singular
moment and upon attaining the trillocycle transpin.

He completed his circumferent inspection tour as the
schedule clerk announced the afternoon break. The circuit
crew was finished with the hookup of section 64 and was
disconnecting the string of readylumes and passing them out
throught the access port. Rosser made sure all the tools were
accounted for and taken out. Then he checked each man out
and crawled through, closing the hatch behind him.

Tripaner stood on the white roof of the gymnasium. His
mind was the center of the tornado vortex. Vast energies
expended in streaks of lightning as he presided over
the direction of the vortex and its form. He kept it from
touching the farmland below as the funnel grew in dimension
and intensity. He was designated as the singular moment.
The opposing realms converged and held together until the
exchange cycle was completed. Surges of working energy in
waveform washed over and around him and for one moment
he would hold three worlds together in one place, holding
them as long as he could until they pulsed with renewed
power.

The tornado broke out of the heavy clouds, a howling black whip scouring the horizon. It did not touch the earth at first, but snaked and wavered over the prairie, threatening yet uncommitted. Silver lightning shattered the boiling under-skirts of hissing clouds as the vortex moved toward the west. Tripaner stood atop the gymnasium searching the funnel with his binoculars. His mind was a part of the storm. He could sense three convergent realms circling each other awaiting and seeking an equation in charm that would allow them to pass through, propel them to a future relationship.

Rosser sensed the timing was correct. While the crews were busy with their hot cups of kiva, he went back to the access port and crawled into the toroid. He shut the hatch behind him and walked in darkness toward a tiny, white pin-light that guided him to a series of two-position selector keys. There was no plan for this keyboard. It did not appear on any pages of the classified toroid circuitry documents. Without hesitation, he activated the time delay and opened the optical wave guide. He didn't know how many seconds he had before the surge would build and override the substa-tions. He turned into the dark tunnel and began to walk clockwise. In his mind, he saw a waterfall and a swift running stream and then he was flooded over with a bright, multicolored wave of light.

Chavan's train slowed and stopped. Trell stood quietly, waiting. Squadrons of soldiers emptied out of the cars and then officers of various rank. Chavan himself stepped down from his private car and walked quickly toward the steel tent. The soldiers appeared calm and deadly, well trained and well paid. Chavan was surrounded by his ministers and generals. Trell said nothing as a carpet was set for Chavan under the steel roof and chair placed upon the carpet. Chavan was not subtle nor diplomatic.

"I have the power now," he stated. "Let your advisors take note. Long have your people resisted us, but no more. I claim this continent as my own. I am King of This World, the One Prophesied born on the waves of the Circling Ocean! I have a power far beyond your ken, Trell. Far beyond a keeper of flocks and animal herds. Gaze you into the desert. I command the power of the sun.''

Trell had yet to say a word and was insulted by Chavan's disrespect. Not even a single cordial greeting. It was an insult to Trell's people as well. He followed Chavan's pointing finger and looked out over the salt flats. Far away, on the distant horizon, a tiny, brilliant spark exploded and began to grow. A ball of fire as bright as a sun swelled and rose and then darkened suddenly leaving a gray black cloud that puffed out thick and ugly.

"General Lo, sieze this nomad and his animal! Put them in my zoo!'' Chavan laughed and his retinue laughed in reflection. A squad of riflemen began to encircle Trell and Hutta. As the soldiers rushed upon them, Trell mounted his stag and spread his arms wide. Light shimmered about them as the rider and his stag became as a mirage and disappeared.

Trell stood on a ledge of sandstone overlooking the railhead and Prince Chavan's retinue. He withdrew his shape from the encirclement and laughed. "Zoo! He would put us in a zoo, Hutta!'' The antelope snorted and pawed the rock beneath his hooves. Trell spread his arms wide and called upon the allies and his ancestors. He saw a vortex of energy surge out of the castles by the lake. He saw a monstrous twisting black storm and he brought the two together. "Here is my gift to Chavan! Yea, you were born upon the waves but you are not the One Prophesied, for that one is yet to arise! Take my gift, Chavan. Into the waters you shall return. The waters of death.''

The tornado broke out of heavy red clouds. It was black and howled like a demon snake and hissed down through a cleft in the sandstone hills scouring the earth and sucking everything loose into its vortex. Chavan and his toy train were consumed in a whirl of rocks and twisting steel. The tornado hurtled down the rail line and red dust boiled up in its wake.

It was four-thirty when Tripaner called home. "Ella! I'm just calling to say, to say I'm going to be a little late today.

Everything all right?" He wondered if such an old man as he was could say, "I love you, Ella," and carry it off. Sometimes he wondered if he was sixty three or twenty three. "Well, I thought you'd be callin'," Ella said. "The tornado went off toward Jenkintown. Blew up a storm out here, but nothing really destructive. Took the screen door off. And your windmill, it got to turnin' so fast it just swooped away into the clouds. One of my nastursiums fell over on the porch. Otherwise . . . what's all that noise? Where you callin' from?"

"I'm in Cal Haver's saloon on River Street. John Tarvey invited me in. He says he's tired of teaching history and wants to go into solar power."

"Harold? What did you do to that tornado? I dreamed you were up in the clouds, you old Wizard. I thought this day was real strange didn't you? Were you ridin' on that storm? You Wizard. Seems like the hours were all stretched out of shape today, somethin' funny."

"I haven't quite figured it out yet," he told her, "but I guess I'll get around to it. Now don't be tellin' folks about me being a Wizard. That's a secret." Tripaner looked at the telephone. It seemed to melt and fall apart in his hand. "Well, don't you be having too many drinks in there," Ella said slowly. "It's enough you were involved with that tornado without being drunk on top of it."

"I love you, Ella!" Tripaner finally got it out.

"Now, I know you're drunk!" Ella said. "You drive real slow coming home. We'll have to fix that windmill tomorrow. Screen door, too."

Tripaner mumbled his goodbyes and returned to the bar.

Trell was dismayed, yet overjoyed, at the continual flood of images that filled his mind. He wandered at the edge of the salt desert following his stag. He sang in strange languages and constructed tall buildings from the changing shapes of clouds. He laughed and the very wind was music to him. The powers of his allies were his to command, yet there was nothing of his world that he would change or work those powers upon. He had destroyed his only enemy by channeling an energy across time and space and he had seen Chavan with his overconfident, ill-prepared vanguard disappear into a swirling black storm that sprouted red and gold lightning as it skipped from one world to another and then to another. He had seen pieces of Chavan's armory and fragments of his toy train fall into a vast, stormy lake partly frozen . . . a lake that was not upon either continent of Trell's own world.

He followed the stag as they sought passage around the Basin of Rocks and thence through the regions of dry grass to the High Plain. How simple life had been before his fated counsel with Baesum: hunting and moving with the herds and the seasons, keeping his tents repaired and his women happy. A new universe had suddenly opened unto him. Yet even with his new powers of mind, he felt like a grain of sand on the salt desert. He called out to Hutta, "Stay, you horned demon! Would you leave me behind? I do not know the trail and I am tired, too tired to ride. I must rest the night." The stag walked slowly back to him. "We camp beneath these cliffs tonight," Trell said. The stag belched and grumbled. "Yes," Trell whispered, "I, too, would rather we sleep upon the tall grass. But that is days away." He loosened the saddle and pulled it down from Hutta's back, then spread his blankets on the sand. He lay down and drifted toward sleep. He saw with the mind of his stag and knew instantly what route he would follow on the morrow, where the grade was less steep, where small watercourses tumbled unnoticed.

He lay wrapped in his fine blankets handwoven by his people, the colors red and purple mirroring the sky, the designs chasing the borders like herds of antelope. Sleep came closer yet a part of his mind was now eternally awake. He saw the ally worlds hurtling away from him on their expansion phase and he knew he could contact them at will, that they were related to his own realm in a manner that he could not give in words. He would make a song of it for his sons. He would make a dance of it to portray his knowing before the Fire of the Elders during the Moon of Snows.

Rosser appeared at the edge of a wide, flat field. The golden masses of slender, clustered stalks lay still under a setting sun. He plucked at a stalk of the grain and examined the fat head of ripened seed. "Some species of cereal grass," he thought. "A cultured planet." He gazed at the sun, a mild, dusty egg settling onto the horizon. "A median star, yellow, somewhat small, not apparently variable. I wonder what they call it here? I need a whole new language." He let his eyes adjust to the slanting sun rays and watched shadows spill over the grain fields, turning darker as the light changed from golden to dull red, as faint purples began to appear in the far distances. "Nice planet," he whispered, breathing in the warm atmosphere through his nostrils. "I'm here, where ever it is. It's a planet. Good air, fair sun. I'll have to move slowly. No reason to startle the locals . . . agriculturalists. Wonder what they call themselves? I'll have to rely on mind paths at first. Then language. Certainly they know measurements. Think slow. No need to start off with distant realities."

A vehicle approached. He sensed it coming down a narrow, black path cut straight through the wide fields. "What's this?" he marvelled.

His sensors reached out, measuring the vehicle, surrounding it long before it reached him, feeling its power source. He laughed at its electrical circuits.

"What is this? It's inhabited!" Rosser sensed the mind within the vehicle and knew instantly he had projected himself to the proper place in his new time/space.

Harold Tripaner drove the Ford on through the gathering dusk toward home. The sun was down, fallen away into the wheat, rolling under the earth. "Gone to the gods," he whispered. "Gone to Apollo in a golden chariot." His mind was overflowing with the continuous mathematics of radiant energy. "In the days of Joshua the people saw the sun stand still in the sky. Time bends," Harold continued. A figure appeared at the far edge of his vision. It stood at the side of the road and glimmered as if it were not quite there. Harold slowed the Ford to a crawl and prepared to stop. He had the sudden feeling that he was keeping an appointment. "Unlikely in random events," he speculated. The figure walked upright. It was a man . . . from somewhere. Not a farmer, that was certain. Harold knew every farmer for miles around and most of the regular hired hands as well. This figure was different, less dense. Harold stopped the Ford, pulled up the handbrake and then set the gears in neutral. He reached over and opened the door on the passenger side. The figure did not move toward the car nor make any signs.

Harold got out of the Ford and walked around in front, approaching the stranger. Suddenly, a bright flash jumped between them, yet there was no feeling. "Photon interaction!" Harold exlaimed. "We've just exchanged photons!"

Rosser was also startled by the flash of energy that illuminated a moment of the twilight shadows. There was a slow silence as he looked at the creature that had just climbed out

of the strange box on wheels. The creature appeared to be a biped somewhat like himself, yet it had large shining, glistening eyes.

Harold adjusted his glasses. There was a faint electrical aura pulsing around the visitor that stood before him in the wheat field. Mind paths began to open and unfold between them. Tripaner imagined a right triangle and stated, "$a^2 + b^2$." The stranger quickly completed the equation adding, "$= c^2$" and then moved the triangle into a dimensional topology, reshaping the lines and curving them. Harold recognized the formation of the sine theorem for sperical trigonometry and he contributed the next sequence in the appropriate cycle of permutations beginning with sin B sin c = sin y sin b. The telepathy between them strengthened and began to develop.

"Earth has gained a deep intelligence here," Tripaner mused. His thoughts became warm colors that appeared and then faded on the established mindscreen. "We cannot, as yet, converse with words, but we share mathematics and it seems that certain thoughts manifest between us in shapes and colors."

Rosser replied to the friendly emmission of light waves coming from his new found associate as softly as he could. The flood of emotions that waved over him took form in several flashes of red and gold. The elation of his successful transfer of energies from one world to another, the years of bitterness and planning that had sustained him at the Vantera, the bewilderment that enwrapped his new existence, all this was transmuted into tremulous formations of light.

"Welcome," Tripaner extended his own ability to communicate in mindspace. "Wherever it is you come from, traveler, welcome. I am very simply a teacher here in Nebraska. Physics. Energy. I know that we have much to exchange. I can learn from you. Teach me and I shall teach you the ways of Earth. If you plan on staying!"

"We can communicate. At the least we have a beginning," Rosser thought. "I am from a place far beyond here.

A different energy level. Yes, Teacher . . . there is much that we can learn from each other.''

Harold retreated and climbed back into the Ford. He beckoned to the stranger indicating that he should follow.

''Close the door,'' said Harold, adjusting his glasses. ''My house is just a few miles up the road, across the river.'' The stranger sat still, looking at him. ''Close the door,'' Harold repeated. He didn't want to reach out suddenly and scare the visitor so he slowly pointed and mimicked the act of pulling inward. The stranger reached out, took hold of the inner door latch and pulled it. The door shut. ''Good, very good,'' Harold beamed. ''We're gonna get along jest fine.'' He put in the clutch, released the hand brake and put the Ford in gear. Rosser started laughing at the sudden sensation of motion. Tears rolled out of his eyes. He thought, ''I've escaped Vantera. I have indeed escaped! I am free!''

The Ford rolled off down the road toward the river, the bridge and the trees.

Introduction to 'The Road To The Sea'

More American sf is translated into foreign languages than foreign sf is published over here. That's unavoidable, perhaps; the English-speaking science fiction community is large enough that most publishers are able to fill their lists quite nicely with domestic product. But sometimes you can miss something that way.

Co-translator Judy Merril, the noted writer, anthologist, New Wave advocate and dreaded "Undoctor" on the BBC's long-running "Doctor Who" series, describes *The Road to the Sea* as:

—one of a group of stories now being translated to make up an anthology we hope will give some perspective on the range and scope of modern Japanese science fiction. In order to convey some of the style and mood, the translation was done "in committee", with the native Japanese co-translator holding final responsibility for the authenticity of the tone of the final draft produced by the English-language co-translator.

The result, in *The Road to the Sea,* is a story of uncommon feeling and poignancy, in any language.

THE ROAD TO THE SEA

Takashi Ishikawa

(translated by Judith Merril with Tetsu Yano)

I must go forth to see the sea!
So the boy resolved. And, the kind of boy he was, no slings or arrows would stop him once his mind was set. Without a word to father or to mother he set out from home.

Which way to the sea? The boy didn't know. But any which way if he just kept tramping along in one direction, he was bound to come to the sea sooner or later. This was the wisdom of a boy just turned six.

The boy had never seen any sea except inside his picture-books.

. . . full of blue water everywhere, the open ocean stretches without end. And in it—there's a whale!*—and a shark—*sea-gills!*—a mermaid and an octopus—kelp, coral, and a* mole! *And over there, and here and here and there again, great floating vans named* "ships" *—and that one is even a* skull-ship *with tattooed pirates* riding in it! *And the horizon out at sea—water, water, nothing as far as you could see but* water*—what in the wold would such a sight look like? . . .*

His mind could not hold on to such a watermuch.

Adrift in dreams of sky-sea-blue, the boy trudged purposefully on.

At the end of the town, he met the old man. This old man was always sitting there by the side of the road, staring at the sky: he was kind of funny in the head.

"Hey, boy!" The old man hailed him, "Where you going?"

"The sea," said the boy, and kept on walking.

"The sea?" The old man opened his toothless mouth and laughed. "That's a good one!" He grabbed the boy by the arm and pulled him to a stop. "Going to the sea? Okay. You'll just have to go to heaven first." He pointed a withered old finger, trembling uncontrollably, at the sky. "The sea is right up there over your head!"

In the clear blue sky there was nothing but the sun, shining bright. The boy didn't say a word. He just pulled loose from the old man and trotted off, pursing his lips a bit and clucking his tongue: *That old man has got too old—his whole head is mixed up now.*

Pretty soon the boy got to a small hill. Standing on the top of the hill, he looked all around him everywhere, but the presence of the sea was nowhere to be sensed. The boy dropped on his haunches and had something to eat while he watched the gradual shifting of ground-shadows cast by the slow passage of the sun.

Beyond the plain was a range of mountains and the sun was just beginning to slant down in that direction. *The sun sinks in the sea:* that's what he had heard, so—*Let's see what's on the other side!*

The boy straightened his back, set his lips firmly, fastened his eyes on the distant hills, and started walking—

Beyond the mountains were still further mountains. Beyond those mountains stretched a plain. At the far end of the plain, another range of hills confronted him.

The boy kept marching along, all alone. Not one town, not one village, not one person, not one living creature did he meet.

His supplies of food and water were getting sadly low.

He did not understand how the sea should be so far away.

The boy kept going. How many times did he sleep on the

ground? It didn't matter. When he was sleeping, when he was walking, he was always seeing his visions of the sea.

He took every shape of the sea. Sometimes he was a fish, sometimes a pirate, another time a harbor, then a sail swelling in the wind—he was always changing from one shape to another; and now—*a storm-toss't ship, bathed in spray-spume, shot through with lightning bolts, pounded on by thunder-claps, just about to sink at last—*

—The boy's legs had stopped walking a while back. Now two moons shed their light on a still small figure stretched out on the red-brown desert sand.

The spacesuit had a two-hundred-hour range before it stopped functioning completely.

The boy was smiling a bit even as his breath stopped. Under the night sky of Mars he lay facing a green star—the sky-floating Earth. The sea was there, but he could never reach it.

Nobody goes back there any more.

Introduction To 'Getting Near The End'

Andrew Weiner is a thirty-one-year-old British expatriate to the sovereign nation of Canada. He is the author of several self-help books based on behavioral psychology: STAY SLIM FOR GOOD, STOP SMOKING FOR GOOD, GUIDE TO INTELLIGENT DRINKING, and PHOBIA-FREE. Beyond that, he says, "I eat too much, smoke, drink a good deal, but have no phobias that I'm aware of." He is currently working as a full-time freelancer, writing articles for Canadian magazines on business, social sciences and the media.

He describes himself as "not a very prolific science fiction writer." He made his first sale to Harlan Ellison, for AGAIN, DANGEROUS VISIONS, when he was nineteen. Since then he has sold two pieces to *Fantasy and Science Fiction* and one to *Chrysalis*.

About *Getting Near The End*, he says:

When I wrote the story, back in 1977, the revival of roller skating was a science-fictional projection (and, I thought, rather a bizarre one at that). Now it's just a social detail. Too bad, because it's just about my only successful SF extrapolation.

GETTING NEAR THE END

Andrew Weiner

They were in the hotel, the singer and the dancer, on the thirty second floor of the hotel which was said to be the finest in the city. They had come to the hotel direct from the airport, through the private subway system. They had been in the hotel for five days, and still they had not yet stepped outside on to the streets of the city. Neither did they plan to.

In the hotel, the singer and the dancer passed the time. They listened to the latest music and screened the latest films and scanned the latest ideas. They ate and drank and played with the singer's child. They looked out at the city through the high wide windows of the hotel and watched the disturbances.

The disturbances were bad. The singer and the dancer had seen very much worse disturbances in different cities at different times, but they both agreed that the disturbances were very bad this year for this particular city. Security forces battled deviant groups, mortars kicked up clouds of dust, ambushed automobiles exploded in mined streets. Sometimes the sky burned red at night. The noise of all this failed to penetrate through the thick, soundproofed windows of the hotel, but the singer and the dancer could see that the disturbances were very bad.

The hotel could have been in Nepal and it could have been in London and it could have been in Leningrad. It could have been anywhere that the big hotels still stood, but in fact it was in New York. The singer and the dancer were in town for the New Year, another New Year in another big hotel. Except that this time the party would be something special. This time the party would be held in honor of the singer, who was about

211

to release her new record album after nearly four years spent in seclusion.

The party would be for the singer, and the dancer was merely tagging along. He would be very careful to remain in the background. The dancer was in reality also a famous singer, in his time even more famous than his current companion. But that was how he liked to think of himself these days, as a dancer. Once, a long time before, his voice had burned, burned deep, penetrated the soul. But now, as he slumped towards his fiftieth year, his voice was to all intents gone, and all that was left to him was the dance. The dance was in his style, in the way he moved, moved through his life, moved on and moved up. It was, in any case, the dance quite as much as the burning voice that the people had paid to glimpse. And that much was still left to him, there was still the dance.

II

The dancer listened to the music playing on the radio. The music was terrible. The music was wretched, strangled, desperate. The music was of its time.

The dancer watched the singer's child play upon the floor, building towers of bricks and knocking them down again. The child was seven years old. He looked something like his mother and something like his father, although the dancer did not know the identity of the child's father. Neither did the child. The child had never seen his father and never expressed any interest in seeing him. He did not know who his father was and apparently did not care.

The child's father was an astronaut, one of the last astronauts. And very soon now he would return to Earth. He would return from Mars. The astronaut did not suspect that he was the father of the singer's child, and she had not chosen to inform him of the fact. The astronaut did not know that the singer had a child, for that matter. He rarely followed the news from the entertainment world, and hardly even recalled his drunken one-night stand with the famous singer. Moreover, he had been off the planet for quite some time now.

The dancer had been travelling with the singer for nearly two years now, moving from one hotel to the next, and still he did not feel that he understood the singer's child, no more than he felt that he understood the singer. The child was a quiet and serious boy, perhaps excessively serious, and he rarely allowed the dancer—or anyone except his mother—to intrude upon his play. Since his birth he had met very few other children, and liked none of them. He seemed to prefer to be alone, or else with his mother. Even alone he was usually with his mother, playing her songs on his Talkie machine, engaging her in deep conversations in which he played both roles.

"Hey, kid," the dancer said. The child's name was Daniel but the dancer usually called him "kid" and the child had not yet objected. "Hey, kid. You want to watch some TV? You want to watch the ship come down from Mars?"

The child considered. "I don't know," he said. "I don't know if that would be very interesting. It isn't going to crash or anything, so I don't know."

He completed his tower of bricks, knocked it down again.

"Why not?" he said.

III

A long three years, very long. Denning yawned, rubbed his eyes, tossed the well-thumbed book of bridge puzzles across the cabin floor. There were still two more hours before his scheduled sleep period. He could, of course, take it earlier than that, but the idea did not merit serious consideration.

Early on, Denning had decided to stick to his schedule, stick to it all the way down the line. Stick to a schedule and you always knew where you were, who you were. But get too loose, let the schedule slip, drift off aimlessly into unstructured time, and you could all too easily end up like Fuller. End up completely flipped out. Because out here, way out here, a man needed something he could hold on to. And he was so very close to home now, it would be tragic if he were to slip up now. One day, he thought. *One day*.

He turned in his swivel chair to scan the instrument panels. Everything, as always, appeared to be functioning correctly. The only major systems failure on this ship had been confined to the soft hardware, to the crew itself.

He yawned again. He got up, stretched, scratched his head. He began to pace up and down on the narrow floor of the cabin. Five paces and turn. Five more paces and turn . . . . A man could use a little more space. But that, as the boys back at the Agency would be quick to point out, was the whole purpose of the exercise. Space. Getting it and keeping it. That was the whole philosophical and economic imperative underpinning this entire mission. That was the thing that had locked Denning and his dear departed buddies into this flying tin can in the first place, and propelled them in a

preprogrammed arc towards the miserable wastelands of
Mars. Space. Nothing less.

Oh, it was ironic. It was certainly very ironic. Denning has
reflected often on such ironies during the long lonely hours of
this voyage home. He has thought many deep thoughts,
engaged in many fascinating speculations about the nature of
man and infinity. And very soon now he would set them all
down in his memoirs for the enlightenment of humanity as a
whole. Memoirs which, he had frequently calculated, ought
to pull in at least a couple of million bucks what with first
serialisation and TV rights. Which was only the beginning.

Nearly home, he thought, so nearly home. If he cared to
turn on the screen, he would be able to see the Earth spinning
around and around his ship, a ball of dirt steadily gathering
size. But he knew that the sight would only make him dizzy.
He could of course kill the spin, slip back into free fall for
awhile, but that wouldn't do at all. Weightlessness played
hell with muscle tone, and he needed to stay in condition.
Besides, floating in free fall always made him feel like some
kind of ghost. He had to hold on to some feeling of his own
substance, existence.

Three years. And quite alone these last six months of the
way home. Plenty of time to think. Too much time, in fact.
He had thought a great deal about Fuller, whether or not he
had been right to kill Fuller. But that was all over with now.
He had resolved that question to his own satisfaction. There
was no question about it, not in his own mind at least.

It had been, after all, practically a matter of self-defence.
There was nothing else to be done. Fuller had needed killing,
that was all, the guy was crazy for it, he went out of his way to
provoke it. There was really nothing else to be done. Denning had put up with all the screaming, put up with all the
ranting. But when Fuller tried to fuck with the controls, that
was really too much. If he hadn't happened to wake up when
he did, they would have ended up in the heart of the sun.

They would surely see it his way, back in Houston, they
would fall over themselves to avoid any further unpleasant-
ness. They would acknowledge that he had acted only in the

best interests of the mission, of which he was, after all, the
acting commander. He had assumed that status after Wyatt
had gone chasing God only knew what shadow out in the
frigging Martian night with only two hours worth of oxygen.

It was really too bad about Wyatt. Denning almost missed
the guy. They had been good buddies once, a long time ago,
so long ago he could hardly even remember the details. They
had been buddies until Wyatt had gone morose and then
quietly gone crazy and taken that long last walk. Looking for
Martians, that was Fuller's notion, and he was probably
right. Fuller was crazy too, of course, but maybe that gave
him some greater insight into Wyatt's behavior. Certainly it
was difficult to explain it any other way.

Wyatt gone. Fuller gone. Leaving only him. Just me, he
thought. The last survivor. The one hero. Jake Denning,
hero. The man who looked infinity in the face and never
looked away, in fact spat right into infinity's eye. The un-
shakeable Jake Denning.

In his mind he reviewed yet again the forthcoming sequence of events: the parades, the speeches, the dinners, all
the riches and fame and women coming his way. It was a very
pleasant fantasy. He worked through it often, changing a
detail here and a detail there, shaping it, perfecting it. What
he would say to the President and what the President would
say to him. Which movie stars he would fuck and in which
rank order, specifying position. Oh yes, the possibilities
were almost endless.

IV

(From: *The Martha Nova Story*, Starline Books, New
York, 199-)

"Levett, her Rasputin, her Epstein, her *personal manager,* grows animated as he recalls the day he discovered the
brightest star in today's entertainment galaxy. His short,

powerful-looking arms stab out like pistons from his stocky body, punctuating his words . . . .

'How did I meet her? I guess you could say that I just stumbled into her. Literally stumbled into her. I was roller-skating . . . this is '89 we're taling about, remember, skating was very big back in '89, especially with the college crowd, that was the year it made its big comeback . . . . I was skating at the local rink and I just stumbled into her.

'Now I was a very good skater. In all due modesty, I have to say that I was good. Skating was one thing I was very good at. I loved to skate, you know, I loved that feeling of doing something *right,* just for once, something strictly my own . . . I was flunking out of business school at the time, and I would cut classes and go skating nearly every afternoon. So I was a very good skater and I wouldn't normally have stumbled. Seeing her, looking at her, that was what made me stumble.

'She had it, alright, she had that *quality.* I don't know what to call it, even now I don't know what to call it. Star quality? No, not that. More than that, much more than that, that doesn't even begin to describe the effect she had on me. There never was a star like Martha Nova.

'Her eyes. People always talk about her eyes, but that isn't it, at least, not quite it. I mean, granted, her eyes are *extraordinary,* but it's not her eyes, exactly, it's *the way she sees.* Her whole way of looking at the world.

'It's hard to explain, to find the words. Detached? Yes. Amused? For sure. But more than those things, she had this whole quality of *vision.* Like she was seeing everything for the very first time. Like she was some kind of alien who had just landed on this earth and was still looking around and observing everything, just checking things out, you know, not making any comment at all. Just looking around.

'That was the way she always was. That was her whole attitude towards life. She'd come from this very small town and moved on to the big city and she was just amazed at everything she saw and heard.

'And I knew she was special. In that very first moment, long before I ever heard her sing . . . . .' ''.

V

The singer's child watched the TV talk show. He watched the talk show host smile.

"Well, Jake" said the talk show host, "I guess it's great to be back."

The astronaut shrugged. "I guess so," he said "I guess I'm glad to be back."

The astronaut pulled back his lips, as if to smile, although the effect was more of a leer. The astronaut's stare into the TV camera was level enough, but there was something evasive about his eyes. He looked tired. He looked worse than tired. He was still painfully thin.

"Tell me Jake," the host said, "Tell me about the Martians. The little green men."

The astronaut stared back blankly.

"I guess you must have been disappointed," the host prompted "that there were no little green men."

"No little green men," the astronaut echoed. "That's right Bob, there were no little green men."

"And did that disappoint you?"

The astronaut looked puzzled. "We knew that already," he said, "we knew that there were no Martians, so we weren't disappointed. We knew that as far back as Mariner One."

"But surely," the host persisted, "surely you *hoped* that all the scientists were wrong. In your heart of hearts . . ."

"Sure," the astronaut agreed, "oh, sure." He shook his head, as if to clear it. He had been drinking all afternoon but he did not feel drunk, only very tired. He had felt that way ever since re-entry. All through the hasty debriefings, he had felt that way, and then again through all these press conferences and interviews. It wasn't a matter of wanting to sleep.

Sleep didn't help at all. In fact it made things worse. "Sure I hoped."

"Well," the talk show host commiserated, "I think we all did. We all secretly hoped. Whatever happened to those Martians?"

Two men dead, Denning thought, and he wants to talk about Martians. They want to keep it light, no doubt, for the holiday season. Well, that's fine too.

"You want to know," Denning asked, "you want to know what happened to the Martians? I'll tell you what happened. They died out. We killed them. We made them dead. There were Martians and we killed them and then it was like they never had been. All there was left was the emptiness, that's all there was left. But there were Martians, alright. Beings like *Gods,* creatures of superior force and power. Or giants, giants at the very least. Old wise Martians, little green Martians, bug-eyed Martians. All kinds of Martians. Living in jewelled palaces, domed cities. With canals, canals a mile

wide, brimming with cool blue water. *There were Martians.*
Until we went there and we killed them and made them like
they never even existed.''

"You're speaking metaphorically,'' the talk show host
said, nervously, "of course.''

"Of course,'' the astronaut agreed.

VI

The singer's child turned off the TV. He looked around the
room. His mother was in her bedroom, dressing for the party.
The dancer was asleep in an armchair.

The child turned on his personal Talkie, which he wore
constantly on a strap around his neck. "I just saw something
terrific,'' he told the machine, "I just saw an astronaut go
mad on the TV.''

"Is that so?'' the Talkie responded, "No kidding?''

"They covered it up afterwards, of course, but there was
no mistaking it.''

The Talkie whirred gently, sifting out an appropriate response, finally settled on a noncommittal, "must have been
something to see.''

"But you can't blame the poor guy,'' the child said, "To
go all that way and all and just find out a bunch of stuff you
knew already.''

"No,'' the Talkie said, "you can't blame him.''

"Like last year,'' the child continued, "when we went to
Niagara, to see the Falls, Mummy and Uncle and me. I told
them before we went, I told them we'd seen it already.''

"And you were right,'' the machine said.

"Sure I was right. But they, or at least Uncle, had this idea
that they were going to see something . . . something *new*.''

"And they were wrong?'' the Talkie asked.

"Sure they were wrong. Because *we'd already imagined
it*. Imagined the water and the spray and the smell of the
hotdogs and the people going *ohhhhhhhh*. We imagined it

and then we did it and then it wasn't new at all. Because there's nothing new, nothing really new.''

''The Donnings-Perkins Building is new,'' the Talkie ventured, referring to the latest skyscraper in the city of Melbourne, Australia, currently an architectural sensation, the tallest building in the world.

''Not really,'' the child objected. ''I mean, that's the whole point. Even more than with Niagara. It wasn't new, because people made it. It was inside us and we put it outside us and now we stand around looking at it, but it isn't *new*. It was in there all along.''

''In there?'' the Talkie asked.

''In our heads.''

''I don't follow you,'' the machine admitted.

''We imagined it and then we made it. It was predictable all along. Like going to Mars and finding exactly what you expected to find. It's all predictable, all of it. That's the whole point. That's what machines are for. To make things predictable.''

''That's very interesting,'' the machine said, guardedly, responding in accordance to its most guarded program, ''that's a very interesting point of view.''

VII

It was nearly ten on New Year's Eve, almost two hours past curfew, and the limousine moved swiftly down an almost deserted Fifth Avenue. From the back seat, Abe Levett peered uneasily out at the desolate streets, through the tinted, bulletproofed glass of the window.

It was more than two years since this current curfew had come into force, more than two years since Levett had been outdoors so late. The downtown area, with its gutted buildings and boarded-up windows, looked unfamiliar in the darkness, like the streets of some other city entirely.

It was, so far, a quiet night, and this was the safest, best policed area of the city. But venturing out after curfew, even with an official city permit on the windshield of the car, caused Levett some little anxiety. Suppose a guard patrol should mortar first and ask questions later. Such incidents were not uncommon. Only the month before, an assemblyperson had been killed near Times Square by a nervous watch detail.

Even with his motorcycle escort, four regular city cops rented out by the hour by Levett's new employers, BK Enterprises, he felt unease. In fact, the escort and the limousine itself served to increase his agitation, to turn him, in his imagination at least, into a moving target. He looked important. And these days, it did not pay to look important.

His anxiety persisted, became more acute. His heart raced in his chest, the palms of his hands were cold and damp, his vision field seemed to narrow in upon him.

Anxious, he thought, I'm anxious. That's terrific. Last week I was depressed and now I'm anxious. Is that an improvement? His therapist would think so. Anxiety, his therapist had told him, showed at least an involvement with the future.

He tried to damp down on his heartbeat, practicing FAMS—Fliegal Autonomic Meditations System—as taught him by his therapist. He tensed and relaxed the muscles of his jaw, stomach, thighs. Some relief came, not much.

It would be bad enough, he thought, just having to see her. Without having the rest of it to try and deal with. How did I get into this, he wondered. How did I get myself into this?

Impossible to say where it began. Maybe in that skating rink, back in Seattle. Maybe in some college classroom, staring out the window, thinking, plotting, planning, scheming. Looking for some way out, some way up, *up* out of the mud. Musing on the poetry of money, the vectors of freedom. But maybe even earlier than that. Because Levett had always stared through windows, always searched for the way through.

But this new episode, it had begun only two weeks ago. Before that, he had thought himself all finished with Martha

Nova, except in his thoughts and dreams. It was more than two years since he had seen her last, since he had settled out of court on the breach-of-contract suit, just before the crack-up.

VIII

Following his release from the institution, Levett had lived in a rented 2 room apartment on West Houston, in a new but fast-decaying medium-priced highrise. Graffiti already scarred the sham wood panels of the elevators, which sometimes shook disturbingly in their ascent and descent. Plaster already cracked and crumbled in the hallways. The door of his apartment was dented, almost eroded, by the carelessness of a succession of medium-priced moving men.

He could have afforded better, on the income from his settlement. But, dulled by his long confinement and continued medication, he had regarded all of it apathetically. It really had not bothered him very much. He had lived there as a man in a trance, somehow suspended in time. A man who had grasped his moment and then lost his grip. He had lived like that until the day the government agents came with their proposition.

At first he had thought that they were Mental Health cops. They looked the part, certainly, in their blue serge suits. And they acted it, too, pushing him back through his doorway into the apartment.

"I'm registered," he protested, "I'm registered with a therapist and I've been taking my medication regularly."

"We're not with the Mental Health Administration," the taller agent said. "This is a national security matter." He flashed identification, withdrew it quickly. "I'm Parker and this is Webb."

Webb grunted. Levett nodded politely.

"The details of this conversation," Parker said, "must remain confidential. You read me? We'll be monitoring you continually from here on in, even if you turn us down. And we can have you pulled in as AP any time we want."

AP. Ambulatory Psychotic. "I'm not psychotic," Levett objected, "I'm depressed."

Parker looked faintly nauseated. "I'm not interested," he said. "That's entirely your own affair."

"In any case, I don't understand. What do you want? What are you doing here?"

"We want you to help us, Levett. That's what we want."

"Help?" Levett was taken aback. "What could I do to help anyone?"

"You can get close to Martha Nova."

"I think this is some sort of mistake," Levett said. He felt dizzy in the head, his knees were weak. He sat down. "I haven't seen Martha Nova in two years. I don't want to see her and she wouldn't see me. I have nothing to do with her any more."

"We're aware," Parker said. "We're aware of the general situation. We know she fired you. But that's alright. We have a cover worked out."

"Cover?"

"You'll pose as a concert promoter, attached to BK Enterprises. You'll go see her and book her for a concert."

"Martha doesn't give concerts anymore," Levett objected. "Not in three years. She doesn't even make records anymore."

"You're wrong," Parker said, "she has a new release scheduled for New Year's Eve. Her record company is throwing a party to celebrate, and we'll swing you an invitation. She'll see you, for old times' sake at least. You should at least get close to her."

"But why," Levett asked, "what for? What do you care about Martha Nova?"

"Oh, we care. We care about everything that goes on in this country. We need information, every scrap of information that we can get. And you're going to get some of it for us."

"I don't follow you," Levett said. "What information. About what?"

"You're familiar," the agent said, "with the ideas of the so-called Nova Children. Specifically, the idea that Martha Nova's songs foresee the future."

Levett groaned. "You don't believe that stuff, do you? That hokum? You don't really believe that she can see the future? That's just PR bullshit, for chrissakes."

"It's said," Parker continued, "that she correctly foretold, for example, the Seattle fire of '79 in her song *Burning*, and again that she foretold the assassination of McWhurter in . . ."

"But that's nonsense," Levett said, "songs full of empty generalities. It's all nonsense, all of it. I should know. How can you possibly . . ."

"It isn't our job to *believe*," Parker said, "simply to keep in touch with all the options. We have to know what she sees, what she thinks that she sees. We have to calculate the effect of those visions upon her followers. We have to be prepared for all eventualities. Believe or don't believe, it doesn't affect the issue."

"Let's get this straight," Levett said. "You want me to spy on Martha Nova. You want me to tune in on her latest predictions of catastrophe. Is that right?"

Webb, the shorter agent, who had been silent all this time, now unexpectedly spoke up. "Don't get excited, Levett," he said. "If you don't want the job, don't take it. Our psych boys were pretty sure you would take it. Make yourself feel important again. Occupational therapy, so to speak. But we don't need you that bad, Levett. It really doesn't matter that much anyway. Fuck it, we're already on our way into dust. Decaying." He pulled a loose thread from the lapel of his coat.

"You sound like a Nova Child."

All this old contempt for the Children, the superfans, welled up. The stupid bastards. After all, he had carefully built the myth. The best promotion job since Hitler, and those creeps had to make a religion out of it. A religion without hope, a religion for the dead.

"But I am a Nova Child," the agent said. "I agree with it all. We are ants on the skin of the giant. Pestilence. Crippled animals. This is nowhere. There's nothing, nothing at all. No life at all."

His voice grew dreamy, faroff. "But we will be released. Any day now. It's coming, coming very soon. Every morning I wake up and turn on my radio and see if it's started yet. Because we're very close now, very near the end. Look at the wars, the shortages, the crime, the vandalism, the desperation . . . The worse things get, the more excited we get. We expect things to get worse. We would be disappointed if they didn't."

"Don't give me that crap," Levett said. "Three years of it was enough for me. Don't forget, I *made* Martha Nova."

"No, you didn't," Parker said, "No, you didn't."

"You agree with him?" Levett asked, "you're a Nova Child, too?"

"A man's religion," Parker said, "is his own affair."

IX

"Why did we go to Mars?" the astronaut said, echoing the journalist's question, "I'll tell you why we went to Mars."

And he would tell him, he would tell this snivelling excuse for a journalist exactly why they went to Mars. He would tell him in exact detail. He was angry enough now to spill the whole show. He was angry with being pushed and pulled and programmed full of answers by the boys at Control. He was angry with people bugging him all the time, grabbing and jostling and tearing away at him. And he was angry when they ignored him, too, the way they were ignoring him at this party, this party for some dumb singer who wasn't, as far as he could recall, even a particularly good lay.

What kind of a world is this, he wondered. A world where an astronaut just back from Mars, *Mars* for chrissakes, Earth's nearest and yet most mysterious neighbor as Bob Milton had so aptly put it on the *Bob Milton People In Town Show* just three hours before, where an astronaut was strictly second-best compared to a lame-ass wimp of a folksinger. What kind of a world is this?

Where, he wondered, where is our sense of values? Where is our pride, for chrissakes? Where?

He hadn't even wanted to come here in the first place, except that Control said it would be good PR and the program needed all the good PR it could get, especially after losing two out of three astronauts on the latest mission, which wasn't good copy whichever way you sliced it. In any case, they had told him, it was New Year's Eve, so what the hell? You deserve a break, you deserve a good party, something to take your mind off things.

Denning didn't care much about good PR, and he was in no real mood for a party, but he had gone along with Control all the same. He was afraid of Control, of what they still might do. Control were not so very pleased with him. They were not pleased about the loss of Fuller and Wyatt, they were not pleased with his attitude, they were not pleased with his behavior on the *People In Town* show. It was possible that Control already suspected the truth that Denning was no longer even sure he wished to conceal, that he was going mad.

So he had come to this party, and now he was playing fill-in for the star of the show. He was Martha Nova's warm-up act, a mere sparring partner for these mediamen as they readied themselves for their real prey. Even while they were asking him their ridiculous questions they kept looking over their shoulders, to make sure they weren't missing the start of the real action.

"I'll tell you why we went to Mars," he told the assembled, knot of reporters. "I did a lot of thinking about that and now I'm going to lay it all out for you. Some day I'll write about it in my memoirs, but in the meantime I'll put it simply. Fear. Fear and hatred. That's why we went to Mars."

"Fear?" the journalist who had asked the question blinked. "Hatred?"

"Hatred. Hatred of what we fear. Hatred of Nature, good

old Mother Nature. Hatred of the Earth and the sun and the moon and Mars and the whole frigging universe.''

"I don't understand you," the journalist said. "You're suggesting that people hate nature? But that's not so. People love nature."

"You're absolutely wrong," the astronaut said. "There's nothing they hate more."

"But the countryside . . . ." The journalist faltered. "The national parks, the campgrounds . . ."

"Simulations" Denning brushed the objections aside. "Simulations of nature, that's something else again. Simulations are safe. Nature is scary. Nature is raw. Nature is senseless, arbitrary, uncontrolled. Control it, and it isn't nature. Pave it over, put electric sockets on the trees, smash your rockets against the sky."

"Technology," the journalist said. "But people hate technology."

"Naturally they hate it," the astronaut said. "That's the whole point. They can't stand excitement and they can't stand boredom. That's the whole point."

"I don't understand," the journalist said. "What does this have to do with going to Mars?"

He looked uneasy. He was, after all, only a showbiz columnist, not a science correspondent.

X

There was a mob outside the hotel, a huge mob, streaming all the way back down the Avenue. Levett had not seen so many people collected in one place in five years. He could not help but shudder.

Around the hotel, squads of city police and state troopers held an uneasy line. A massive violation of local curfews, a completely illegal assembly, and yet the security forces seemed helpless to enforce the law. There were just too many

of the Children. And this was their big night. Nothing would
stand in their path tonight.

Tonight, in this hotel, at a very small and most exclusive
New Year's Eve celebration to welcome the coming mil-
lenium, year 2000, Martha Nova would make her first public
appearance in three years. She would communicate with
representatives of the international media, in order to pro-
mote her long-awaited new album. The party would be tele-
vised around the world. A very big night.

As the limousine moved towards the hotel checkpoint, an
arm of the mob swung away, wrapping itself around the car.
Faces pressed up against the darkened glass. Momentarily,
Levett was terrified, certain that they would tear the car and
its occupants apart. But then, disappointed, they fell back.
Clearly they did not know that Martha Nova was already
inside the hotel, had been for some days.

Nova Children, usually so calm, so quiet. But tonight they
seemed over-excited, as if expecting something enormously
significant to happen, more significant even than a new
album by Martha Nova.

Levett pressed down the button to roll open the side-
window a little, to get a closer look. The Children appeared
happy, smiling, full of joy. They were singing. The whole
crowd was chanting, Levett realized, chanting the same thing
over and over again. *"Getting near/Getting near the end/
Getting near/Getting near the end . . . ."*

The chorus of an old Nova song, one of her most famous.
Dimly, Levett remembered her writing it, back in their old
beach house at Malibu, back before the whole thing got out of
control.

The chanting, soft and eerie and compulsively repetitive,
disturbed him. He rolled up the window.

"There's going to be trouble," Levett's bodyguard muttered beside him, "trouble out there tonight." He shook his
head from side to side. "New Year's Eve is always trouble.
But this is going to be worse. I don't understand it. I don't
understand why they don't do something about these . . . .
Children."

The bodyguard was a big, slow man, a patrolman moonlighting in plain clothes. Clearly he feared for the safety of his buddies, out on the street.

"They're not violent," Levett pointed out. "In fact, they're against violence. Which may be why the Government tends to leave them alone, if not actively encouraging them."

"But it's crazy," the bodyguard said. "I just don't understand it. All for some *singer*."

"It's not the singer," Levett said. "It doesn't matter who the singer is." He realized, as he spoke, that he was trying as much to convince himself as the patrolman. "It's just a hunger, a great hunger. A hunger for religious ecstasy. That's what it is."

He had read that in a magazine once, and it had stuck in his mind. *A hunger for religious ecstasy*. That was really a pretty good way of putting it. He couldn't do better than that himself.

The limousine passed through the checkpoint and down into the underground parking facility of the hotel. Here, Levett immediately felt safer. He boarded the express elevator to the penthouse floor.

XI

The hotel had been built in another time, a time of great confidence and expansiveness. Levett walked awed under the high ceilings on the thick carpet, hardly worn down.

There was a time, when Levett had been moving up, when he had himself exuded an enormous confidence. When the interviewers came to call, to marvel at his art collection and his sunken bathtub and his tropical plant house, he would answer their unspoken question this way: "You want to know what it is I do? Do to deserve all this? I'll tell you what I do. *I feel the changes*. That's what I do. I feel these . . . . *movements*. Out there. And I go with the flow."

But that was a long time ago and Levett no longer felt the movements, no longer moved with the flow. If the changes

reached him at all, he was not prepared to deal with them. He
stood by the wall and watched the people mingle, ebbing and
flowing across the floor. One man, who was talking very
loudly and emphatically and could well have been drunk,
was attracting some attention. He seemed to be talking about
Mars. A second knot of people had formed around a famous
singer of a previous generation, whose style Levett had
overtly despised as an adolescent and secretly admired, a
performer with a genuine kind of class.

New Year's Eve, he thought. The year 2000. Jesus Christ.

He was seized by a sudden panic.

The lights dimmed. A man who looked like a record
company executive stepped to the front of the small stage,
framed by spotlights. He picked up the microphone.
"People," he said. There was quiet. "Usually," said the
record company executive, "people are slow to recognize
greatness. Michaelangelo. The Wright Brothers. People
don't usually approve of you until you've got where you're
going, or else been and gone.

"But to every rule there is an exception. And tonight
RealTime Records are proud to present the first new product
in three years from a very exceptional lady. We're really
getting behind this one, and we hope that all you folks out
there will get behind it too. Ladies and gentlemen, I give you
songs for a new century, I give you Martha Nova's latest and
greatest masterwork . . . *End of Time*."

Still milking that decay *shtick*, Levett thought, that whole
doom-and-gloom number. Which surely by this time is getting sort of threadbare, even if her fans do still eat it up. It's
time that she progressed, moved on. She has the talent, even
if she doesn't have the motivation. She needs someone to
guide her, someone to push her to think some new thoughts,
sing some new songs. If I was still her manager . . . .

But he could not afford to think those sort of thoughts. Just
being here, in this hotel, so close to her, was disturbing
enough, it ate him up inside. How did I get into this, Levett
wondered again. How did I get myself into this?

A promotional film was showing now, a collage of photo-

graphs of Martha Nova, at first silent. And then the music
began, began and swelled and filled the room. There was no
sign of Martha Nova, just her photographs on the screen and
her voice, rising and falling through the giant speaker system.

The music was familiar and the music was strange. It was
as though he had never heard anything like it before, but also
as though he had been hearing it all his life. Levett shivered,
in the grip of profound apprehensions.

The music was more electric than before, a full electric
band fleshing out the previously spare vocals and guitar. But
it was a sweet kind of electricity, sweet and soft and insinuat-
ing, rolling and shuffling around the voice. *"Dance . . ."*
the voice said, and Levett strained to make out the words. *"Is
this a dance or is this still a dream?"* And later: *"And who is
dancing?"*

A dance tune, he thought. She cut a dance tune. The
desolation shuffle.

He closed his eyes, and it was as if he could see the dance
moving across the nation, the slow undulating dance. Beginning in the streets below with the Children, snaking its way
across the city, across the country.

XI

The brightness of the film hurt the astronaut's still-
sensitive eyes, and the music bothered him, too. The music
was too cool, too slithery. The music was like being in space.

He pushed his way through the crowd to the door. The
corridor outside was deserted except for a small boy, who
looked perhaps six years old. The boy was staring out the
window.

"Hey kid," the astronaut said, "what's happening?"

He followed the child's gaze down into the streets below.
The streets were choked with people. Denning had not seen
so many people in one place since the launch, since more
than one million people had surged into the Houston area to

watch their boys take a shot at Mars. Those crowds had been incredible, just incredible. And now it had come to this.

It must be a New Year's Eve party, he thought, turning away from the chaos below. Like they used to have in Times Square. Anyway, he was too tired and too aroused to make any sense out of it.

"Some party, huh, kid?" he said.

"It's not a party," the child said. He did not look back from the window. "It's a transformation. Can't you feel it? Can't you feel the transformation?"

Denning did not follow the child's meaning at all, although it disturbed him at some level he had no wish to explore.

"Look, kid," he said. "You want my autograph?"

This time the child turned around and studied the astronaut with little apparent interest.

"I don't collect autographs," he said, "I collect snowballs. You know those glass balls with cities inside and snow when you shake them up? I collect them. I have snowballs from thirty-six cities."

"That's terrific," the astronaut said.

The astronaut did not much like kids in general and he was not sure that he liked this one in particular, but you had to try and be nice to them, you had to try and reach the children. The children were the whole future of this country. The children were what this thing was all about.

"You know who I am?" the astronaut asked. "I'm Jake Denning, the man from Mars. I just got back, you must have seen me on the TV. I bet you just can't wait to tell all your buddies how you met the man from Mars."

"I saw you on TV," the child agreed. "I saw you go mad."

He turned back to the window, to watch the coming transformation.

XII

As the music played on, Levett picked his way through the room, easing his way towards the door that led backstage. He had come to this place for a reason which no longer seemed to him to make any sense, if it had ever seemed to make sense, but still he might as well go through with it, he might as well try and reach Martha Nova.

In the backstage area, a group of musicians were setting up their instruments. A stage crew moved around quickly and soundlessly. They were watched by a famous singer of a previous generation.

A security officer blocked Levett's way. "I'm sorry sir," he said, "this area is restricted."

The famous singer, who liked to think of himself as a dancer, observed the incident. He waved at the security officer. "That's alright," he said. "You can let him through."

The dancer recognised Levett from his old photographs in mass circulation magazines, although he had never met the man. He was curious about him, curious about anything connected with Martha Nova.

"Mr. Levett," he said. "I'm pleased to meet you."

They shook hands.

"It's an honor," Levett said.

"You've come to see Martha?"

"That's right," Levett said. "I have a deal I want to discuss with her, a business deal." It sounded ridiculous to him, but he persevered. "I'm with BK Enterprises," he said, "these days."

"Is that so?" the dancer said. "BK Enterprises?" His voice showed no recognition.

"We billed 10 megabucks last year," Levett said.

"Really?" the dancer responded, "you must have quite an organization."

"We do," Levett agreed. "And we want to talk business with Martha. A coast-to-coast tour."

"Coast-to-coast?" the dancer echoed. "That's quite a proposition. Especially for someone who hasn't toured in four years."

"We think," Levett said, "that the time is right."

"That may be so," the dancer agreed. "In any case, Martha isn't here right now. She'll be down soon, but I doubt that you'll get the chance to talk to her in any depth. She's going to sing."

"Afterwards . . ." Levett said.

"Afterwards we're flying to Madrid," the dancer said. "But maybe you could come along with us. Or it might be simpler just to go through Martha's management . . ."

Levett shook his head vigorously. "Oh no," he said. "I have to talk to Martha."

What does he want, the dancer wondered. Obviously not to make any deal. What does he really want?

Levett's anxiety was quite apparent. His face was streaked with sweat, his voice trembled as he spoke.

"I thought," the dancer probed, "that you were pretty much retired from the music business."

"I was retired," Levett said. "But I'm making a kind of comeback . . . Like Martha, in a way. The inactivity, it gets to you after a while. And I guess this business gets in your blood . . . ." He trailed off.

The dancer tried to recall the circumstances surrounding the break between Martha and Levett, the circumstances surrounding his crack-up. Something that had happened in Las Vegas, when Martha was playing a season in one of the big hotels, a deal Levett had himself set up . . . Something about Levett running out into the streets, into the heat, into the traffic. Among the cars, the cars, hard white and smooth, under the signs that burned all night.

"How did you like it?" the dancer inquired.

"I'm sorry?"

"The music. The new album."

"Oh," Levett said. "I don't know. I don't know if I like it."

"What do you think?" the dancer asked. "Do you think her audience will go with it?"

"They'll go with it," Levett said, "I don't doubt that."

The dancer looked at his watch. "Eleven thirty," he said, "Martha will be down soon. She's scheduled to start at midnight. Why don't you stick around?"

XIII

"How come you're not listening to the music?" the child asked the astronaut. "Don't you like the music?"

"No," the astronaut said, "I don't like the music."

The music, in fact, still echoed somewhere at the back of his mind, down deep somewhere he could not dislodge it. In his mind the music played on, and it made him shiver. There was something spooky about that music. Just as there had been something spooky about the singer, that one night he had spent with her, something that had cut through his drunken haze, something he would have much rather forgotten all about. There was something very spooky in the way she looked at a person.

"If you don't like the music," the child said, "you're not going to enjoy what comes next." He did not elaborate.

"What do you mean?" the astronaut asked. "What do you mean, I'm not going to enjoy what comes next?"

XIV

The astronaut had dreamed of the fire, dreamed of it in deep slow dreams that oozed with heavy colors, dreams that surrounded him and enveloped him and cradled him and carried him through his most terrible nights. He had dreamed of the fire, and now, as the capsule began to tumble, he remembered his dreams.

"I'm in a spin," he told Control.

"Say again?"

"I said, I'm in a spin."

The heat increased, became unbearable, as unshielded surfaces caught fire in the terrible friction.

I have failed, he thought, failed re-entry.

He fell. Slipping and sliding, he fell. Fell through the web, through the space and through the time, he fell, all the way down, he descended to earth.

XV

Emerging from the elevator, the singer saw the astronaut talking to his only son. She had previewed this scene, of course, imagined it in exact detail for many years, and still it brought her very close to tears.

The singer was thirty five years old. She had made six albums in the last eight years, every one of them certified as better than platinum. She was sometimes said to be the most popular singer in the history of the world. The singer sang about what she saw, and what she saw for the most part was decay, dissolution, the end of all things. The singer had reason to believe that what she saw was the future. She had been seeing the future since she was four or five years old, although she had never subjected her talent to any objective test procedure.

"Things will be different," her son, Daniel, was telling the mad astronaut, his father. "Things will be very different."

XVI

Memories. The memories engulfed Levett. Standing frozen to the spot in the backstage area with the stage crew swarming around him, waiting for Martha Nova, Levett

understood at last how it was that he came to be in this time
and place.

Since his breakdown, Levett's memories had been patchy
at best, and in any case he rarely liked to reflect upon the past.
His official therapist had clearly outlined for him the concept
of repression, of a conditioned forgetting, and Levett could
intellect what the man was talking about even though he
could not personally identify with it. The holes in his memory did not seem to bother him very much, and when he
thought about them at all he was more likely to ascribe them
to the effects of the ECT.

In any case, the memories were back, there was no question about that. He remembered the last time he had seen
Martha Nova. He remembered the last thing she had said to
him. "I'll see you later," she had said. "I'll see you at the
party."

And then he had run out into the street, out into the heat.
He had run from their suite in the hotel, the superbly air-
conditioned hotel that stood alongside the other hotels in the
middle of the desert.

And he remembered why he had run. He remembered his
moment of recognition.

They had been arguing about the show, about Martha's
choice of material. Or rather, Levett had been telling Martha
why the show was lousy and she had been listening the way
she always listened, like she knew everything you were
going to say and it wasn't going to bother her in the least. So
you couldn't really call it an argument because an argument
ought to have at least two sides.

"You don't care," he had told her. "You just don't care."

And then it had hit him, the recognition. He was stunned
by the weight of the insight.

"You don't care," he said, "because you heard all this
already. You saw the fucking future."

Well, there had been clues all along, so many clues, and
there was really no saying what had finally tipped him off,
but suddenly he knew, he was consumed by a certain knowledge.

"It's no hype," he said, "it's the inside story."

Without realising it, he was backing away from her, setting a greater and greater distance between them. He was terribly afraid.

"It's alright," she said. "Take it easy. You're tripping, that's all. Just tripping."

"I'm not tripping," he said. "I don't do drugs. You know that."

"You're having a flashback," she said. "A quick flashback. To when you used to do drugs."

Her face seemed to recede away from him. His vision became blurred.

"You saw the future."

"Stop it," she said. "Concentrate and you'll be able to stop it."

"You can see the future," he said, "the whole thing. Every last detail of it. You can see me die."

"No," she said. "I never saw you die."

"You can see me die," he repeated. His heart hammered in his chest. "Tell me how. No, wait. Don't tell me."

He backed all the way to the door.

"How can you stand it?" he asked. "I couldn't stand it."

"You get used to it," she said. "It isn't as bad as you think."

And then he had left, run from the room. And she had called after him. She had called, "I'll see you later. I'll see you at the party." But he didn't think much about it as he ran out into the heat.

XVIII

The singer saw the future only up to a certain point, a point in space and time beyond which she could not move. And now she had almost reached that point. She had concluded some time ago that this point must mark the moment of her own death. She presumed that her death would be very sudden, since she was unable to preview that exact moment.

Her last memory of the future left her frozen on stage in the middle of a song and after that, nothing.

The singer believed that her son had something of her own talent, although she had never discussed the matter with him. She listened carefully to the conversation between the child and the astronaut, even though she had overheard it many times before.

"What will be different?" the astronaut asked. "How will things be different?" It seemed to him very important to hear the child's answer, even if it would do no more than confirm his own train of thought.

"Everything," the child said, "everything will be different. The whole world will change. There will be a transformation. And before that, there will be a burning."

"A burning what?" the astronaut asked. "And what does this have to do with the music?"

"The music precedes the transformation," the child explained. "The music imagines the transformation."

"What the hell does that mean?" the astronaut asked.

XIX

The future spoke through her. And now they were getting very near the end.

"Hello, Jake," she said.

The astronaut turned.

"Are you coming to see the show?" she asked.

The astronaut and the child followed behind her, silently, as she walked through to the backstage area. The child glanced backwards out of the window. Down below, in the streets, the dance had already begun.

XX

"Martha."

She had expected to see Levett, she had been expecting it for a long time.

"You said you would see me later," he said. "You said you would see me at the party."

"That's right," she agreed. "I said I would see you at the party."

"You look good, Martha," he told her.

"Thank you," she said.

"This is the end," Levett said. "Isn't it? Isn't this the end?"

"That's right," she said. "This is the end. This is it. The last party. Be sure to enjoy it."

She picked up her guitar and began to check the tuning.

XXI

"*We are home,*" Martha was singing, "*We are back home . . .*" A new song or perhaps a golden oldie, Levett could not quite recall, as he left the party. He picked out an unlocked car from the parking lot underneath the hotel and drove out slowly, through the crowd of Nova Children. Martha Nova was projected onto a giant screen on the wall of the hotel. Her voice echoed away down the Avenue.

The Children were dancing. The Children were celebrating the coming transformation.

"Things end," Martha had said as she stepped up to sing. "End and begin and end again. A beginning from every ending." And then she had started to sing.

XXII

Sometime later, the burning began. Out on the Turnpike, driving fast, Levett did not notice it at first. And when he did notice it, he paid it no attention. He drove on, along the burning highway, while the radio played its sweet soul music. He drove on, on and on, through the fire, on that very last night. He drove on, as if in pursuit of some promise, shining always just out of reach, that he would never quite define.

Introduction to 'Certain Fathoms In The Earth'

Jean E. Karl brings to her writing more than twenty years' experience in the publishing industry, primarily in the line of children's books. She is currently Vice President and Director in Charge of the Children's Book Department at Atheneum, a hardcover house justifiably well-known for its many award-winning children's titles.

Her novel, BELOVED BENJAMIN IS WAITING, is currently available from Dell and she has a new work, BUT WE ARE NOT OF EARTH, coming from Atheneum this spring.

They say you should write about what you know, and in *Certain Fathoms in the Earth*, Jean Karl has done just that. But better yet, and the mark of the true writer, by the end of the story she is writing about something we all know . . . .

CERTAIN FATHOMS IN THE EARTH

Jean E. Karl

Mercy Warren stood up the minute Lederle came into her office. There was no place for him to sit, and she was not about to have him looking down at her, making her feel like a child in a schoolroom. But even so, the conversation got out of hand.

"You're an anachronism!" he said, finally.

"Has this department ever lost this company one two-cent piece?"

"No, but the same money invested in a more acceptable product could bring in a bigger gross."

"You can't prove that! And a better gross doesn't mean a better net. You'd better look at the last line before you do something you'll regret. And besides, it's in the original merger agreement. You wanted the Phoebus textbooks, but you had to promise to keep a department for the new literature, the experimental ideas."

"Not if you retire and there's nobody to take your place. Nobody can make us continue, if there's no fool to do it. Just run that over. And let me know when you plan to go."

"You can't force me out. Not by the new laws. Not if there's no one waiting to take my place."

"I can make it damn uncomfortable for you to stay."

"It's been damn uncomfortable. And I intend to stay."

Mercy slid into her chair as Lederle stalked down the hall. Over for another week, or, if she was lucky, for another month. The nerve of that man. There was no department in the whole of Eastern and Warberg that turned in a better net. She saw to that, even if it meant prices were higher than she liked. Year in and year out she made money. She had to. So she shouldn't let him upset her. But she was furious as usual. The blindness of some people. Of most people. She wanted to put a tattoo on Lederle's forehead that he'd have to look at every day when he shaved. "You can't live on the ideas of the past," it would say. Subliminal advertising at its most persistent. Well, hardly subliminal.

She sighed and turned to the manuscript in front of her. *Signifying Nothing.* The title seemed appropriate. That's what the fool Lederle did: signify nothing.

But the truth of the matter was that she couldn't hang on much longer. She was seventy-five. She didn't look it. At least that's what kind friends said. But sometimes she felt it. And she wanted a chance to do something new. Her friends all seemed to be resting in the sun, or running with the wind, off into the world. She wasn't sure what she wanted, but more than this three by three hole. That much she did know. She'd stick it out, though. She had to; there were too many counting on her.

Why was that old woman looking at her book? Betsy wondered. It was the second morning this week, waiting for the elevator. It wasn't as if the title showed. She had it wrapped in a carrying case, so nobody could see the cover. And what if they did?

Certain Fathoms in the Earth. That was the title. And why should it matter that no one would recognize it. That it wasn't a classic. That it certainly wasn't a best seller or on any of the approved lists. It made her mad. Why should she feel so sneaky? Just because she liked books that other people didn't read. Why couldn't she be different? Who said that "they" were always right? She sighed. Everybody said so, and that was the problem. Everybody but her. Fortunately nobody knew how she felt, because she'd always had sense enough to keep still. Kari would look at her strangely, if she knew, maybe even make her move out of the apartment. And she was pretty sure none of the men she saw would come around any more if they knew.

It wasn't, she reflected, that anything would happen to her

or to anyone for reading what she read. Or for thinking what she thought. There were no laws against reading the kinds of books she liked. It just wasn't done. It wasn't the thing. You didn't.

But she did.

The elevator came, and she got on. So did the woman, still staring at the book. Well, let her stare. The book didn't look so different. It was like some of the classic reproductions. Even if most people read film in mini-micros, there were still bound books around. Especially in paper like this. There were even some for kids. And if it was OK for kids, who could question? Certainly not some dried-up old female on an elevator.

The elevator stopped on five and Betsy got off. The woman stayed on. So much for that. Good-bye for another day.

It had to be *Certain Fathoms in the Earth*. Mercy was willing to admit that she didn't recognize every book she'd been responsible for, just from the top. But her books did have a certain look. People would say she was crazy—they did anyway—for thinking that she could tell a book when she couldn't see the title. But she could tell. It hardly seemed possible, though, that one of those mass-produced, computer-oriented, plaster-cast editors on the fifth floor would be reading one of her books. They were screened too well for that. All the attributes of normalcy. That's what Eastern and Warberg wanted. Even peas in the same pod were more different. If peas still grew in pods. She doubted it. They probably grew in computers, too, so they could be equalized.

The phone rang. Mr. Boston, she was sure, and she wasn't quite ready for him. She'd promised him *Signifying Nothing* this morning, and she didn't have it quite finished. She sighed, remembering the days when she'd had a secretary, a copyeditor, a production person, even a designer—all working for her—all at her disposal. Now she was alone. Well, she didn't do so many books anymore. That was for sure. But what she did, she did more carefully. She had to because it was so important.

She answered the phone, waiting for the voice on the other end to speak before she did. "Good morning, Mr. Boston . . . . No, I am sorry. I know you've saved time for me . . . . I know you're the only typesetter and printer in the city and you're busy . . . . Look, I also know you care. And you've got to give me the time I need . . . . This afternoon . . . . Yes, only a few more pages to go . . . . No, nothing wrong with it. The problems are all mine. It's the old hassle. And I've been worried . . . . Say, you don't know anyone who could take my job, do you? . . . No, don't get upset. I have no intention of quitting. But they do get insistent. I have to find someone, have someone ready to take my place . . . . OK, let me know if you think of anyone . . . . Well, send your man over about fourteen . . . . yes, I'm sure I'll be ready then."

The phone rang again. Always when she was busy. Better pick it up. You never knew.

"Mercy Warren here. Oh, Webster . . . You've been talking to Boston, I can tell . . . . I know, Webster, that you need an editor. Every one of the authors I publish needs an editor. For one thing, not one of you can spell. Not that it matters, I guess . . . . No, I do not intend to give up. Don't worry. Boston is a worry freak . . . . Well, of course, I can't go on forever. I'm seventy-five. I've never kept that from anyone. I couldn't . . . . I know I need someone. But where am I going to find it? . . . Man or woman, who gives a damn? Just so it walks. Just so it cares. Just so it can edit . . . . Well, ask around . . . . You may know a few I don't. There has to be someone, somewhere . . . . OK, well sure, good-bye."

Why didn't they leave her alone? She knew that they all counted on her: the authors, the printer—no matter how impatient he got; Mr. Kositz downstairs, who did all of Phoebus Division's shipping and billing without a computer (how he managed, she'd never understand); the network of bookstores—most of which sold old books and mixed in the things that she and the few others like her did; and, of course, the readers. They all knew each other, whatever they did. Just as the vast mass of most people seemed to clot together, those who were different belonged—to each other, though they were not alike. But their group was small.

She remembered back in the 60s and 70s when minorities were the big rage. Now there were no minorities—only the vast unthinking, computer-TV oriented majority, who read and thought and did what "they" said. Not because they had to. That was the grim thing. But because—well, why because—a latent herd instinct, maybe. It was beyond her.

Yet there was that minority. Her minority, the differents. And they read the kinds of books she published—in their old fashioned paper bound formats. Issued and billed the way books were issued and billed more than thirty years ago, sold only by a cheap catalog. Someday maybe she'd try to slip one of her books on the computer-feeder downstairs that beamed things out to the bookstore computer-receivers. Wouldn't those bookstore know-nothings who simply pushed the right buttons to get the mini-micro films out of the computers for their customers be surprised if they got one of hers? Ah, well, they'd never know, except that they wouldn't understand it. It didn't have pictures.

"Don't be cynical, Mercy," she muttered.

Her way was best. Keep quiet and do what had to be done. And find someone to take her place before it was too late.

There was that woman again. Betsy hugged the book, so the old busybody couldn't see it. Why was she so damn curious?

The elevator door flew open, and Betsy pushed in. Back into the corner. But some dope had dropped a pencil calculator. She fought to keep her balance as the slender cylinder rolled under her foot. The book fell. She grabbed it up. But not before the woman had seen the pages as they opened. Could she tell? Well, let her. Though, of course, if she worked for Eastern and Warberg, there might be a problem.

Oh, bother it all! The whole business was nonsense.

The elevator started up before she got herself calmed down. She hoped someone had pushed five. Good. Corinne was on. She would have pushed it.

The woman was still looking, half turned to stare at her. And she'd have to pass her going out the door. Blast the luck Three . . . Four . . . The door opened at five. Corinne pushed out, then she followed.

"Look at the last page. Mercy Warren on six."

Betsy hurried down the hall. What was that! The old woman had said something. She was too old to be working. The old witch, what was her problem? The last page. And someone on six. Mercy. Well, she, Betsy, would certainly need mercy, if that old monster said anything.

She whipped into her office and closed the door. The partitions didn't go to the ceiling, but you could close the door and be unseen.

With a shaky hand she turned to the last page of *Certain Fathoms in the Earth*. Something in very small print. She

squinted and got into a good light. "Pheobus Division—Eastern and Warberg © 2001.''

Betsy fell into her chair, ignoring its contours, sitting rigidly. Here—and just last year! She had never known. What was Phoebus Divison? That woman must know. What did she have to do with it? Did she know where there were other books? The bookstore was in such a weird part of town. She hated the thought of going there again, but she wanted more books. If she could get stuff here . . .

Would the girl come? It was a good thing *Signifying Nothing* was done. The whole thing made her as nervous as a bee in a plastic garden. She laughed. That's what she was, a bee in a plastic garden.

She pulled out a pile of submissions to read, knowing she couldn't concentrate on anything else. How people knew to send things to her, she could never wholly figure out. Except that they were a group, and people found out what they needed to know.

It was after twelve when she heard footsteps in the hall. Lederle again? No, too soon. And the steps were too light, too hesitant. Could it be the girl? She could hardly credit the idea. And besides, her office was hard to find, hidden down the hall behind the general accounting computer bank. She looked up, hardly daring to hope, yet wanting to believe that the girl might come. Why had she never seen her before? Maybe because she hadn't been desperate enough to look!

"Your name is Mercy?" The girl stood at the door, shy, hesitant.

"Yes. I'm Mercy Warren. And you?"

"Betsy. Betsy Lederle."

"Lederle!" The name gave her a jolt.

"Yah. What's—oh, my father. Well, don't worry about him. I won't tell him you're here. We don't really get along. I don't live at home any more. But he said I had to work here. You know. It's sort of expected. And I like it. Except all that stuff we do is so stupid. It would be OK if it wasn't so, well you know, so kind of all alike. But I guess that's the way it is.

It's that way all over. Except, of course, in some books." she stared defiantly at Mercy.

"Come in, Betsy. I'm sorry there isn't room here for an extra chair, but you're agile enough to sit on the desk, aren't you? Let me close the door."

What was she getting into? Did this woman know her old man? This woman was even older than he was! How could she know what it was like to sometimes need something different? Well, just let her try to tell people around here. There were ways to shut people up.

"My dear, you may be an answer to prayer, as they used to say. I guess some groups still do. It's still accepted. But, be that as it may, let's begin at the beginning. I thought it was *Certain Fathoms in the Earth* you had when I saw you earlier this week, but I wasn't sure until today. You saw that Eastern and Warberg published it."

"Yes, but how . . . where? What's Phoebus Division? I never heard of it."

"Let me explain."

Fifteen minutes later, Betsy sat with her mouth open and her heart pumping. She had never dreamed of such a thing. She looked at the woman in front of her and longed to reach out and touch her, just to see if she was real. And yet she knew she was. And the story Mercy Warren told was true. It had to be.

"You really mean that—about wanting someone to take your place?"

"I do. I'm seventy-five years old. I've worked long enough. Your father thinks so, and so do I, though for different reasons. Yet, I can't give up, not until I'm sure that what I'm doing will go on. To be sure of that, I have to have a successor I can trust. Somebody who knows the publishing business, who's willing to take a chance, to be different, who doesn't care about getting ahead or being one of the crowd."

Yah, she was right. You couldn't do this job and be one of

the crowd, not if the crowd knew what you did. Weirdo. But Mercy Warren was no weirdo.

"You wouldn't be alone, you know. We're a tight-knit little group—the world around, I guess. We see each other, those of us who live close. And we certainly hear from each other. We exchange ideas, talk about what we read in little groups."

"But you don't see other people, the regular ones."

"We see them. It's just that they don't see us. We're the invisible minority. Besides, they're dull."

"Yah, I guess. But what about people like me? I didn't even know these crazy groups existed. I just found the book-store by accident—down on 6th Street."

"Mr. Doomer's."

"Yah, that's the place. You been there?"

"Yes, he has little group meetings now and then. If you'd gone back often enough, you'd probably have been invited. He doesn't take people in easily. But he takes in those he knows are serious, the ones who keep coming back so he knows they care."

"Could I—could I go sometime?"

"I'll take you to a meeting next week, if you like. If you really want to do it. In the meantime, think about what I said. It's asking a lot of you. It means giving up life as you know it for a hope, in a way, for a dream; it's selling yourself to give new ideas, new ways of thinking, a chance. It's a big step. You have to be sure. Don't make up your mind either way in a hurry. Give it time. And come up to talk if you feel like it. Just don't let your father know what you're doing, or what you're thinking about."

Betsy laughed. Her coming here would be the ultimate— the final joke on him. And Mercy Warren knew it. She gave the woman a quick look. Knew it better than anybody.

"Yaah! I really liked that meeting. And they weren't all old either, the people there. I thought they might be."

"Oh, there are a lot of young ones. The author of *Certain*

Fathoms in the Earth, for example, isn't much older than you are.''

"You mean it? And if I took this job, I'd meet him?''

"You probably would. But don't take the job just to meet Webster Pinkus. That won't do. You have to take the job for you. Because of what you want, what you believe, what you are willing to do.''

"How do I know I'd like it? That I could even do it?''

"You could come up and try it, during your lunch hour, say. Would anyone wonder where you were?''

"No. I generally eat at my desk. I lock the door and read. It's the safest place I've found to read. You know, the only place except the bathroom that you can really lock up.''

Mercy Warren howled with laughter. At first Betsy just looked at her. And then she saw how funny it was. Locking the door to read at a publishing house. They laughed together.

"OK. I'll come up every day—for, say, half an hour. I don't think anyone will notice. I'll take the stairs. And no one in the computer department ever sees anything.''

"I'll look for you then. And, Betsy, if you should decide to come, begin to think about your father.''

"I am.'' She smiled.

"Ms. Warren!''

"Mr. Lederle?''

"I have called to the attention of the Board of Directors the fact that you will be seventy-six in three weeks. They feel that even under the new laws, no one is compelled to keep an employee beyond his or her seventy-sixth birthday. Surely you realize that this is for the best. It is for the sake of employees that such rules are made. We do not want to exploit the willingness of our older workers. They deserve their years of rest and enjoyment, years they have earned by devoted service.''

"Nonesense. However, I'm perfectly willing to leave, so long as I know that the terms of the Phoebus merger will not be violated—that this department will not be eliminated.''

''My dear woman, we do not violate agreements in this firm. We make agreements and keep them when we can. But, of course, in this case, no one will want so unpopular a position, so unpromising a career, one so isolated from accepted modes of thinking. There is, of course, no future . . .''

''But I have found someone.''

Lederle looked doubtful and Mercy nearly laughed.

''Well, of course, in that case. But it would have to be someone qualified. Someone with experience, preferably with this company or another like it. I can't imagine . . .''

''But I do have such a candidate. Would you care to talk to her, or should I go through personnel?''

''Another woman. I might have known. No man would be so foolish.''

''I have plenty of male authors.''

''Fools. Fools. All of them. Aberrant thinkers. What kind of parents did they have? No sense. No proper education.''

''Well, you're right there. None of them can spell.''

''The candidate. A fool. But I will see her. I warn you, I won't take someone unknown, untried. I will have to know her full background.''

''You will. You will.''

''How soon will he be here, my father?''

''Another five minutes. Nervous?''

''No, just scared, I guess. But he won't talk me out of it. He knows me better than to try, I think.''

''Here he comes. Early. He always pounds like that when he comes down this hall.''

''Ms. Warren. Ms. Warren. Must you close your door?''

''Oh, do come in, Mr. Lederle. Fine. Now I want you to meet my replacement. Actually, you have met, I think. And as you know, she's been employed here for some time. She's had a superior education. Well, you know her background; but she'll be glad to fill you in on anything you don't know. She's been working with me during her lunch hours for several months and has come to know the work here quite thoroughly. I'm quite satisfied."

"Yes, Daddy, I'll be glad to tell you anything you want to know. I really want this job. I've never done anything so exciting. It's all so different. You know I got so tired of that stuff downstairs. It was like a drug—or a couple of drugs. I'm grateful to you, though, glad you insisted I come here. Without you, I'd never have known Ms. Warren and lots of other nice people I've met through her. You do think I'm qualified, don't you? I took my application blank for the job to personnel yesterday afternoon, and they thought it was all right. They felt there was no question but that I had the qualifications, if I really wanted the job. And if Ms. Warren approved. They said I could start here full time next week. That is OK, isn't it?" She stopped abruptly, feeling she'd rambled on too long.

Lederle's answer was silence and a stare. Then he turned his back and strode down the hall.

The two women looked at each other and laughed, as they had so often before. It was fun, being on the outside. It was so much better than anything else available. And it was a good thing they both felt that way because the work had to go on. It was important. Somehow, they both knew, the future depended on it.

Introduction to 'Drift Away'

Nicholas Yermakov is a study in extremes.

As many authors have, he's worked at a number of jobs to support himself while waiting for editors to recognize the worth of what he was throwing over their transoms. Few other writers, however, can match the variety of his meal-tickets; he has been, at various times and with varying success a rock musician, a disc jockey, a radio production expert for the UN, a salesman of aftermarket chopper accessories for Harley-Davidson motorcycles, a private rent-a-cop in Beverly Hills, a bartender, a professional actor, and a nonfiction writer for a range of productions from ''Broadcast, Programming & Production'' to ''Rider.'' He was also, once and only once, he emphasizes, an undercover conservative published in William F. Buckley's ''National Review.''

Since starting to hit with his fiction he has sold more than a dozen short stories and four novels—in less than three years. His first novel, JOURNEY FROM FLESH, was published by Berkley in February; his second, LAST COMMUNION, will be released this June by NAL.

DRIFT AWAY

Nicholas Yermakov

Lilah left me. She never even said goodbye. But then, it had always been her way to avoid any sort of confrontation. She left no word, no message. I simply came home one night to find that she had gone. She had taken all her clothes, all her possessions and a few of mine as well, and disappeared. I had no idea why. There was no reason, that I could think of, why she should have suddenly become unhappy with me. Not that we had ever been, looking back on our life together, deliriously happy. As we'd floated by each other on the seas of time, we happened to drift together for a while. We shared a home, saw to each other's needs as best we could—well, at least, I like to think that I tried my best—and each of us was able to put up with the other's small peculiarities. If anyone had asked me, then, if I loved her, I would have assured them emphatically that it was so. Yet, now, I had to admit that I did not. And I don't think she loved me, either. Neither of us knew the meaning of the word, although we pretended that we did.

But, be that as it may, I came home one night to find her gone. It didn't take me very long to realize that she was never coming back. After all, she had taken everything. She never would have done that unless her decision had been firm. Looking back, again, I must admit that I was not shattered, although, ideally, I should have been. I wasn't hurt. I wasn't angry. I wasn't even very sad. At first. No, my initial feeling was a brief pang of regret. Not a very large pang, just a small one. And some small degree of puzzlement. But it was really too much to deal with. I poured myself a drink and settled down before my Panasonic CinemaVision, where a slice of someone else's life was waiting to take the place of mine. I wanted something different for a change, not one of the programs from my library. Perhaps, if there was anything good on, I'd tape a new one. That way, I wouldn't even have to pay very close attention. Once it was in my library, I could always come back to it to pick up on what I'd missed.

I checked the listings, to see what new visions were available in my box of solitude. There was a brand new remake of an old, traditional swashbuckler. I debated, for a moment, whether or not I was in the mood for feeling ocean spray upon my face or whether or not I could stand the pitching motion of a slippery deck, or the tangy smell of burnt powder. No, that was a little much. I needed something more relaxing. Something to take my mind off Lilah's undramatic exit. There was a space drama; that held some possibilities, although I already had several of those in my library. There was a love story, one of those "lusty, brawling sagas" of a family torn apart by illicit passions (as if there were any such thing), no, that wouldn't do . . . .

What the hell. I decided to simply switch the TV on and drift until I found something to my liking. I settled down into the contoured couch, finished off my drink, rested my hand lightly on the console and, with a shrug, switched it on. There was that old familiar hum, so nice and soothing. Then the heather was bending to the wind and rustling. In the distance, I could hear the triumphant song of bagpipes. It was coming closer. Then I saw them, coming up over the hill, resplendent in their highland regalia.

I switched the channel to see what else was on.

I found myself inside a cave. It was dark, but a shaft of light shone through an opening in the rock above. I could hear seagulls in the distance and I could almost smell the briny odor of the sea. As my perspective shifted, looking at the mouth of the cave, the silhouette of a woman became visible. As she came closer, walking slowly, seductively, I could see that she was naked. As she came closer still, I could see that her hair was soaking wet. Little rivulets of sea water ran down between her breasts. And she looked a bit like Lilah. I got angry and hit the console just a bit too hard, I guess. I had meant to switch the channel but instead, I broke it. I broke something, anyway, or perhaps it broke itself, just at that precise moment, I don't know. But the result was a sibilant whispering of snow and a crackling of light, refracted. I stabbed at the console, trying to adjust it, but it was hopeless. I shut it off.

Just what I needed. The unit was not a new one, by any means, but still, the store I bought it from had told me that it was guaranteed for years of trouble free service. The only trouble was, I had no idea what I had done with the guarantee and besides, it was too late to call a repairman. It looked like, for the first time in I could not recall how long, I would be without my TV for the night. I felt mildly irritated. Well, all was not totally lost. I could still relax and dig some music. Relax with some wine and Brian Eno.

And it was only then that I saw that Lilah had made off with my stereo as well. I began to feel spiteful. Not only had she left me, but she must have *planned* to do so, for she would never have been able to move it by herself. I imagined the smirks on the faces of the moving men as they helped a woman leave her lover. No doubt they had laughed at me. Well, this was too much. That sound system was *mine*! I didn't mind so much that she took some of my other things, but the Marantz! Had she been able to do so, she probably would have taken the CinemaVision as well. Or perhaps, she had sabotaged it in some way and that was the cause of the malfunction. I wondered why she did it. Had I done something wrong? I could not recall. She had left me simply no choice, it was an intolerable situation and I would have to press charges. I didn't really want to bother, but it would have to be done.

I was beginning to grow excited and the last thing I wanted to do was to endanger my health with strong emotions, so I went to my cabinet, in search of something appropriate to take. Only Lilah had already taken everything. I stood there, looking at the empty cabinet—empty, that is, except for some mild pain killers, a tube of toothpaste, my toothbrush and my shaving kit, and I wondered why she had done it. I must have done something to make her angry. Possibly not, though. She might simply have taken all those things because she wanted them. And the CinemaVision might simply have broken by itself. Either way, there was no point in dwelling on the matter. She was gone, my things were gone, and it was not my bedtime yet. I had to find something to do to kill the next two hours.

Which was how I met The Captain.

The broken TV had put me off and just listening to the radio would only make me miss my sound system, so I decided to go out and buy some drugs. Some quaaludes would do just fine, I thought, I'd just pop a couple and lie down, experiencing rigor mortis as my limbs and then my body gradually grew numb until I could no longer feel anything or see anything or smell anything or think anything. Just blissful nothing. No muss, no fuss, no *tsuris*. And no thoughts of Lilah.

The Captain was sitting on the floor of the lift as I got in. I didn't pay him any mind, at first. Just some old guy, sitting on the floor with his eyes closed. No concern of mine. His trip and he looked harmless. I hit the button for the lobby. But we never got there. It was a night doomed to mechanical failure. The lift ground to a halt somewhere between the fortieth and thirty-ninth floors. I punched a few more buttons, but it didn't seem to help. It seemed that I was stuck. I stood there, looking at the unresponsive panel, wondering, vaguely, how long it would be before we would start moving once again. I shifted my weight from one leg to the other. Then I tried the buttons once again.

"That won't do any good, you know," the old man said. I didn't turn around. "I said, it won't do any good." I continued to ignore him. "It won't do any good," he said, again. He repeated it twice more and I decided that I should make some form of acknowledgement or he would likely say it again.

"Yes, I heard you."

"No, no good at all," he said. His eyes remained closed, as he sprawled there, on the floor. "We are becalmed within the vortex."

"Yeah, sure."

"A most curious phenomenon. Most curious, indeed." His eyes popped open and he stared at me, white showing all around his eyes. I wondered if, possibly, he was not as harmless as I had thought.

"I guess we'll be moving, soon."

"No. The ship is drifting, but it's going nowhere." He continued to stare at me. I don't think I saw him blink. He had a very deep voice, very sonorous and clear. "We are beached upon the shores of time, until the pendulum starts swinging once again."

"Uh, yeah." I tried the buttons to see if anything had changed.

"Avast! Belay that!"

"What?" I backed off a step.

"Don't fuck with the buttons, stupid."

"Sorry."

"I am The Captain here." He said it that way, with capital letters. "I give the orders on my ship."

He closed his eyes again. I pursed my lips and looked at the buttons again. The red one should have done something, but it hadn't and I wanted to try it once again.

"I've got a lot of ships, you know," he said again, as if there had been no pause in the conversation. "All over, I've got ships. That's 'cause I'm The Captain. I'm on this one tonight. It has no name. I used to give names to all my ships, but there are too many of them now. I keep getting new ones." He opened his eyes once again and leaned forward, slightly. "I get a lot of boarding parties, you know." He swept his hand out. "All over. All my ships. A lot of boarding parties. They never talk to me because they know that I'm The Captain. You're not supposed to talk to The Captain, y'know. Some of them are not too friendly. I don't repel boarders, you know. No, that's the crew's job." He frowned, slightly. "I wonder what happened to the crew. I haven't seen them in a long spell. On the other ships, I reckon. I don't like that. I'm The Captain, you know. No crew should be without a captain."

He lapsed into silence once again, closing his eyes. I licked my lips and wondered if anyone knew that the lift was stuck. I had never been stuck in a lift before. Especially in a lift without music. The music had stopped with the lift. I was beginning to get upset, what with Lilah and the lift being stuck and all and the old man talking crazy and I didn't want to get upset.

"That's mostly what I do, y'know," the old man said. The eyes snapped open. "I try to get around to all my ships. That's The Captain's job. To get around to all the ships. Only it's a tough job. That's because there are so many of them. So many ships and just one captain. Although, every now and then, I lose a ship, y'know. Yes, I do. Ask me how."

I decided that I'd better ask him. "How?"

He leaned forward once again. "Hostile boarding parties!

You know what they tell me?''

"No, what?''

"They say, 'Get out, old man!' That's what they say. So I have to walk the plank. That's because my crew is not around to repel hostile boarders. If I had my crew with me, it would be a different story, I can tell you! We'd clap all of them in irons! The boarders, that is, not the crew. In irons! But only if they were hostile boarders. The ones who show proper respect, they're welcome on my ship. They understand that I'm The Captain. Sit down.''

"What?''

"Siddown, God damn it!''

I sat.

"You stick with me, kid. You want to be my mate? I'll make you my first mate, what do you think of that, eh?''

"Thank you very much, captain.''

"*The* Captain. If you're gonna be my mate, you gotta learn to address me properly.''

"Thank you very much, The Captain.''

"There! That's much better.''

"Uh, The Captain, sir, as mate, shouldn't I see about getting the li—the ship moving once again? I'll try the red button once again . . . .'' I started to get up, but he screamed at me.

"Will you sit the fuck down and forget the frigging red button? The God damn lift is stuck and that's all there is to it!'' I sat, quickly, realizing that I was in the presence of a possibly dangerous schizophrenic.

"When you're sailing the swirling vortex, in the eye of the hurricane, there's nothing to do but ride it out. Y'see?''

"Aye, aye, sir.''

He nodded. "I'll bet I know what you're thinking. You're thinking that you're in the presence of a possibly dangerous schizophrenic.'' He nodded, sagely. "Well, y'know what? I don't give a shit.'' He closed his eyes.

I swallowed, heavily, wishing I had some pills. *Any* kind of pills. Or some music. Anything.

"You'll be climbing the walls pretty soon, there, mate. I

can tell.'' The eyes opened once again and he winked at me. ''You know why?''

''No, why?''

''Because the ratlines have parted beneath ya. You've fallen overboard. And you know what?''

''What?''

''You drowned.''

''Oh.''

He closed his eyes once again and leaned back against the wall. We sat for a long while, in silence. It started getting to me, after a while. When was someone going to fix the lift? I wanted to yell and hammer on the walls, but I was afraid of The Captain. But, having drowned me, he seemed to have forgotten all about me. So much for my promotion, I thought. His own first mate drowns and he doesn't even yell, ''Man overboard!'' I smiled at that, in spite of myself. More time passed. I didn't know if he was asleep or just sitting there, with his eyes shut.

''I just stepped out to get some pills,'' I said.

His eyes flew open. ''Hark! A voice from the past!''

''I was all out of pills. Lilah had taken them all.''

''Ah!''

''I don't know why. Maybe she was mad at me.''

''Over the side with her.''

''It's too late for that. She's gone. She left me.'' I shrugged, feeling foolish, but talking to him was better than sitting there and doing nothing.

''You gonna tell me the story of your life?''

''Well, no . . . . I mean, I was just talking, you know?'' I shrugged again. ''I mean, I just thought, long as we're here, you and I, we'd talk. Sir. The Captain, sir.''

''Suits me fine. We'll lash the wheel and shoot the breeze a spell. You want to tell me the story of your life, feel free, I don't give a fuck.''

''Well, I wasn't going to tell you the story of my life, I mean, hell . . . . I wish they'd get this lift working or get us out of here or—''

"Forget the lift. We may wind up being here all night. Go on, what's on your mind?"

"All night? God, I hope not, I—"

"You know what you're doing to yourself? You're getting yourself all wound up." He lifted his foot and smashed it down onto the floor. "*Straighten up, boy! Straighten up and fly right!*"

"Yes, sir!" I was beginning to get pulled into his fantasy. I couldn't help myself. He was quite compelling, in his way.

"You think I'm crazy?" he asked.

"Well, no, I didn't say—"

"Bullshit! Tell the truth now or I'll keelhaul ya!"

I gulped.

"You think I'm crazy, don't ya? Don'tcha?"

"Well, I—"

"Goddammit, say it, boy! I'm crazy, right? Say I'm crazy, say it!"

"All right, all right, I think you're crazy!" I half expected him to jump me.

"Oh yeah? Well, I don't give a shit!" He stuck out his lower lip. Then he sniffed and rubbed his beard. "You know what your trouble is, fella? You and all the other sad cases in this city? You're all too sane, that's what!" He slumped back against the wall, thumping his head. "Who's Lilah?"

"What? Oh. My wife."

"Left ya, huh? Lowered away the longboat and took off? How come? What'd you do to her?"

I shrugged. "I don't know. See, I didn't really want to think about it, because if I thought about it, I knew I'd get upset. So I figured I'd just watch some TV, only the damn thing broke or maybe she sabotaged it, I don't know. Anyway, she took my stereo. And all my drugs. So I was on my way to buy some more when this happened . . . ."

"Best thing in the world for ya."

"Getting stuck in the lift?"

"Well, no, not that, exactly, but that, too, yes, that's a point well taken. I meant, your box getting busted and your wife taking off with that stuff. Good for ya. Ask me how.''

"How?''

"Glad you asked. I'll tell ya. Take me, for instance. How old do you think I am? Go on, take a guess.''

"I don't know. Sixty-five?''

"I'm eighty-six years old.''

"You're kidding.''

"Nope. Don't look it, do I?''

"No, not at all. You seem quite fit, for a man your age.''

"Didn't used to be that way. Ask me why.''

"Why?''

"I'll tell ya why. Because I was a consumer, just like you. I did nothing but consume. Ask me what I consumed.''

"What did you consume?''

"Myself!'' He nodded, for emphasis. "Ask me what I mean by that!''

"Okay. What do you mean by that?''

"I'll tell you. What happens when you've got a good sized fire burning, only you stop adding wood?''

"It goes out, eventually.''

"Ah! It *burns* itself out!''

"Oh, I see, it consumes itself, eh?''

"There, y'see? I knew you were a clever fellow. That's why I made you my mate. When you've got a good and faithful crew, nothing on this earth can stop ya! Look there, we're in Tahiti!'' He pointed at the wall. I looked.

"What do you see?'' he asked, his eyes open wide and gleaming.

"For a real good time, call Sheila, 762—''

"Avast! Belay that, swab!'' He frowned. "Just for that, you'll stand the dog watch!''

"I apologize, but see, it *does* say . . . .'' I stopped when I saw the look on his face.

"Look again, lad. Can't ya see the palm trees?'' I looked at the wall. "Ain't it beautiful? Palm trees gently swaying in the wind, and over there, look, there's a graceful barkentine at anchor, with her sails all furled up tight and proper. Ah, this is the life, eh? What say we settle down here, stay in this

sleepy little lagoon forever? Nothing but warm sun and island girls with fresh hibiscus in their hair, eh? Aye, that's the life for us!''

I felt like an idiot, staring at the wall.

"You can't see it, can you?" he said, a trace of sadness in his voice. I smiled and shook my head. "Ahh, y'see, I was right; you drowned."

He leaned back against the wall and closed his eyes. For a long while, he didn't say anything and I felt regret at having disappointed him. Perhaps I should have tried to see Tahiti. I reached out, hesitantly, and touched him on the knee. Then I leaned back against the wall, beside him.

I sighed. "You know," I said, "I think maybe I can see a little bit of Tahiti, after all."

His head swiveled around and he looked at me. "No, you can't. We're not there any longer."

"Oh." It was getting stuffy in the lift. "Where are we now?"

He sat up straight, very suddenly. "Avast! We're in a squall, lad! You and I are in for it, for sure! Look how black the sky has grown! And, lo, the lightning crackles and the thunder roars! St. Elmo's fire dances on the masts! Quick, mate, climb up the rigging and take in the sails, else we're bound for Davy Jones' locker!''

"Aye, aye, sir!" I sat up straight, beside him. He was looking up, at the ceiling.

"That's it, lad, climb aloft! Hold on, ya bastard, or the wind'll tear ya from the ratlines!''

I followed his gaze and looked up at the ceiling, as well. Evidently, I was up there somewhere, swinging from a precarious perch.

I raised my voice a little. "Shall I . . . furl the sails, sir?''

He squinted up at me. "Nah, forget it. It's all over. We're drifting in the vortex once again."

"Well. That was quick."

"Yeah. Sometimes, it's like that, yes, it is. Like with your Lilah."

"Who?"

"Your wife, peabrain."

"Oh, yeah. What about her?"

"Departed on the howling winds."

"Hmmm. Knowing Lilah, she departed not with a howl, but with a smug little chuckle."

"Hey, that's not bad, you know? Not with a howl, but with a chuckle. I'll write that in my logbook."

"Thank you."

"Don't mention it." He paused. "I'm sorry I called you peabrain."

"Rank has its privileges. Wish I had something to eat."

"Here, have a mango."

"Why, thank you." I took the fruit he offered me. "Wherever did you find a mango out of season?"

He jerked his thumb over his shoulder. "Back in Tahiti."

"Ah."

"Eat hearty, lad. We sail for New South Wales within the hour."

The mango was delicious. We shared it. It wasn't quite so stuffy on board the ship anymore. I thought the wind was picking up.

"Hey, are you all right down there?"

"Hark!" said The Captain.

"Hang on, we're coming down! The lift's stuck, we'll have you out in a jiffy!"

"Did you hear them request permission to come aboard?" The Captain asked.

"Not me."

"Me, neither. Could be trouble, lad."

I heard a thump overhead.

"Stand by to repel boarders!" The Captain bellowed.

"Aye, aye, sir!" He handed me a boarding pike, then stood to the helm. As the first man came up over the side, I jabbed at him with the pike.

"Hey! Jesus, are you crazy?"

"We'll let em have a broadside," The Captain shouted, as I ran along the deck, freeing grappling hooks and tossing them over the side. "That'll blow 'em well away from us!"

"Hey, Ed! Call the cops, these guys are freaking out in here! One of them just jabbed me with a boarding pike!"

I felt the ship shudder as the broadside let loose. The boarders never had a chance. The Captain and I had met the enemy and they were ours. The wind picked up and filled our sails and The Captain brought her up into the wind. I felt the pitching of the deck beneath my feet and ocean spray upon my face.

"Well fought, lad!" cried The Captain.

"Thank you, sir!"

"Aye, we survived our baptism of fire in this stout ship and garnered our first victory!"

I felt exhilarated. "Don't you think that we should give this ship a name, sir?"

"Aye, that we should. We'll call her *Lilah*."

"Good a name as any." I smashed a bottle against the bulkhead, christening her.

"We're bound for New South Wales!" called The Captain.

"Do you think this fair wind will hold up?" I asked him.

"Aye, that it should. Just don't go playing with the frigging buttons."

Ursula K. Le Guin

10705	**City of Illusion** $2.25
47806	**Left Hand of Darkness** $2.25
66956	**Planet of Exile** $1.95
73294	**Rocannon's World** $1.95

Available wherever paperbacks are sold or use this coupon

POUL ANDERSON